TIME & TIDE

ISBN: 979-8-218-67372-7 (Paperback)

ISBN: 979-8-9991857-0-9 (Hardcover)

ISBN: 979-8-9991857-1-6 (eBook)

Cover by Sand Dollar Designs.

Stuart Island map image by Madison Richmond

First Edition 2025

Island Thistle Publishing

For all the girls,
but especially my girls Addie and Norah...
and Taylor too.

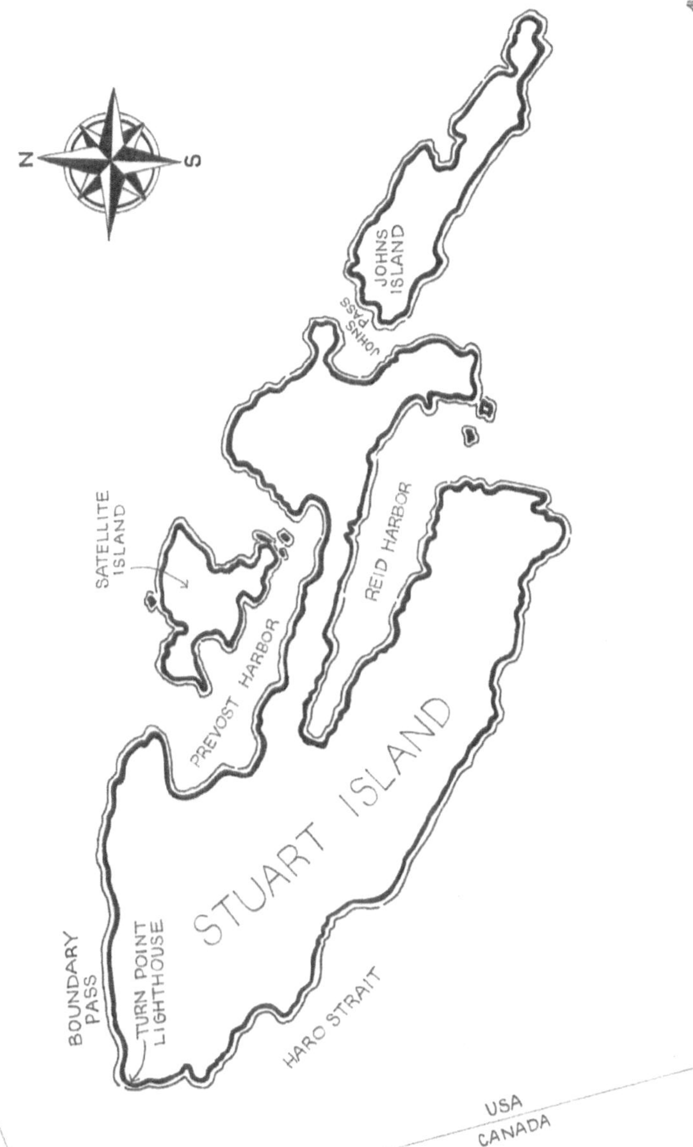

N
S
CANADA
USA
JOHNS ISLAND
JOHNS PASS
SATELLITE ISLAND
PREVOST HARBOR
REID HARBOR
BOUNDARY PASS
TURN POINT LIGHTHOUSE
STUART ISLAND
HARO STRAIT
USA
CANADA

1

Curious Child

Looking back on the timeline of my life it's hard to pinpoint the inception of events, the story lines blur and swirl to such an extent that the beginning is hard to say, really. After navigating its course, after fighting the relentless currents of time and station, any linear construct of how I arrived here, or even who I am now, feels impossible to capture. It's like trying to mold water into a shape, of course you can hold it in your hand, but the slightest manipulation creates cracks and holes, and the water slips right through your fingers. Like water and my will, there was no amount of force or determination that could bend either to conform to the holder's designs— they flowed without regard for other's notions of what they ought to do. And any observer would be hard pressed to characterize the shape of the water, as it evaded and schemed and fought for its independence through the hands of its captor. I suppose the most sensible place to start is back in Virginia, some 2,500 miles away from the island that would almost claim my life and would also breathe life back into me.

We had come to our new duty station of Portsmouth, Virginia only eight months prior. My mother had settled the house in record time, improving her domestic efficiency score with each new duty station. We had been assigned officer's housing on post and had accepted a large red brick brownstone on the end of Liggett Street. The house was deceptively large and seemed to swallow up the mixture of heirloom pieces from my grandmother's family, along with furniture we had purchased when we arrived in Portsmouth from San Diego. My father had recently been promoted, and the house was more formal and imposing than the previous military housing assignments we had accepted. Our former home in California was a newer style and had felt breezy and modern, in stark contrast to the formal East Coast grandeur that came with my father's new position. My mother had been disappointed when my father told her about Virginia, although no one in the family knew about her disappointment, aside from me.

My father had been second in command of a Coast Guard vessel off the coast of California that monitored the border between Mexico and the United States. He was often gone for days at a time, sometimes weeks, and it was during this time that I developed a new appreciation for my mother. Perhaps it was the newfound lens of adolescence that I was viewing her through, or the absence of my father, that illuminated her finally as a person to me and not just a mother. Regardless of the mechanism, it was there in California that I witnessed the initial glimmers of hope and sadness and real life behind her perfectly coifed hair and pink stained lips. She transformed that year into more than a mother, personified under the hazy orange and soft pink glow of West Coast summer evenings. We spent most of our time, nearly two summers ago, walking the sandy coastline and dipping in and out of the waves. There was a lightness about her then, or maybe that isn't the right word, an easiness was there, between us that I had never seen in her before, and for that matter, seldom saw after leaving California.

My mother had always had a sense of urgency about her, a military-like precision in conducting the business of running a household, she would always be the last person to bed and the first one to rise in the morning. She was one step ahead of everyone in the house, anticipating a need before one of us even knew we had it. I learned to see past my mother from an early age and mistake her precision for something machine in nature. It wasn't until that summer that I experienced the heartbeat and the lightness and the humanity of her. I remember fondly those sunset stained evenings where the light hangs out over the water, fending off the day's end, suspending time. A far cry from the frost filled windowsill of November in Virginia where my room felt heavy and dark. The cold wood beneath my feet brought the weight of the present sharply back to the forefront of my mind, and the water and the lightness and memory of color faded.

The rhythmic click of my father's boots echoed down the hallway. His cadence was forceful and deliberate, and his brisk steps created a wake of soft rattles and glass clinking from the hutch as he marched past it. My father had risen particularly early that morning, and my parent's muffled voices carried up the stairs. The sun was just coming up through the window of my room and the smell of breakfast wafted under the small slit of light visible along the door's edge. The hum of morning activities was beginning to thrum outside my door, and I begrudgingly accepted the inevitability of my circumstance, outstretched my arms, and drew in a resolved breath.

I slipped into my neatly pressed school uniform that my mother had carefully laid out. The cold buttons and starched fabric slipped over my skin as I dressed in the dark. My father's steps repeating more aggressively now as he moved throughout the house below. The clinking of dishes intermittently interrupted the chorus of muffled conversation and the cadence of my father's step. I hurriedly gathered my things, ensuring I was not a source of delay and disruption to the household morning routine.

Descending the stairs the overpowering odor of my father's aftershave enveloped the living room. It permeated the entire downstairs and smothered the kitchen air like a persistent fog. The sun was now just over the horizon and was reflecting through the frosted kitchen window. My father looked up at me only briefly before resuming his stiff stance near the fireplace. My mother whirled past me to the other side of the kitchen where she was assembling lunch bags for my brother and me.

"Good morning, Willow." She rattled off the greeting automatically as she assembled sandwiches next to an array of sliced fruit for lunches. I slid into my chair and spread bits of butter and jam onto my toast. My father approached the table and sat down across from me. He looked up at my mother as he sat, expectantly staring at her to serve him. My mother dropped the cheese slices and hurriedly shuffled to pour his coffee and deposit the morning paper on the table. My father sighed as she approached and began reading the paper intently. I knew better than to remove my gaze from my toast, let alone speak in the morning. The toast crunching in my mouth and the paper rustling across the table filled my ears and the void. I chewed faster knowing it was the only thing standing between me and a release from the tension, a tension I was all too familiar with in the morning. I gulped my orange juice and thanked my mother for breakfast. I grabbed my lunch and quietly slipped out the door into the cold Virginia air.

The school was located a few streets down. I had been granted permission to walk to school as it was located on the military base and deemed safe by my father. He seldom approved of me going anywhere alone, even though I was graduating that year and would be fully on my own by autumn. I had come to cherish the short walk and time alone, despite the bitter winter weather. The tension of the morning slipped slowly away the further I walked from home. I wondered about my mother and if she felt the same when my father departed for work each morning.

The school was an old brick building built sometime after the war. Its architectural lines were harsh and more fortress-like than a school ought to be. They were a reminder of another time and another mindset that I didn't fully understand at the age of eighteen. The thick walls and small windows of the facade suggested an impending attack, and the imposing structure was a constant reminder of the harsher nature of men and power. The only visible sign of children were the outlines of a few art projects taped haphazardly to a small corner window on the far side of the building.

School was a kind of escape for me, but never a fully satisfying one. I immersed myself in books and my studies, but attending school on military bases my entire life meant the pressures of rank structure and military expectations were always looming. My friend choices were limited as my father was an officer, and fraternization with children of enlisted ranks was not done, regardless of the base we were on. I felt the weight of my father's career in every test question, introduction, and interaction. He had impressed upon us at a very young age that everything we did was a reflection upon him and his ability to lead and command. Every B earned was a dirty smudge on his otherwise perfect record, every social interaction an opportunity to climb the class order for future promotion.

I hadn't made many friends this go-round, much to the anguish of my father who knew I was in the same grade as his commanding officer's daughter, Inez. Each day he would inquire at the dinner table, not so subtly, if I had secured a relationship with her and if she would be coming around the house soon. I resented his bleed into everything in my life. He was everywhere, permeating every part of my life and I couldn't bring myself to befriend someone in such a disingenuous way. I knew the sooner I invited her over, the more cause my father would have to insert himself in my daily routine.

I ascended the stairs to the school and pulled the heavy double doors open into the building. The soft yellow light gave a dingy glow to everything it illuminated. You could always tell a military school from any other old building; they had a certain bleakness to them that became familiar and almost comforting if you weren't careful. As I walked toward the classroom, the warm dry air felt like an assault to my senses, and I fought the urge to inhale. I quickened my pace, not wanting to be late, unknowingly picking my nails down to the quick as I walked.

"That's all I need," I muttered to myself.

I pushed past the interior steel door and found my seat. My eyes traveled around the room, taking in the same people doing the same things, the same voices, clambering over one another to be heard. My mind slowly drifted, lulled by the predictable pace of the morning, and I wondered how truly happy they were. I thought about the happiest person in the world, and if they still had moments of sadness. I think they must feel *some* sadness, right? Would the world then dismiss their inevitable moment of sadness by simply knowing they had reached the zenith of happiness? And then how terribly alone must they feel at the inescapable gaslighting about being human— expressing an emotion every other person is allowed to feel... except them. And I found myself feeling sad for the happiest person in the world, and I hoped that they never knew it.

The scream of the morning bell snapped me out of my existential spiral, and I was reoriented into the fluorescent light of the yellow classroom. The people in the room now visibly apparent, leaving me aware of my body, cheeks flushed and exposed. Nobody seemed to notice I had been someplace else, or even in the room for that matter. I tucked that flicker of light, the truest part of myself back into its neatly pressed shell and kept it safe from the prying eyes of Virginia teenagers. The morning announcements creaked through the loudspeaker, and I steeled myself for another day of formal learning and calculated interactions.

That afternoon I walked home from school in the cool winter air and felt life slowly seep back into me. I lingered for a few moments near a pine tree and rubbed the needles and slowly breathed in their scent. *I was happy*, I thought to myself... *Definitely not the happiest person in the world though... Thank God.* I smiled at the absurdity of that relief and knew it to be entirely true at the same time.

As I passed the front hedge of the property I drew in my last deep breaths like a diver before their descent into the cold underwater world, wrapped in armor against the elements. The outdoors was life, and I clung to each inhale before going inside. A long gasp of fresh air entered my lungs, and I resolved to be the brave, front line soldier in the family army. I wasn't entirely sure I knew what I was fighting for these days, other than my father's reputation and my sanity, often on two opposites sides of the spectrum.

Dinner was routine in that my father seemed preoccupied with anything other than his family and my mother pretended not to notice. I retreated to the confines of my room and waited out my time in the safety of my own space. The cold rushed in as I cracked the window for a moment. If I looked hard enough, I could see the shimmer of the moon reflecting off the water in Batten Bay and I wondered if anyone else was looking out at the water from their window tonight.

The weather had been bitterly cold this season and its icy impression made remembering the way the outside world looked in the summer harder and harder to recall. It seemed mythical that the endless sea of barren sticks rising from that void of white could ever return to life. I held on to the idea that buried beneath the harsh and jagged landscape was the certainty of lushness and green— that dormant color and light lay patiently waiting to awaken. I clung to the faint whispers that the bleak landscape held a secret of future warmth and life, and the promise of spring would be renewed again. That seemed like something I remembered.

The first few days of spring passed by much like the last few days of winter. You could feel something happening in the air, a palpable change, but everything looked the same on the surface. I first sensed the change in my father. He was always gruff and preoccupied, but he seemed to possess a harrowed look to him these days as if something had its grip on him and the pressure wasn't releasing. My father was always an absolute force; he had a way of making people and things bend to his will and seeing him grapple with distress was foreign to me.

There were only glimpses at first, stolen moments he quickly rectified and covered when he sensed I was on to him. It made me pity him and then resent the pity immediately. I wanted very much to hate him, but it felt too simplified when I attempted it. I admired the way he took what he wanted, and I also despised him for it. He was ruthless and imposing, but so are bears and I know I would still cry at the sight of one struggling in a trap unable to free itself.

My mother was better at concealing her emotions; to be fair, she had also had much more practice. I could always tell when my mother was troubled because she threw herself into her daily tasks with an intensity that rivaled a drill sergeant. The less my mother sat down, the more worried I became and the more cracks I saw in the ice that this family was nestled on. Both of my parents were shaken by something, but other than the uneasiness that grew in the house, they hadn't disclosed the source to me.

That ice finally broke one afternoon in March of 1926. It had been particularly warm for the last few days and the air was heavy and damp. It made the school building smell like an old book that had long been abandoned in a musty basement. The sun shone through the dingy windows and landed in geometric patterns on the desks and floor. Through the rays of scattered light, dust particles suspended in the air were illuminated and quickly vanished once they cascaded past the speckled beam of light. I saw a small note on the floor that was folded into a haphazard rectangle, and I wondered how long it had been there amongst the other shapes in the sunlight. I looked around the classroom scanning for the author or recipient to lay claim. Most of the class was engrossed in their workbook, eyes averted from me or the note. Quickly, I slid my foot past my chair and over the top of the note. I drug it back to within my grasp and slid it up from the floor. I gently unfolded the note and instantly felt my heart sink and my throat tighten. It read:

"*L-,*

Can you believe it? I am so mortified for her. Her father's career is over, and she doesn't even look scared. Their family is so strange! Glad I never became friends with her; she certainly didn't last around here. Where did they come from? California or something?

-Inez"

My heart quickened and a lump began growing in my throat. My mind raced to a hundred different scenarios and my heart pleaded with my head to make it stop. This message was about my family, but I fought that idea with every fiber of my being. This note was the point of no return; I had left the safety of land and was now floating in a sea of unknown depth and distance. My life was on the precipice of change and as much as I wanted my life to change, I couldn't bear the thought of what was to come. The devil I knew was just fine, thank you. My thoughts began to spin. *But what had my father done? Did he break the law? Was it an affair?* Thoughts ebbed and flowed through my head, surfacing rapidly. The room swallowed me up and swirled me around with each passing scenario. I felt weightless then heavy and tossed around like a boat in a squall. As I processed the possibilities, my stomach sank and rose rhythmically, but to a rhythm I was unfamiliar with. Fear swelled uncontrollably and snatched my insides, only to release its hold and drop me back down to reality. I spent the rest of class being pulled into the rip tide of my father's situation, fighting it, knowing full well the only way to escape it was to let it take me out to sea.

My mother never wavered from her initial explanation that my father was reassigned and had the 'opportunity' to fulfill a duty assignment at an outpost in the Pacific Northwest. She kept it simple, and technically never lied to her children; I just hope she never lied to herself. I secretly wondered if they knew that we understood that something big had happened, or if they thought they had spared us from the truth... but when you are young, everyone assumes that you know nothing. We packed up our belongings and fled the Virginia cold before April and the promise of spring could unfold. My parents left their secret frozen in the ice, locked into the Virginia landscape, and looked unwaveringly to the West for their revival.

2

The Water's Rough

The train doors opened onto King Street station to a palpable moisture, a freshness, that was unique to Seattle and the Northwest region. It was the kind of moisture that felt cleansing and crisp and inviting. I drew in a hungry breath of salty air and felt like I had the summer I learned to dive for pennies in the city pool. I felt as though I had penny in hand, bursting through the water, seconds from drowning, and felt the air fill my lungs as I surfaced. Seattle smelled clean and new, and the city felt more alive with every breath I pulled in. The cool breeze invigorated me after the humidity of the East Coast that I had become accustomed to. The air in Virginia had a way of seeping into spaces and sticking to everything; the kind of air that could slowly suffocate someone. If it had tried to close in on me, I had escaped and took my first breath of freedom. It felt new and bright and airy out West— almost elusive, like I was chasing it, and not the other way around.

As my family and I walked towards the pier for the ferry terminal, the sound of gulls playing in the wind muffled the sound of passengers disembarking the train. A sliver of swirling blue and green began to ascend from the city street horizon as we walked down King Street toward Elliott Bay. Tall brick buildings acted like blinders temporarily obscuring the unfolding view of the water as we walked. The slow reveal of the surrounding bay felt like a beckon with each peekaboo glimpse. A few blocks down, a busy port hummed with life, and ships sounded distant horn blasts as they crossed the Puget Sound. I felt the draw of the blue grey water and the palpable pull toward the sea even as we were surrounded by cars and vendors and the thrum of a thriving port city.

My father told us to wait as he approached the ticket booth. I walked to the edge of the pier where it met the city sidewalk and looked down into the water. The waves swirled in a beautiful aqua near the wooden pilings, so unlike the grey black currents of the Atlantic. My brother chased seagulls as they perched on the railing looking for handouts. In the distance I could see the faint outline of snow-covered mountains across the water and trees as far as the eye could see. I wondered how far away our final destination was, and where the blue green water would take me.

"Willamina, it's time to go," my father insisted as he tapped my shoulder, "we missed the evening ferry to Friday Harbor, so we'll have to stay in town tonight." He fumbled with the packaging as he loaded his pipe with bits of tobacco and looked back toward the city streets. He puffed aggressively on his pipe and the smoke wafted out over the pier and disappeared as quickly as it had formed.

My mother chimed in as she overheard our conversation, "Well I don't know about you, but I am starving, and I smelled something amazing coming from up the street! Let's get freshened up at the hotel, set down our things, and have a proper meal together before our big journey to the island tomorrow." She placed her hands on Kyle's small shoulders, and he looked up at her sweetly.

My mother had always tried to put a positive spin on our situations. She treated every duty station change as an exciting adventure and put her best face forward. I firmly believed part of her was truly that adventurous, but I also knew there was a part of her that longed for belonging somewhere... the kind of peace you could only get because you hadn't moved in years.

With that announcement, my mother quickly turned on her heels and set off for the hotel district a few streets up. We all followed in turn and walked back up the hill. My little brother scurried up to my side and started asking every question that he had been holding in for the day.

"How long will it take to get to Stuart Island tomorrow?" he asked, ignoring the fact he was out of breath to continue his line of questions. "Can cats talk to each other? And if so, do dogs speak cat? Will there be cats on Stuart Island? How many pets does the President have?" We chatted all the way up the hill, and it was a nice distraction from all my own thoughts.

We sorted ourselves at the Hotel Sorrento and walked back down the street towards the bay. We finally settled on Merchants Café, after my mother had skillfully convinced my father to walk the twenty minutes to the restaurant, 'so we can be familiar with our route tomorrow.' When really, she had chatted with a few ladies in the lobby and wanted to sample West Coast salmon. She clasped my arm as we scurried through the city streets and whispered that the restaurant was also rumored to be haunted. Every few blocks she would poke me and wail like a ghost in my ear. "Willlowwww, I'm coming for youuuu!" she would whisper and chase me like a mischievous child. We both giggled and it felt nice to feel so light and free with her, given the heaviness of our circumstance.

We rounded the corner just before the restaurant door and as my mother turned to playfully poke me again, she ran straight into a tall spectacled man. She was caught off guard and stumbled as she recoiled from the impact. My mother instantly apologized as she righted herself from her near fall and the man laughed and caught my mother as she leaned uneasily off the walkway.

"That's quite alright my dear," he proclaimed. "If only I was having that much fun tonight, please carry on and enjoy yourselves."

His blue eyes twinkled behind his spectacles and his dark hair framed his face as he chuckled. My father stepped in and apologized again for my mother's carelessness and introduced himself. The man smiled politely and introduced himself as Paul McMillin. He winked at my mother and told her to "Try the oysters, they're my favorite." and he walked off into the night. My mother blushed and my father noticed. He seemed annoyed by the harmless fun and scolded my mother and me for the scene we had made. As we opened the restaurant door, the smells and the warmth came billowing out like a deflating balloon, and with it our playful moment passed.

Inside, the restaurant was humming with the sounds of people talking and dishes clanging. A group of women in sparkling gold dresses brushed past us toward the back of the room. They were giggling and gesturing, and completely unbothered by who was watching and the space they held in that large room. I couldn't take my eyes from them and the shimmering glow of warmth and confidence they had about themselves. It felt so foreign, but at the same time so familiar and inviting. I wanted to run to them and be known by them. I envisioned waving my gloved hand in the air as I laughed with my head thrown back. I wanted to drink Rosé and tell people what I thought about things. Those girls were so far removed from who I saw looking in at myself. They were so self-assured and airy, like nothing held them down, free to float and drift in both opinion and form.

Watching them made me consider what my life might have looked like if I had grown up as they had, away from the military, and away from the anchor of expectation and rigidity. I daydreamed about an alternate life, one where I had been raised in the city, free to explore, given the opportunity to build my own life. I knew firsthand that a life like that would never be mine, at least not anytime soon. Instead, I would be stuck on a remote island, at a military outpost, far away from the Seattle scene and society. I sunk deeper into my melancholia as I envisioned the next year of my life, almost enjoying the self-pity I was compiling over the evening.

Morning came quickly after the whirlwind of Seattle nightlife before. The city was already buzzing with life as I opened my eyes and remembered where I was. Rain drops softly hit the window as my eyes adjusted to the room and I gathered my bearings. Today was the day we would leave the mainland behind and head North into the islands. I clung tight to my pillow and pushed my face into the cold sheets unconsciously, almost as if I could stop the inevitable flow of space and time by gripping onto the bed and anchoring myself to this spot like a barnacle.

"Willow, it's time," whispered my mother as she floated by and grazed my arm with her hand.

"You can't make me," I muttered back and pulled the sheets in tighter. My mother laughed and my father scowled and went back to his newspaper.

"You know what they say Willow, time and tide... they wait for no one," he said as he scanned the paper and took a sip from his coffee. "The ferry doesn't wait for indolence."

I begrudgingly rose from my safe harbor and slowly walked to the window. The sky was grey and fog hung stubbornly to the tops of the buildings. I watched helplessly as small wisps of cloud clung to the rooftops and were unwillingly pried from their occupancy, one by one, and flung into the drifting morning air. I watched the last tendrils of clouds morph and shapeshift in the early morning breeze as they took on their new forms and floated out to sea.

The ferry landing was filled with people and teeming with morning activity. Vendors were loaded down with supplies and carried crates onto the pier in front of us. The façade of the pier had a wooden front, and the building structure spanned a great length out over the water. Inside, a domed waiting room and large tower sat on the end of the pier for passengers. Ferryboat and steamship operations had experienced a boom in the last couple decades due to the Gold and Timber Rush. The pier bustled now with the steady stream of business and urgency only a new port town knows. A place where rugged beauty is monetized, and progress grossly barrels ahead. The pier felt smug and sure of itself, but the sound of the waves lapping against the pilings reminded me of nature's persistence and that time inevitably always won in these scenarios.

Looking out past the bustle, across the water it seemed unlikely that people could ever deplete the vast bounty of the Northwest or conquer the surrounding sea, but the topside of the pier hummed in unison this imperial directive. It was hard not to get caught up in the frenzy of it, but I didn't like the idea of a gold rush truth be told, the suddenness and impatience of it all. It brought the worst parts of humanity churning up to the surface and left a scum that choked out everything below it. This veil of greed and so-called progress left little room for anything else, let alone the delicate balance of light and life.

We boarded the steamship that morning and I stood on the stern of the ship watching the Seattle skyline slowly shrink as we bobbed up and down with the current and tide. As quickly as we had entered the city, it slipped from sight, and we were enveloped in a thick curtain of fog. The only thing visible was a small stretch of water surrounding the hull of the boat and the rest of the sea disappeared into the grey. Distant ships sounded off with their horns as we cut through the water and headed North. I settled into a booth and pressed my head against the cold glass of the window. My brother was nestled next to my mother and my father was writing in his notebook deep in thought.

I suppose I had better get used to grey and nothingness as far as the eye can see, I thought to myself. I slowly traced shapes and outlines in the condensation of the glass pane as we sat silent that morning. The images superimposed on the grey stillness out the window gave a respite from the reality that I felt looming like the fog. I traced outlines of trees and a river with buildings along the banks. I began to daydream about how I would one day take this same ferry and go somewhere very, very far from here, and no one could stop me. Someplace where I would be witty and beautiful and effortless like those women in the restaurant. So ethereal that doubt and duty and expectations wouldn't be able to take hold, they'd just float right through me like they were never there. A smile began to take hold of the corners of my mouth as I pictured myself grown, surrounded by interesting people who thought I was also interesting.

"Tell us more Willamina... we are dying to hear about your travels!" they'd say, or "You're the bravest soul, living alone in Paris— You do know that you're simply the best thing at this party!" My mind reeled off into my make-believe life of glamour and helped pass the hours and eased the sting I felt of being so out of control of my life currently.

We pushed North up the Salish Sea and had a fairly uneventful ferry ride, save the crossing of the Juan de Fuca Strait. We had the current against us for most of the journey, but the farther North we travelled the stronger the pull became. As soon as we left the security of the Southern Puget Sound behind us, the open water from the Pacific came rolling down the strait and created a washing machine effect which is exactly like it sounds. The waves and wind and opposing currents all converged and produced a churning monster of water that threw our boat wildly around for over an hour. I didn't get sick like my brother did, but watching the sea transform into that powerful turbulence gave me a healthy respect for the ocean and Mother Nature.

We pushed into Friday Harbor just as the sun was setting. It didn't look like much, save a few dozen boats in the harbor, several industrial wharfs, and a long pier for steamers like us to dock. At the shoreline sat a row of small businesses, canneries, houses, and a lumber mill. As I took in my surroundings the harshness of our situation started to take hold. Fuel tanks lined a long pier adorned with nets and stacks of fish traps. The harbor felt a world away from the hectic pier we had just left in Seattle.

"This is the *large* port we were coming to, before we transfer to the smaller one?!" I chirped to my mother. Not worried about overdoing the sarcasm due to the actual shock of the remote port unfolding in front of me.

"It will all be fine, it looks lovely, doesn't it Kyle?" she quickly regurgitated aloud what her mind must have been creating to calm her own self down. We pushed closer toward the Starboard window, craning our necks to get a better view of the landing. My father gathered his belongings and stood up near the corner of the booth to straighten his suit, away from the window and away from our commentary. We lunged forward as the ship made contact with the dock and slowly swayed back into a stationary position. I longed to get off that boat, second only to my little brother who ran ahead and attempted to push through the crowd of people gathering to exit.

Once off the steamship we were told a smaller boat would be coming from Stuart to collect us, but our ship had made port early. We were advised we should have dinner and orient ourselves to the town while we were in port waiting for the Coast Guard boat. The officer retrieving us was named Ensign Joseph Cail and he would come find us on Spring Street in the few local shops or the restaurant. This would be the closest civilization point for our family for the next few years, visited only for special occasions and for shopping trips. We followed the small group of travelers up the pier and onto Front Street. A newly constructed stone wall emerged from the wooden landing and acted as a buffer to the adjacent working port town. As we ascended onto Front Street proper, we were greeted by a small circular park with a bench and a monument to the locals who fought in the World War. We walked a block slowly up the hill along Spring Street and stopped at the mercantile on the Northeast corner.

The store front was made of wood, and two small benches stood to the left and right of the door. Billets were posted haphazardly to the storefront advertising everything from cannery workers wanted, to sheep stud services. A large poster was positioned centered between the door and the bench. It dwarfed the other billets in both size and production quality. It was a recruitment posting for Roche Harbor Lime Kiln across the island. I turned away from the postings when a small group of immigrant workers came noisily past us toward the harbor docks. They were speaking a language I was unfamiliar with, and I strained to listen to the unusual inflection and rhythm of speech. Some of the women carried baskets of fish and vegetables, I assumed for their evening family meal. A young woman close to my age smiled at me as she passed.

I sat on the bench and waited outside for my father to finish his business. The air was pleasantly cool and damp, and the smell of fresh cut timber and salt air was the perfect remedy after a long passage in rough water. Fisherman and cannery workers passed up and down the street and I tried to place the different languages many of them spoke. Friday Harbor was fairly new as far as port cities go, and for such a remote area, there seemed to be an eclectic population. Many of the locals were beginning to assemble and file up Spring Street now from the canneries and docks, making their pedestrian commute home. They traveled in small family groups that became larger as more people filed in. The feeling of being an outsider steadily grew as I stood there alone, and not because of anything they did. I watched them trudge up the road to their homes, together, and it made me think about my new home and how I would fit into island life.

My stomach grumbled and brought me back to my immediate needs. I pushed open the door of the mercantile to find my mother and persuade my father to eat. The store was warmly lit and was much larger inside than it appeared from the front. A long wooden counter spanned the left side of the store, and rows of wooden cubicles were filled with a variety of things from candy and ammunition to glass floats in all manner of size. My father was heavy in conversation with the shop keep and my mother and brother were all the way in the back of the store engrossed in the taxidermy collection that hung along the back wall. My brother was enthralled by the numerous pelts and horns that hung where he could reach them. There were several fish that were mounted on wooden plaques with scientific names and their length and weight. Most of these creatures we had only read about in books, but here, a life-size Dall Sheep looked Kyle directly in the eyes. He pet the sheep like one would a dog and traced the large looping horns with his finger. My mother studied the collection with awe and slight disdain. She was never one for senseless killing for sport, as often these trophies represented.

My father appeared behind me as I approached the back of the store. "Are we ready for dinner?" he asked everyone, seemingly in a much-improved mood from earlier. Kyle raced to the front of the store, perhaps the only thing that could tear him away from the animal exhibition was the promise of food. We walked a few doors down to the saloon and ate hot sandwiches that settled our stomachs after the long journey. We had just finished dinner, when a tall man in uniform came through the door. The light filtered in behind him as the door flung open, giving dramatic flair to his entrance. His face was confident, and he instantly caught my attention as he searched the saloon for someone. His eyes met mine suddenly and he smiled the most gorgeous smile I had ever seen. I was momentarily lost in the ocean of blue as we locked eyes across the open room. He shifted his gaze to my father and began immediately walking toward us. He effortlessly pushed chairs out of his way, while keeping eyes on my father and plowed through the area with a confident finesse. He could not have been more than a few years older than I was and the closer he came the more intrigued I became.

"Captain Donovan? Hello Sir!" he projected as he continued to clear his path of obstacles to get to my father. His outstretched hand made it to my father before the rest of his body had. He squared up to my father and introduced himself as Ensign Joseph Cail.

"I apologize for the delay; your ship wasn't supposed to come in so early and I've been back on the island getting things ready for your arrival," Ensign Cail reported.

"Not at all Ensign, not at all, no worries indeed," my father said as he visibly stiffened to add an inch of height to his stature.

"I have already secured your personal effects from the steamship. We are ready to depart for Turn Point when you are, Sir," he said as he snapped back into a more formal posture after reading my father. The slightest corner of my father's mouth turned up, for a split second, after the ensign's change of demeanor. I'm not sure anyone else caught it, but I did.

"After you Ensign Cail," he softly replied and gestured towards the door, releasing the young ensign from attention.

We walked back toward the water, and I followed behind the rest of the group a few paces. Dusk was setting in, and a mist began to materialize in the harbor. The smell of wood smoke and fresh fir mixed with the salt air and added to the untamed feeling of these wild lands that encircled us. My heart rate quickened as we descended the steps from Spring Street as the ensign offered his hand to steady me. He looked at me intently and with purpose, if only for a few seconds, and I don't think I had ever had anyone look at me that way. I couldn't say anything to him, to that face; I was momentarily paralyzed as he told me to watch my step and smiled up at me. His eyes were a blue grey that matched the color of the water perfectly and contrasted with the deep blue of his dress coat. Short whisps of blonde hair poked out from under his hat and I had to refrain from tucking them back in unconsciously.

We walked in step down the pier for a short distance until he quickened his pace and assumed the lead to the awaiting boat. Tied to the dock was a smaller power boat with Coast Guard markings and a massive light just forward of the helm. We climbed inside as a seamen greeted us, most likely another one of my father's subordinates who had been left behind to collect our belongings from the ferry. The two quickly shoved off and we slowly motored away from Friday Harbor. My father stood next to the ensign as he manned the helm, and they became engrossed in boat specifications and military things that held no interest to me. The changing landscape and coastline of this Archipelago were much more interesting than hull displacement when the boat was fully loaded.

As we edged out of the harbor, I studied his countenance while he simultaneously conversed with my father and skippered the boat. He seemed to look right past me now as we headed for Stuart Island. He was fixed on my father and wouldn't meet my gaze when I tried to catch his. My mind drifted back to that first smile, and I became determined to recreate it. The boat picked up speed and shifted effortlessly through a maze of crab pots and small skiffs. His hand steady on the helm as he navigated the anchored boats in the harbor. He moved with an efficiency and confidence that made me feel at ease about this leg of our journey. The smooth lines of his jacket outlined the contour of his shoulders, and I felt myself blush as I realized where my thoughts were wandering. *I bet I could get you to stop thinking about this boat if you looked over here...* I thought. I smiled unconsciously and turned to see my mother grinning that grin that told me she knew exactly what I was thinking about. She turned her face quickly after our stolen moment and I wrapped my shawl around my head in hopes it would cover my tell.

As soon as we left the harbor the current became stronger. The water began to swirl and churn around the rocky shoreline in the distance. A large island lay directly in front of us off in the distance and I asked if that was where we were going. My father and Joseph answered in unison, "No, that is Spieden Island." Joseph smiled and my father turned back towards the rear of the boat where we were seated, delighted to have a captive audience.

"That island was named by the same man during the same expedition as Stuart Island," my father reported, as he tucked his hand into his jacket waist. "It was Captain Wilkes, if I'm not mistaken," which we both knew he wasn't.

"During the Wilkes expedition of 1838 to 1842 I believe, named after the ship's purser William Spieden. Stuart Island was also named by Wilkes, after his clerk." He cleared his throat for effect. "Devil of a man, or so I'm told, not a favorite of the crew, he ran a tight ship back in those days."

My father looked out past the bow of the vessel and gestured importantly out toward the water, "Stuart Island is just Northwest of Spieden, and larger, it's as far as you can go and still be in U.S. territory— the mainland you'll see is Canada from our front door."

My father turned back to Ensign Cail and began asking questions about the vessel traffic in the area once he realized he had lost his audience. After our history lesson I fixed my eyes on the horizon and admired the rugged beauty of the surrounding islands. The loud engine thrum slowly drowned out their voices as the light bounced off the water with the setting sun. My mother gently stroked my brother's hair as he lay sprawled out on the bench next to her. I admired the utter faith and trust he had in the world at this age. He was curled up soundly sleeping and I couldn't stop thinking about what would be waiting for me at what seemed like the edge of the world.

A low fog started to creep in as we left the shoreline of Spieden Island behind. The water began to calm its steady push up the channel as slack tide approached. The boat skimmed gracefully over the water now and through the settling fog I began to make out the outline of land. The island was a sea of grey and green and looked uninhabited through the mist. I could make out large rock outcroppings along the coast that were topped with trees towards the center of the island. It looked as though an act of God had forced the sea floor up through the water and then violently set the island down. The fog clung to the rock outcroppings and softened the rugged edges of the coastline. The island was scattered with tall fir trees and some kind of tree I had never seen before. The trunks were twisted and contorted and were a beautiful burnt sienna color. They grew in the most unrelenting and unapologetic way I had ever seen. They seemed to cling to bare rock and hung precariously over the water with no regard for how a tree ought to grow. They had large shiny green leaves that rustled in the calm sea breeze. I had never seen anything like it and stared out the window in awe of the natural, almost mythical, beauty.

As we motored along the shore, each bend and stretch of coastline revealed another pristine natural landscape, hiding small coves and rock formations. Sections of the island rose up out of the water and revealed striated patterns of rock that presented different layers of the sea floor, pushed up and then turned sideways into their final resting spot. In their slumber, small patches of native grasses and lichen had taken hold in meager pockets of soil and taken root. It was fascinating to see such grit in Mother Nature, despite these harsher elements. Several seals popped their sleek heads out of the water as we passed and quickly vanished below the waves as we approached their vicinity. Life was abundant here amongst the craggy sea cliffs in the wind-swept channel.

The island looked ethereal as we motored through the mist, and I felt instantly drawn to its natural allure. Something about it felt so familiar, yet I had never seen anything like it in my life. It was mysterious, yet inviting and dear. Like a word I couldn't recall that sat waiting on the tip of my tongue. We pressed on along the Northwest side of the island as daylight waned. I made mental notes of island landmarks, hoping to retrace my passage from land, and visit some of the small beaches and vistas above during the coming months. The island overhead looked navigable from what I could gather from below and thankfully, didn't seem to be inundated with thick underbrush like some of the landscape I had seen farther South. The water had a beautiful green hue to it surrounding the island and it looked almost out of place with the dark blue, almost black, water from the strait waiting just offshore.

A small point became visible as we rounded the mid-section of the island, and a beam of circular light spun out from our immediate destination. I followed the segment of light as it made its rotation out over the water and illuminated a small linear tract of the channel as it spun. The sun was dropping just as the lighthouse had come into view. As we drew closer, a massive sea cliff that looked as if it had forced itself up from the outer belly of the island dramatically appeared. I craned my neck to see the top, but it was covered in a thick blanket of fog concealing the complete effect of its impressive stature. The tidal movements below the cliff came to a screeching halt where the stone met the water and circled and spun out in different directions. Kelp beds clung to the small outcroppings of rock at the shoreline and made a lapping sound as the boat pushed through them. A small dock appeared just below the lighthouse beacon, and we made landfall just as the last glimmers of light were peaking below the horizon. The boat made a heavy groan as it pressed into the dock, and we swayed back and forth slowly while the men tied off.

A seaman with a fantastic red bushy beard came bounding down the steps to the dock and greeted us as we were helped out of the boat. He looked much too young for a beard of that magnitude, and I had to look twice to make sure it wasn't a prank of some sort. Kyle was first out of the boat and ran squarely into the gentleman. He caught Kyle staring up at his beard speechless. He bent down and gave him a slight wink and tugged on the bottom of his beard. I laughed out loud at the gesture and chuckled how he had instantly read our minds. His eyes sparkled mischievously, and I knew I liked him immediately. Kyle was grinning ear to ear as the man slapped him on the back and said in a thick brogue, "Dinna fash lad... your beard is likely coming in next summer, what with the salt air and big salmon dinners we'll be havin'." He introduced himself as Seaman Sam MacDara as he rose to his feet, but my father had already moved on toward the cargo area of the boat.

My father had begun to bark orders to the awaiting men and sent us up to the main house to get settled. We climbed the steep steps away from the water and the main house came into view. It was surprisingly beautiful and well-kept in a way I hadn't expected, given its remote setting. The house was painted a soft white and had big wide swept steps leading to a large covered front porch. A wide gable sat atop the porch and drew the eye upward toward the green trim and shutters. Thick columns interspersed the porch and framed the front entry. My mother was visibly delighted, and I could see a small weight lift as she surveyed the property.

The soft glow of light beckoned from inside the windows, and we hurried inside as the cool night air set in. We opened the solid wood door and stood together, all three of us, for a moment taking in what would be our new home, at least for a while. A carved wooden staircase lay directly to the right of the entrance and the sitting room to the left. A hallway laid directly in front of us and must have led to the kitchen by the smell of it. We all took leave in different directions, eager to explore our new home. My mother headed straight for the kitchen, Kyle to the sitting room where papers and charts lay strewn over a large table next to the fireplace. I made my way to the staircase and admired the character of the wood as my hand reached for the railing.

At the top of the stairs was a small landing and a few bedrooms and bathroom. The floorboards creaked underfoot as the space unfolded. The first bedroom was painted a robin egg blue and was sparsely furnished with a small bed and wooden dresser. Atop the dresser was a small porcelain box and metal brush, as well as an oil lantern for light. The objects were unique in an otherwise impersonal space. I reached to examine the curious artifacts of the room's previous tenant and heard a soft patter and a chirpy purr from under the bed. I instantly got down on the floor and lifted the bed sheet. Staring me in the face was a massive orange tabby cat completely unbothered by my sudden appearance so close to him. He slow blinked his golden eyes and gave a slight swish of his tail as I admired him.

"Well, hello handsome," I said to him. "aren't you a magnificent creature!" He yawned as I continued, "You're absolutely gorgeous, aren't you?"

He lifted his chin and made another chirp as if he understood and agreed entirely with my appraisal. He rose from his spot and threw out his massive front paws for a stretch. "Well now you're just showing off," I told him as he sauntered out from under the bed. He rubbed his whole body-width against my legs and sat and stared up at me expectantly. He went limp in my arms and licked his lips, completely relaxed as I hoisted the animal off the floor. He flicked his tail and looked up at me and I couldn't wait to show the others. I sauntered off, back down the stairs eager to show everyone the best part of the house.

"Mom, Kyle, you aren't going to believe what I found upstairs! Oh... and the blue bedroom is mine now!" I shouted as my new friend rode happily sprawled out in my arms toward the kitchen. Kyle was first to see the cat and shrieked like a mouse when he saw him. The big tabby turned towards Kyle and flattened his ears slightly. My mother came around the corner and he swished his tail in mild annoyance at the package deal that seemed to be unfolding. She smiled a wide smile and laughed at the sight of that massive cat being held like a baby.

"I wonder if he belongs to the other seamen stationed here?" she questioned. "I wonder what his name is... a cat of that stature must have quite a name... I think he looks like a Thor or a Zeus."

"He looks like Shere Kahn!" Kyle added and moved toward the cat with outstretched hands.

"What do you think Willow?" she said as she tousled his massive head.

He squirmed at the sudden rush of attention, and I immediately set him down on the hardwood. "I think he will tell us what it ought to be." His feet hit the floor, and the massive animal scampered down the hallway and out the front door without so much as a backward glance. My mother looked at the clock and rushed us to get washed up and settled for the evening. After all we had a big day coming tomorrow and we knew full well what day one of a military station move was like.

3

No Compasses, No Signs

The next morning my mother was already in the kitchen, hard at work. I rolled over and wrapped myself tighter in my blanket, hoping to delay the eventuality of move-in day for a few more minutes. As I pulled the blankets in, I heard a gentle chortle towards the door and was startled to see my new feline friend. He was sitting on the dresser by the door with his tail neatly curled around him. He had come sometime in the night and now sat staring at me silently. He sat unblinking for several moments and with no warning let out the loudest meow I have ever heard in my life. I bolted up in bed and he remained like a statue. We locked eyes again and the slightest tail flick preceded another massive yell. The sound emanated like a trumpet or a war cry, and again the massive cat did not move a muscle or blink in the aftermath. The resonant song extracted me from the bed, and the animal broke his stare and sauntered off down the hallway towards the stairs. He stopped on the landing and looked back at me in a way that made me believe I had better follow him if I knew what was good for me.

35

As soon as he was sure I was following, he pranced off down the stairs pleased with his morning accomplishments.

The morning of a move in day is always organized chaos. My mother was everywhere all at once and the to-do list was Herculean. Our belongings were being carted in by several seamen and my mother was directing traffic and giving orders in a way that rivaled my father's level of intimidation. I had been tasked on settling my brother and I, and we were thankful to have an eagle eye view away from the battlefield below. My mother had a way of snatching idle hands and putting them to work in her domestic army and we both knew how to avoid being captured. A poor young seaman named Jack had unwittingly walked in to welcome my mother to the island and was now alone in the parlor unboxing books and lining the shelves. His face conveyed the confusion of his own situation, but he kept lining the books up like a good soldier.

Kyle and I decided to risk the chance of being captured for a chance to survey our new surroundings. He was the first to bolt down the landing and I proudly watched him bound down the porch steps on his way to freedom. I cautiously peered down the banister and tiptoed down a few steps. My mother materialized out of nowhere and said,

"Willow, there you are…, please go out to the cellar and see if my groceries have been delivered, and then go ask your father if he has seen where the men put the coat rack, and then take this box upstairs when you're finished."

I jumped when I saw her and muttered, "So close…" under my breath.

I walked out on to the porch and stood in awe of the unfolding view. The Haro Strait surrounded us on both sides as green foothills and islands rested on the horizon line above the water. There was no sign of civilization anywhere, only untamed natural beauty as far as the eye could see. The front yard sloped down gently to the sea and disappeared where the blue of the strait met the green and yellow grass. Clover bloomed haphazardly in the grassy expanse near the house, the first sign that spring was breaking loose on the island.

The lighthouse lay directly in front of the main house perched on the edge of the sea near the dock. The dock was hidden from the main house, sunken under huge rocks that the main yard sat upon. We were deceptively high up from sea level and there was not any visible beach to the point. As I walked toward the lighthouse, the steps down to the dock came into view. My eyes focused on Kyle at the end of the pier chatting with one of the men about the boat that was sloshing around tied to the dock. Standing outside the door to the lighthouse was Joseph who had one leg up on the door frame and was leaning casually back with his arms folded. He looked up grinning a devilish grin when he saw me approach.

"Good morning, sunshine," he said to me as I floated in his direction.

"Good morning yourself, sailor," I replied and flashed him a casual side smile. He kicked his leg off from the building and rose up to meet me. I almost took a step back he came so close and instantly made me flush. The clean cut of his jaw was visible in my periphery, and I felt drawn to his physicality inexplicably and turned to face him. His broad shoulders circled me, and I spun the opposite direction to meet his blue gaze.

"How do you like Stuart so far?" he asked as he walked next to me toward the dock.

"I haven't really had much of a chance to see anything yet," I told him. "but, my first impressions are mixed; I'm both in awe of its beauty and also slightly terrified of its solitude."

"Most beautiful things need to stay hidden from the world in order to stay beautiful." He lit a cigarette he had pulled from his pocket as he spoke. The smoke billowed out of his mouth as he turned and stared out into the strait, pleased by his cynicism. "People have a tendency to ruin everything... horrible lot," he smirked. The smoke rose into the air as he spoke forming visible veins that intermingled and then disappeared into the grey sky.

We walked back along the shoreline toward the house when my father spotted me, and I remembered my mother's ask. "I have to go Joseph, but I'll see you around, I'm sure." I smiled.

"Oh, I'm sure," he quickly retorted and walked back toward the lighthouse.

There was something about him that kept my mind racing back to our run-in throughout the day. I was taken by his cool confidence, not to mention his impressive form. I found myself looking through the house windows so I could set eyes on him again, intrigued by his first impressions. He had definitely made the move to the island more interesting, and his presence was a welcome distraction to the laundry list of tasks I had been asked to accomplish. He seemed to be curious about me as well, if I was reading him right. I spent the rest of the day daydreaming, lost to idle fantasy, about a blossoming love affair like Romeo and Juliet, without the family drama and suicide of course, emersed in the make-believe love story in my mind. I was unknowingly grinning when the front door flung open, and Sam and Joseph entered the parlor with my father. My cheeks flushed and a warmth crept through my body. I felt flustered and exposed like my mind had been broadcast on one of those new picture shows for everyone to see. Joseph looked up at me on the stairs and smiled for a split second and quickly shifted his attention back to my father. I composed myself and I walked casually down the stairs, jolted back by my father's tone.

"It is a matter of national security as far as I'm concerned," my father asserted.

"But Sir, the bloody government has only given us five men at full strength for this post, you'd be lucky to catch a fish, let alone a rum runner in these waters with a crew that small," Sam countered.

Joseph was quick on my father's heels as he paced the front window like a faithful hound on his master's heels. "I have to agree with you Sir, this waterway goes completely unpatrolled and I for one, won't stand idly by as illegal items just flow freely past our post."

"I'm glad to hear it ensign. You'd do yourself a favor, Seaman MacDara, to follow in his stead," the captain said, as he pointed to Joseph.

MacDara appeared stoic and formal, but as my father and Joseph turned to the window together, a smirk appeared on his face that had not been meant for my eyes. The cat had followed the gentleman into the parlor and was circling Sam MacDara's feet as he stood at a sort of modified parade rest. He weaved in and out of Sam's feet and perched his large body precariously on Sam's shoes, rubbing his face on Sam's knees. The massive cat looked absolutely ridiculous and had no idea. My father turned back toward the parlor entry as he heard my footsteps down the stairs.

"Willow, would you so kindly remove this infernal cat from the parlor? Devil of a thing, always underfoot."

Sam and I both lowered our eyes ever so slightly at my father's callousness towards the creature. The cat remained unbothered and looked at both of us expectantly and proudly. I swiftly walked over to him and in his defense retorted, "He's the most beautiful creature in all the islands, isn't he?" as I looked down at him hoping he was not offended at my father's descriptor.

"Looks like a useless fur coat to me," Joseph muttered, and my father chuckled.

"Seaman, to whom does this animal belong?"

Sam snapped into a more formal position after successfully dislodging the cat from his boots. "All of us, I suppose. This cat has been in this home for as long as I've been here. The fellows before us said he was here when they arrived as well. He's as much a part of Turn Point as the actual lighthouse."

"What's his name?" I eagerly asked Sam, hungry for all the details of his life here on Turn Point.

Sam responded, "His name's Oliver, but we call him King. It's on account of the famous trumpet player King Oliver. That cat has a meow like an Archangel's trumpet and his favorite time to play is in the wee hours of the morning."

I laughed remembering my first morning on the island and Oliver's feline version of Reveille. The name was absolute perfection. At that, I scooped up the King and carried him out of the parlor as his tail swished and he clung to my shoulders, looking back at the men left standing around the large table. The rest of the day was spent under my mother's regimented schedule, ensuring quick order, and no room for chance encounters with Joseph.

Early the next morning I woke to the dappled light flickering through the tree canopy behind the house. My bedroom window looked out over the cellar and into the woods that led into the interior of the island. Oliver sat perched in the sill, chasing a small ladybug through the curtains, sending beams of unwelcomed light onto my face. I laid there in the quiet, watching Oliver track the tiny creature until it slipped through the cracks of the window and escaped into the morning light.

My mother had received a welcome invitation for Kyle and me at the schoolhouse that morning, and she intended for us to walk there today to make our introductions. It was an odd feeling to finish out high school walking to a one room schoolhouse with my younger brother. There were no graduation parties, or dances, rather I had regressed into a small child again. Here I was at the mercy of my father's career, away from civilization, and most likely going to spend my last few weeks of high school playing nanny to the other island children.

I so badly wanted to be ill-tempered and feel sorry for myself, but as soon as Kyle and I stepped onto the windy uphill road I couldn't help but be pulled into the beauty and mystery that surrounded us. The treetops towered over the road ahead creating a kaleidoscope canopy of green and gold. The forest floor was covered in moss, grass, and lichen and the canopy was alive with small chipmunks and birds chirping as they worked. The gnarled twisting of the tree trunks rose out of the lichen and moss and behaved like contortionists twisting their limbs into impressive shapes and positions. Interspersed through the vegetation I could see a variety of rock outcroppings, in all shapes and sizes, that pushed through the thick moss. Patches of tiny white and purple flowers were tucked intermittently into the recesses of the rocky crags like miniature bouquets.

Further ahead the island floor exposed more of its stone underlay where moss could not grow. Large boulders were set into the sides of hills as if they had been rolled there and then forgotten. Small caves and crevices were created where groups of boulders were left behind as the hillside eroded and evolved. It looked like something out of a fairy tale, and I was enchanted with each bend in the road. As we neared the top of the hill the water was again visible through the trees. I hadn't noticed how far up we had climbed until I looked out at the strait and the looming island chain in front of me. I called for Kyle to follow me as I noticed a small footpath leading off the road to what promised to be an up-close lookout point over Haro Strait.

"Come on!" I said, "I wonder if we can see the lighthouse from up here?" I shouted as my voice trailed off from halfway down the path.

Kyle was soon right on my heels and giddy with my burst of energy and the promise of adventure. Despite the age gap we got along famously, and I often wished we had been closer in age so he would have had more of a playmate in me. We scampered down a large, buried boulder, embedded in the hillside, and stopped short in the nick of time. The trail ended on a cliff high above the water. I inched closer to the edge of the cliff with Kyle holding onto me for dear life as I did. There was a small tree near the edge of the cliff, and it appeared to be firmly rooted into a large crevice of the rocky sea cliff. I grabbed hold of the smooth trunk to stop the uneasy feeling I had in the pit of my stomach, being up so high and so near the windy cliff face. Looking down from our new vantage point I surmised this must have been the sea cliff I had seen the night we came to the island.

Kyle and I sat in silence and stared out at the water for a few moments. We were both in awe at the spectacular beauty of our surroundings, also both grasping the scope of our circumstance, and how truly remote we really were. I looked down the sea cliff, as close as I could get and leaned over the edge. Kyle still held onto my hand refusing to let me lean any further than I had. The water below met the rock sea wall and huge kelp beds swirled in the currents. I could see massive logs forced up on the small rock outcroppings below that had floated by in a storm and been set down during heavy seas. It was both beautiful and brutal and I was both frightened by it and drawn to it at the same time.

Kyle pulled me back after what he deemed an appropriate amount of time for surveillance. "What did you see down there?" he asked as he pulled on my arm and patted my back.

I told him about the kelp beds and the big logs and rocks, and then I grabbed him by his waist and tickled him as I shouted about a giant sea monster that eats little boys. He squealed and squirmed and we ran back out to the road to the school.

We walked and chatted aimlessly as the road wound slightly downhill. A small farm became visible at the end of the road as we entered a clearing. We both were excited as it was the first sign of actual human life on the island, aside from the few of us. We picked up our pace and made guesses as to who lived in the farmhouse as we drew closer. The house was set back from the road near the water, with a large pasture separating the house and the road. In the far-right corner of the pasture was the outline of an old man working a plow. A small black and white dog lay a few yards off in the grass who had been aware of our presence across the field, long before we knew of theirs. He offered a wave from the far side of the field as the dog alerted, and we waved back to the man from the road. He went back to his field work, and we proceeded on down the road together chatting in the sunshine.

A big red barn was situated simultaneously on the property line and the road, and the large door split and creaked as we walked by. A soft bray came from inside the doors and a man could be heard gently coaxing the animal from somewhere inside. Kyle and I giggled at the sound of the donkey's protests as the man unsuccessfully attempted to gain the animal's cooperation.

We continued up the road past a few other farms and homesteads and at last came to the schoolhouse. It was nestled in a small clearing and was set just past a small pond and a grove of apple trees. The building was small and white and had a few steps leading up to the door that hung open to the morning sun. As we approached, a tall woman in a long flowing skirt and button up blouse walked across the doorway. She turned and faced us and lit up when she saw us walking up the road. A few other children of various ages stood in the doorway and peered out from inside. Behind her another form rapidly appeared and jostled the older woman for position down the stairs. It was a young woman who looked to be about my age beaming from ear to ear as she jogged toward us. She was dressed in a maroon blouse with cape sleeves that came together with a large bow knot at the front. She was a blur of crimson as she pushed past the sea of tan and white pupils who had begun to gather. The girl had a short dark bob that curled up around her ear and large brown eyes. Her lips must have had some kind of rouge on them to make them that color, but it was just a sweet enough red, it made you wonder. She was all smiles as she ran up to us out of breath.

She grabbed my hand and threw her arm around me like an old pal would do as she guided me toward the waiting woman. "I'm so happy you're here!" she exclaimed as she chewed on a piece of spruce gum and tousled Kyles hair. He looked up at her in wide eyed amazement at her brashness.

"I'm Marjorie Borcher, of course, and you are Willow and Kyle, of course!" she said as she gestured with her hands.

She resembled a high fashion model or one of those young flapper women you see in magazines. She looked completely out of place given the setting, but also the look suited her so perfectly I couldn't imagine a watered-down version of her. She wouldn't let anyone get a word in, although I don't think either of us tried, as we were too enamored with her persona to participate in the conversation or stop the show. She began detailing certain people on the island, places you had to see, and had almost covered world peace itself by the time we made it over to the schoolhouse steps and the awaiting woman.

"Thank you, Marjorie. You are our enigmatic welcoming committee of one, aren't you?" Marjorie curtsied at the woman's descriptor. "Well, I suppose with that kind of welcome, one member will certainly do," the older woman teased.

"Hello and Welcome Donovans!" she said as she outstretched her hands for Kyle and me to shake.

"How do you do ma'am? I politely responded.

Marjorie jumped in and fielded this question without even blinking, "Oh Miss Katie, they are simply grand, do you know they haven't even met the Eriksens, or the witch... oh Willow, I must tell you all about the island witch..."

Miss Katie stopped Marjorie in her tracks and hurriedly reassured me there was not, in fact, an island witch, but a very old spinster woman who lived in a cottage on the other side of the island and just because she kept to herself does *not* mean she was a witch.

Marjorie mouthed "witch" to me as Miss Katie spoke and I had to look down at the ground to stop from laughing and giving her away.

Miss Katie guided us up the steps and through the doorway into the schoolhouse. It looked inviting and cozy and smelled of old books and new lumber. Several small desks lined the front of the room, along with a stove in the back, and several rows of books. Miss Katie had a larger desk in the corner of the room that was neatly appointed with the tools of her trade. A small collection of wildflowers that had been neatly arranged sat in a small copper vase as well. Several canvases hung on the walls depicting seascapes and wildflowers. There was an easel in the back corner of the room along with a small shelf of oil paints, watercolors, and brushes. There were two other boys inside and they eyed Kyle cautiously until Miss Katie intervened and introduced them. She gave the boys a bag of Jacks and a small ball, and after some small talk and they hurried out the door together thick as thieves.

Miss Katie asked about my plans for next year and I told her I was hoping to attend a state college on the mainland, as that seemed to be what everyone wanted to hear. I actually wasn't quite sure what I wanted to do, but that answer staved off the vultures attempting to marry me off to their next eligible single cousin, nephew, or pastor's son.

Marjorie offered to walk us home, which was really more of an assertion rather than an offer. One of the other boys in the schoolhouse turned out to be her younger brother and we all set off together up the dirt road towards the lighthouse. Marjorie's family home was just past the schoolhouse in an almost straight line through the woods in Prevost Harbor. The road to her house, however, was not direct and it connected to Lighthouse Road along our path home. Her father was a fisherman, and she had four older brothers. Her mother had died in childbirth with her younger brother, and she would often be left home with Charles to care for him and run the home during fishing season. She told us that her family had been out on the boat for a few days and weren't due back for another day so she and Charles would not be missed.

She seemed mature beyond her years, yet also childlike in her effortless ability to find joy and excitement all around her. As we walked, she would point out butterflies and skunk cabbage and rattle off delightful tidbits of information about the things she knew. She delighted in the world around her, and it was infectious watching her wild joy uninhibited. Marjorie was a kindred spirit, and I was again surprised at the island's offerings and welcomed this unexpected gift into my life.

My mother was the first to see us walking down the hill back to the house. She was hanging washing on the line in the yard and stood with her hands on her hips and waved us over. She looked so relieved to see us with people our own age, and in the few moments it took for us to reach her I swear she looked like she had set down another heavy load. Her smile and the creases between her brow softened. I hadn't noticed she was worried about us having friends until I saw the burden lifted from her. She hurried us toward the house for lemonade and a front porch chat. She wanted to hear all about our first day and get acquainted with our new friends, Marjorie and Charles.

My mother had a knack for judging character, and for making the right people feel welcomed. She had a guardian heart for others, and I always puzzled at her inability to apply that protection to herself. As we walked back up to the house, I noticed Charles' innocent eyes following her every move and it made me feel for their situation. I couldn't imagine growing up without my mother and the countless ways she smoothed the road with my father for my brother and me. My mother also sensed Charles enamored gaze and focused her attention to him. She asked him questions about school and the island, and he lit up like Christmas morning with each passing minute. Marjorie took it all in and I could tell by her soft eyes toward my mother that she had gained a loyal following before we had even hit the porch steps.

"Come on up you two!" she said as she put her arms around them both and ushered them up the house steps. She planted them in the wicker rockers next to the door and told them not to move a muscle while she fixed everyone a quick bite. Marjorie perched on the edge of her rocker and grabbed my hand and squeezed it three times quickly. It was such a swift, unconscious action, but it meant the world to me in that moment. I felt seen and not so alone. It was nice to have a friend.

"So, tell me everything Willow, and I mean everything. Don't leave out one single detail of your entire existence," she said as she gestured grandly like she was delivering the closing line in a three-act play.

I laughed and told her, "We might need to pace ourselves, after all we have nothing but time these days."

She stood up in defiance at my assertion and grabbed my hands and pulled me from my chair. She twirled me around and started pacing out Waltz steps as she threw her head back and sung the words, "Time, beautiful, wonderous time!" as she spun me around a half step behind her. Her positivity was contagious, and I couldn't help but be pulled into her joyful mood.

My mother came hurriedly through the door just then with a tray of lemonade and lavender biscuits and Charles and Marjorie flocked to her like the seagulls I saw at the ferry terminal in Seattle. Charles grabbed a biscuit and unapologetically sat down in my mother's lap. My mother always had a tin of her signature honey lavender biscuits ready for drop in guests. They were a delightful cross between a standard flaky biscuit and crumbly shortbread, and were infused with a honey lavender flavor, that had just the right touch of sweetness. She slowly wrapped her arms around Charles as he leaned into her and began asking Marjorie about her life. I sat back and marveled at how at ease she made people feel and how fortunate I was for today's events. We chatted until the sky turned paper pink and orange and the sun started sinking into the horizon.

My father was returning from the dock and waved to us on the porch. He ascended the stairs and quickly asked for introductions. Charles leaned into my mother as he approached, and the captain shook Charles' hand.

"Good evening my boy, I'm Willamina's father, Captain Donovan," he proclaimed.

"Hello Sir," Charles said meekly. "I like your biscuits and jam, Sir," he squeaked.

"Your face gave that away son," he announced as Charles wiped the jam from his face with his sleeve. "And who might this young lady be?" he postulated as he took large slow steps over to Marjorie.

She stood to meet his gaze and proudly outstretched her hand before my father could. "Pleased to meet you Sir, my name is Marjorie Borcher, my family lives down the road in Prevost Harbor."

"Hmm...That's quite a walk home for you tonight, and the sun is sinking quickly, allow me to drive you children home." Marjorie scowled slightly at the descriptor, and my father walked toward the outbuilding before waiting for a reply. My mother started tidying up the porch, her unfailing tell for when she felt awkward tension, or uneasy with something my father had done.

My father was seldom excited about anything, but he had a true love of automobiles. He had purchased one back in California and it had followed us to every duty station since.

It was a beautiful blue Buick that he had purchased new off the lot. It was a favorite conversation topic to anyone who would listen, and we would sometimes catch him staring out the window at it for long periods of time. He had refused to sell it when my mother suggested it, reminding him of where we were headed. The Borchers eyes lit up as they realized they would be riding in an actual automobile today. I hadn't thought about it until just now, but I had only seen a couple of them on the island since we had arrived.

The captain pulled the machine around and Marjorie hugged me and told me that she would meet me at the corner by the MacDara farm, where Lighthouse Road met Southside Road, and we would walk together to school. Charles jumped down the steps as Marjorie reached for his hand to get in with my father. I watched them slide across the cream-colored bench seat and marvel at the driver's gadgets and the luxury of the interior as they settled. We waved from the steps, and I softly hugged my mother as we walked into the house together that evening.

The next morning, I awoke to what felt like a Labrador Retriever walking across my chest, only to open my eyes to a massive fluffy tail brushing across my face. King Oliver had resolved that I had rudely decided to sleep right in his only path of travel, and he was not about to let my resting body get in his way. He walked back and forth, and halfway, decided to slam his head into mine and purr. He plopped down on my chest and stared at me with only a few inches between us. I scratched his head and told him I was very cross with him for being so rude, but also that he was exceptionally beautiful this morning and a good kitty.

School was a nice distraction from the continued work happening at Turn Point and it had brought me a wonderful friend in Marjorie. Miss Katie had turned out to be a brilliant teacher and a truly kind individual. She kept all the children engaged in learning by knowing each one personally and what made them tick. Marjorie had been tasked with leading music for everyone, and she positively lit up when she was at the piano. Her voice was angelic and the way she spoke life into the songs she sang was intoxicating in every way. She made old songs new again and I found myself singing along without even knowing it.

Miss Katie had the group of boys identifying and classifying marine animals they had compiled in their class field journal. I found myself enthralled as well by the bounty the sea held in the cold waters of the Pacific Northwest, and I joined the boys at the table. I ran my hands over the specimens that were neatly displayed. There were sea urchin exoskeletons, sand dollars, clam shells and mussel shells. There were colorful kelp pieces that hung loosely drying over a wooden dowel. A small bone that Charles had said belonged to a seal sat next to the collection of feathers they had gathered that school year. Charles was very excited about the bone because it was splintered about three quarters of the way down. He ran his fingers over the fractured area as he showed me the teeth marks carved into the bone fragment. He recanted memories of the times he had seen the resident Orcas hunting seal and salmon around the island. He said Turn Point was one of the best places to see them, but islanders couldn't go there since the lighthouse went up. He said his father had told stories of sitting on the rocks where the lighthouse now stood as a small child. I felt guilty knowing something so communal for the island was now inaccessible and vowed to bring it up with my father when I had the chance.

My days in the schoolhouse consisted mainly of exam preparation, as I had completed all the course work for graduation before leaving Virginia. Miss Katie did her best to quiz me and keep the things I had learned over the year fresh in my mind. Marjorie attempted to help me as well, but most of the time she'd be tearing through Miss Katie's stack of magazines and travel books. Marjorie would never go to college, and she knew it. It had been a special gift to continue her education as long as she had, truth be told. Her father had a special soft spot in his heart for his only daughter and Marjorie had said she resembled her mother very closely when she was her age. Her brothers had left the schoolhouse to fish and earn money for the family years before graduation. Her father had wanted more for Marjorie than what he was able to give their mother, and he ensured she stayed in school and was educated.

Marjorie was enthralled with the idea of city living and exotic places. She had big dreams, and in my heart of hearts I knew she was going to do something incredible if she got off the island and out into the world. To listen to her stories and to hear her sing was magic. She could transform all of us to different times and feelings. Everyone loved her musical storytelling; she was a mastermind of timing and delivery. I invited her to sleep over this weekend after begging my mother for a reprieve from getting the spring to do list completed. When I promised we would both help with the garden planting, she knew she'd been beaten through her own necessity.

The boys had decided to stay after school to play jacks, and we were excited to chat away from prying eyes. As we walked home from school Marjorie gathered grasses and wildflowers as she walked and wove them into beautiful floral crowns for us to wear. She was the most creative person I knew, and I relished every new idea she made me consider, and every new opportunity to see beauty in everyday things. She told me all about the island inhabitants and the family skeletons that were passed down in small town living like genetics. The island was rare in that it was so small, yet so diverse. There were immigrants from Europe and the Hawaiian Kingdom, there were fisherman and farmers, and several first and second-generation families working the land here, some of whom rarely left the island, let alone made it to the mainland.

"Did I hear you say there was a MacDara farm on the island the other day?" I asked Marjorie.

"Yes, it's right where we meet for school in the morning, by the big red barn near the road."

"One of my father's men is a MacDara, I wonder if they're related?" I said as I twisted a rye stalk around my finger.

"He's a cousin of the family. I know he'd requested this duty station to help when his aunt died last year," Marjorie said, "his name is Sam, I believe."

"Yes, Sam MacDara, with the big red beard."

"That's the one," she chuckled. She grabbed a stick from the side of the road and started speaking in a thick Scottish brogue and said, "Aye lassie, give it a tug and I'll flash you a smile!" as she swung her stick sword and pretended to tug on her imaginary beard.

"Margie! That's indecent!" I laughed and playfully slapped her on the shoulder.

That night at dinner my father seemed mildly annoyed, but that didn't surprise me. It was nice to have Marjorie in the house and both my brother and mother had fallen under her spell like I had. We hurried through dinner, as we had plans to play cards and look through my mother's magazines she had promised to Marjorie. She had been positively overjoyed at the thought of something new to read, let alone fairly current. Marjorie had been obsessed with the recent new trends in fashion and the associated liberation of women's expression of femineity. This past fall she had cut her hair, much to everyone's dismay and reveled in the fact that she was the talk of the town while simultaneously being on the cutting edge of women's fashion. She had had a marvelous time turning heads and making people talk.

She had a phonograph in her house that her father had rebuilt for her last year, and it was her most prized possession. She had a few new records she had scrimped and saved for and would spend several of her nights alone passing the time creating dance routines and radio shows in her mind. She idolized Sophie Tucker, Josephine Baker, and Clara Bow. Marjorie had told me all about the later, how she had come from a poor family, with a tragic backstory and a dead mother, just like herself, and made it into a real motion picture after winning a contest. Marjorie poured over the pages absorbing all the glitz and glamour she could.

Marjorie's family wasn't well off financially and new clothing wasn't a luxury her father invested in. He would from time to time bring Marjorie home a bolt of fabric for her to sew with. She made all her own clothing and quite creatively fashioned an impressive closet out of the fabric allotment. She had used what she had, an even made her own dye and patterns, with Miss Katie's help, after learning about local tribes of the Pacific Northwest and their use of Salal berries and flowers for dye.

We retreated to my bedroom and Margie stood admiringly in the doorway. I gave her a grin and told her, "What's mine is yours." Margie headed straight for the dresser, grinning from ear to ear.

"Look at this cardigan, it's my favorite!" she exclaimed as she took the garment unfolded from the drawer. She pressed it onto her body and gave it a giant hug. "And look at this blouse, it's such a nineties trend... but you know how red never goes out of style. Those puffed sleeves are sublime Willow!"

She placed the red blouse back in the drawer and grabbed a matching scarf that had been gently folded on the top of the dresser. She skillfully draped it over her head and tied it neatly under her ear. She put one hand on her hip and pointed the other in the air and began to shimmy and kick her legs in a chorus line fashion. I rolled on the bed with laughter and Margie collapsed next to me finally breaking character.

Marjorie looked over at me playfully and then asked, "So when were you going to tell me about the absolute catch that's been eyeing you every time our paths cross?" She flashed me a devilish grin and looked back to the magazine pile in front of her. "Don't pretend you don't know what I mean either." she said as she flipped nonchalantly through the next magazine.

"Oh that...it's nothing, or at least nothing yet..." I smirked back. "Honestly, he is absolute perfection to look at but

I'm not sure he would understand a girl like me. He feels too...practical."

"I *fully* know exactly what you mean by that," she nodded in agreement, "please do remember every single detail of your first kiss when you do it though. I think I might die when it happens, I'm afraid." As she said the last word, she let out a breathy sigh and then pretended to faint on the bed next to me.

4

Warm Winds and Frozen Swims

The days were growing longer and getting warmer by the week. Marjorie and I had become fast friends, and I couldn't imagine living out my new island adventure without her. Marjorie had planned to take me out to Satellite Island for a picnic, she said she had something to show me. Her family owned a small skiff she was allowed to use, and we would row across the harbor and spend the afternoon together. We set out as the sun broke over the tree line and talked about everything we felt at that particular place in time. Marjorie talked about her mother and what her home life had been like before she died, and the sadness after. I talked about my time in California and how I never really felt like I belonged anywhere. I felt like Margie had this incredible gift of empathy tempered with a strong sense of self and it amazed me how she could sometimes articulate what I felt when I, myself, couldn't find the words. She guided me but never directed me. Our closeness grew as we walked under the trees and followed the little road to Margie's house.

I don't know what I thought Marjorie's house would look like, but it certainly wasn't what I had expected. The far side of the house was pushed up next to the water's high tide mark and the yard looked like a graveyard of boats and fishing equipment. There were remnants of a small garden at some point in time but had long since been lost to the sea of nets and fish traps that were stacked up as high as we were. Netted glass floats adorned the old wooden steps that led up to the front door. Pieces of driftwood no doubt collected by Margie and her siblings were strewn over the porch area and the old flower bed. The house had been weathered by the salt air and anything metal was now an orange rust color amongst the neutral sand and whitewashed wood. The house was windswept and appeared defiant as its base met the rocky shoreline. A larger fishing boat was anchored in the harbor, as well as a few small skiffs and a dilapidated old sailboat that looked as if it hadn't left its mooring in quite some time. Farther down the beach a large dock stretched out into the water that held several fishing vessels and a large Ketch rigged sailboat.

I heard the door close, and Marjorie came bounding out with oars and a small blanket in her hands. "And we're off!" she said as she untied the bow line from a large piece of driftwood and sauntered down the pebble beach to the waiting skiff. The boat was pulled up quite a distance from the water and she threw the items in the small boat, including the line, and told me to get on one side of her, and we would drag the skiff to the water line. Margie directed me to get in and hold on as she pushed the skiff through the water and leapt onto the boat, at the last minute using the momentum of the push to keep us off the rocks. Her left foot just grazed the top of the water as she nimbly navigated the wobbly boat. Margie grabbed the oars and began pulling us slowly toward the island across the harbor.

She pointed to a small sandy beach at the entrance to the harbor that was a favorite of hers when she wanted to be alone. She told me about a driftwood shack she had made years ago, that she spent a lot of time at, after her mother died. A few years ago, some local boys had come across it and torn some of the frame down and she had spent weeks watching the beach shoreline for skiffs through her bedroom window, fantasizing about what she would do if she caught them. They never returned to the scene of the crime however, and her attention shifted back to her music and happier things than revenge. I watched her sinewy shoulders pull the oars and marveled at her grace, and her strength. She had endured so much in her life, but it had made her beautiful and wise and I was proud to know her. The water was calm that afternoon and several small seals poked their heads up, investigating our approach, as we the passed through the harbor toward the beach. I felt happy and alive, and grounded to the present as we made our way to the other side of the harbor.

The boat glided into the sandy shore and softly came to a halt. Marjorie leapt from the bow with the line in hand and jumped onto the sand. With a tug she dragged the boat a few more feet in and I was glad I hadn't stood up yet or I'd be going for a very cold swim. The forward half of the boat was rested firmly on dry land and Marjorie held out a hand for me to make the leap. I nimbly jumped from the bow like she did, bypassing the outstretched hand, and turned to face her proudly after I had gracefully landed. She grinned and told me I was a fast learner.

We had grown up with small sailboats as a child. My father was a fourth-generation seaman, and we would spend summers out on the water for as long as I could remember. Boats were not new to me; they just represented a structure and formality I had grown to rebel against. We walked up the grassy hill toward the interior of the island and to Marjorie's hideout. The driftwood shack was perched on a relatively flat rocky hilltop, protected from view from Stuart Island, but exposed to Haro Strait. There was a small open doorway and a low makeshift window frame. The roof was constructed of slats of weathered driftwood of varying shapes, and chunks of sea grass growing in the small pockets created by the uneven wood pieces. It stood around six feet high, and we had to duck inside the eave to enter the dwelling. The floor was hard stone and had been covered by sand to make it more navigable and somewhat level.

"Margie... this is magnificent!" I said as I looked around at her creation. There were three small chairs and a low table near the window with a candle and a glass vase. Glass floats hung from the far roof line and dried wildflowers were tucked into the gaps of the roof line near the floats.

She hugged me beaming and said, "I knew you would love it; I knew you would see it the way I do."

We ate lunch at the small table together and she told me about how this had been a special picnic spot for her mother and herself. They would go together and watch for the boat to come back to Prevost Harbor with her brothers and father. The two would keep watch and make wreaths and crowns to give to the family on their safe return from fishing in Boundary Pass and the Strait of Georgia. Her father had a secret code to let them know it was him if the boat arrived after night fall. He would signal E, B in Morse code for Eugene Borcher, with the lights as he approached the island. Her mother would rush to the edge of the water signaling with her lantern in return.

She told me how she had come out to Satellite Island often after her mother died. She had felt lost and would look out at the strait hoping for some kind of sign or signal meant just for her, that would tell her all was well, and everything would be ok too. "Which brings me to my next activity, Miss Donovan," she proclaimed.

"I'm going to go for a swim," she announced.

"Is there a lake over here?" I asked.

"A lake?" she laughed, "Oh Willow, who needs a lake when you have this big, beautiful sea to swim in?" she gestured out to the water as she ducked out of the shack and into the sun. I swiftly followed her back down the grassy hill to the beach, which was in total shade, due to the time of day.

"Margie, you're mad, you'll die in that water if you go in!"

Margie was already peeling off clothing and skipping towards the water as she laughed at me undeterred. She walked right into the water undaunted and sank her body into the frigid water, out past where her toes could touch. She turned and floated on her back and asked me, "Aren't you coming in?" I could not believe she was so calmly submerged in the icy water. I dipped my hands and toes in at the water's edge and recoiled them instantly when they met the bitterly cold water.

"Margie, you're going to drown in that water! You just ate!" My head reeled with all the reasons she shouldn't be swimming farther out into the harbor. Around the point the current was ebbing swiftly, and I became more nervous with each stroke she took. Margie was floating on her back now, and she could see my worried face on the shore. She started back for the beach, and my hands unclenched as she drew closer and closer to safety.

"Goodness you're a nervous Nellie!" she said as she rose up out of the frigid water and walked to shore. I quickly wrapped the picnic blanket around her and told her she was crazy for going out in that water. She looked at me solemnly and said, "Willow, that water saved me. You don't get it." She sat down on a rock as the sun finally poked its way over the hillside and the light caught her face. I could see her slightly deflated. I felt guilty for not trying to understand her and jumping to conclusions. "I can take care of myself just fine, you know. I've been doing it for a while now." she said as she looked out over the grey and blue water.

"I know you can, you're the strongest and bravest person I know Margie, but I was scared. I really thought you were going to sink or drown or die out there. I've never seen nor heard of anybody swimming in waters this cold and..."

She cut me off and said, "well my family and I do, so now you have, so there's that," she stiffened.

Her demeanor towards me had changed so visibly and so quickly. It was like the current had actually carried her away from me, and I was left on the shore with no way to reach her while she bathed in her brokenness. The distance built between us with each passing moment, and I stumbled over my words trying to wade into the troubled water to be reunited with my friend. I put my hand on her shoulder, and she turned to me, eyes teary and flashing. She was so hurt, and I had caused it, but I didn't know why.

"Oh Margie, I'm so, so sorry for whatever I did… please forgive me, I should have never questioned you," I stammered, "I should have gone in, I should have…"

Margie's eyes softened and she grabbed my hand and laughed as tears fell from her face.

"No, I am sorry. You hadn't a clue about any of this and what it means to me. I was unfair to you," she said as she wiped away her tears with the blanket edge and forced a pained smile.

"I hadn't been for a swim with anyone else since my mother died. I come here and swim now, but it's always by myself. This is where I go when the grief gets the better of me and I can't put it down. The sea and the cold always take it. It's honestly been the only thing that's kept me sane after she passed. My mother loved swimming in the sea. She taught me how to breathe, and how to go in and stay in, to make peace with the cold," Margie said.

"I *can* tell you I was never really a fan of it when she was alive," she chuckled as she wiped another tear away and looked up at the sky and said, "I didn't need it then. I really am sorry. Being here with you— and everything came back, and I just miss her so much and I don't know… it just overwhelmed me, and I had to go in Willow. It's the only thing that brings me back and stops the hurt."

I put my hands on her icy shoulder and pulled her in tighter, trying to carry the weight of our rift. The cold bled into my ribs and legs as I pressed my body next to hers. The sun was fully on our backs now and as we sat and talked. We looked out at the water and let it heal the both of us in a way each of us needed. I wanted to be brave like Margie, and I wanted to meet her in her grief as well. I grabbed her hand, and with the most resolve of my life, I walked toward the water.

"You don't have to!" Margie pleaded as she saw me marching down to the water's edge.

"I want to," I said undeterred by the escape clause Margie had presented, dropping her hand.

I marched into the icy water. It nearly took my breath away as I lowered my legs in and kept moving forward. When the water hit my torso, it did take my breath away. Out of fear of backing out, I threw myself like a sacrifice into the cold water gasping for breath as I popped back up.

"Now who's insane?!" Margie yelled as she dove in to meet me. We swam out together and after the shock of the cold wore off, I felt the magic she talked about. I felt alive and fully present, strangely at peace with my place in the world. The frigid water demanded my attention, and my mind couldn't possibly wander anywhere else but this precise moment. I watched my feet kick in the clear water, suspended over the cold sea floor. Margie swam over to me, and we bobbed in the water, grinning at each other. We spent a few minutes floating in the water and then swam for the sandy shore. We walked out of the water together and I reached for Margie, and felt her pain fit perfectly in the palm of my outstretched freezing hand. She looked over at me the same way she had looked at my mother, with a new loyalty and appreciation, the kind that is only reserved for kindred spirits.

5

High Tides

School was wrapping up on the island for the season and there was talk of a community wide social to kick off summer. An air of excitement permeated the household as the event drew near. All of us eager to have an excuse to get dressed up and meet many of the other islanders we had only heard mentioned. The dance was all Marjorie could talk about, and she already had raided my closet and selected multiple outfit prospects for both of us. Joseph hadn't made mention of the festivities, and it wasn't clear if he was interested in going, let alone with me, but I was determined to find out this week. I had volunteered to help my mother with summer plantings and would be outside the house all day in plain sight, in the event a certain gentleman was to want to enquire about a date.

I ran down the steps as my mother called for me, ready to get my hands in the soil and make the house our own. She looked up the staircase with a sly grin and told me how wonderful I looked. "Willow, I think the asters and the dahlias are undoubtedly going to appreciate the length you went to today with that hair," she joked. I gave her a wry smile and headed out the door as I fastened my apron tight. She nudged me with her elbow and leaned into me as we walked down the steps. I laughed and slapped her hand away playfully as she saw me scanning the area for the ensign. We worked together all morning tending to the flower beds, planting the new season's flowers. I was so intently working a particularly stubborn dahlia tuber from its small pot that I hadn't noticed my father approaching. Joseph was walking just a few steps behind.

"Willamina, I have some news," he announced. I straightened up and brushed the dirt from my apron and tried to look as nonchalant as I could. "One of our neighbors is hosting a summer social next week and I have enlisted Ensign Cail here as your escort." Joseph flashed a confident grin in my direction, and I was visibly irritated.

"Well... isn't that lovely," I replied.

My mother didn't need to be brought up to speed, she flashed a look to my father that seemed to say, *Way to go blockhead.* My father didn't catch my mother's facial clues and continued looking pleased with himself as he continued to lay out the day's events. We would all drive together in my father's car and my parents would return on foot to the house after the picnic portion of the evening. My father would leave the car, and Joseph would drive us the short distance home after the dance.

I was annoyed that my father had yet again decided to orchestrate every aspect of my life down to the minute. I was also annoyed at myself for being annoyed, as this was exactly what I had wanted, just not how I wanted it to happen. I had romanticized being asked to the dance by Joe, I didn't want my father assigning him to me like a charge. I felt more like a ward of the state, rather than a love interest. My father dismissed Ensign Cail and started to talk to my mother about canned salmon stores in the root cellar. She just looked at him with pursed lips and said, "Way to go Raymond." and my father looked bewildered and then annoyed as well.

"What are you talking about?" he snapped.

"You couldn't let the boy ask her himself? Is this really something you needed to manage? Let the girl be a girl and the boy be a boy for God's sake," my mother said as she shook her head.

The captain began to load his pipe with tobacco and told her that she was overreacting. My mother walked away from him and made a deep sigh. I heard him mumble as he loaded his pipe, "Of all the infernal..." his voice trailed off as he walked back to the dock and away from my mother.

I picked up the stacked pots and walked back toward the house replaying the confusing events in my head, ultimately thankful that I was going to the dance with Joseph. Afterall, we would actually have time alone, away from my father's gaze, to finally get to know each other. I concluded what mattered was the outcome, and not the delivery. I kept recounting his face as my father delivered the news, and I couldn't quite understand it. He didn't seem nearly as uncomfortable with the idea of my father handling his affairs as I did. He must have been in a terrible spot, with my father being the captain and all.

The next morning, Margie and I met at the corner where we always did, and the boys ran off ahead together up the road. Margie looked incredibly energetic this morning as she walked next to me slapping me playfully with a stalk of rye every few steps. "Ok out with it!" I said and grabbed her hand mid slap.

"Sam asked me to the dance!" she said as she giggled and then smiled smugly up the road.

"Sam?... as in Sam MacDara, Sam?"

"That's the one!" Margie beamed.

Happiness emanated out of me for her happy news. Sam was one of my most favorite people and if anyone deserved a heart like Margie's, it was him. They were both spirited, lively people that had similar nurturing qualities that had endeared them to me from the start. Margie told me she used to have a crush on him from the time she saw him last year on the MacDara farm. She didn't have occasion to visit Turn Point, and until I had come along, she had never been invited. Now that she frequented the lighthouse, her and Sam had had the opportunity to talk and get to know each other over the past few weeks. It was the sweetest thing to witness. Sam would find any reason he could to be out on the dock and offer Margie a wave or sneak away from his work to say hello. Last week he had brought her a lavender soap made of sheep's milk from the family farm and every morning since I have smelled just a hint of lavender in Margie's hair.

"Well, I have news as well," I said as I took a deep sigh. "It didn't go exactly how I wanted it...but I also have a date for the dance, Joseph."

"Tell me everything Willow!" Margie said as she tore into a biscuit my mother now religiously packed for her and Charlie each morning. I told her about how my dad had been involved, and how it complicated things having him smack dab in the center of my love life. I told her how I couldn't read Joseph's feelings about it when it happened. If he had asked me himself, I wouldn't be wondering if he wanted to go with me or if he had been ordered to take me. I also told her about how, if I had to guess, he didn't seem bothered by the whole situation. Margie nodded in solidarity as she ate her biscuit and walked alongside me.

"You're going to have to try and get him alone before then," she said with a full mouth. "Find a chance to talk to him and see what he says. Or I can ask Sam to find out?" she winked at me.

"Both good options," I nodded back, "let's see what I can find out this week and then we can bring in the operative." I joked.

The next afternoon proved fruitful in opportunities for a chance run-in. The men were back and forth from the house grabbing charts and old logbooks. There was a lot of activity on the dock as well, as they moved the larger boat closer to shore and the smaller boats to the end of the dock. Supplies were loaded onto the smaller boats and tarped immediately. It looked as if they were planning to mobilize quickly if possible and I asked my mother what was happening. She told me it was just my father trying to make a name for himself again, and not to worry. There was no danger, and they were just being prepared for anything out on the water.

After having mint iced tea with my mother and Kyle on the porch, I decided to walk along the West side of the shoreline that ran parallel to the house. I was hoping my movements wouldn't go unnoticed and Joseph would take the opportunity to catch me alone. The grass met the rocks and sharply dropped off into the steep sea cliff about forty feet from the water's edge. The currents were so swift around the point it pulled at the kelp beds rhythmically, and they waved in opposition. To the left stood the massive sea cliff where Kyle and I had first played on our inaugural trip up the road to the tiny schoolhouse. It looked massive from this perspective. I could hardly make out the small tree atop the cliff from this vantage point.

The waves below the grassy expanse churned as they neared the point. Closer in, the squeaking of the dock kept time as the smaller boats were pushed and pulled in the fluctuating tidal currents. The new positioning of the boats on the dock meant the smaller boats were out farther in the current and banged against the dock with a symphony of groans, squeaks, and sloshes. A large log floated past the point, its speed accelerating as it migrated. The water looked deceptively slow farther out in the channel, but it carried the log quickly past and out of view. I found a relatively flat rock and decided to sit and watch the water below. The kelp beds undulated with the flowing current, seemingly pushed and pulled in all directions. I wondered how they hung on in such a turbulent landscape. I wondered if they had ever known peace, or if they ever would, living in that relentless current.

High above the water a group of cormorants made their way across the island inbound for the nesting season. Their calls rang out as they floated overhead, out shadowed only by their impressive wingspan as they glided and caught the air currents with their large wing sails. The birds would suddenly lift from an air stream without so much as a flinch, hardly expending any energy as they soared through the air.

The bird's adaptability and fortitude were admirable. We would often see them soar out over the strait and dive deep into the water, contorting their body into a sleek compact bullet before hitting the water. It was remarkable watching the transformation happen midair. Kyle had told me he had found one of their nests destroyed on the far side of the lighthouse. The chicks had been nearly old enough to hatch and something had torn through the nest crushing the life out of everything.

"What's got you so deep in thought?" Joseph whispered as he approached from behind. I smiled and told him, "Just the island talking to me, telling me its secrets."

"Well, what does it say?" he whispered.

"I wouldn't be a good friend if I just up and told you her secrets, now would I?" I moved over on the rock and made room for him to sit, despite my declination of his inquiry.

"We are very much alike, you and I," he said as he sat on the rock beside me. "You come from a good family, you understand military life... well, you even have an affinity for the sea." He took out a small trinket and fidgeted with it in his hands. He closed his fist around the object and I wondering where he was going with this conversation. Out of everything I knew about myself, this was an interesting list of qualities to hear from a love interest.

"Well, I'm happy to hear my resume is up to standard Ensign Cail, just what exactly is the position I have unknowingly interviewed for?" I asked.

He ignored the slightly playful tone in my voice that would have signaled to more attentive people that the desired outcome would not be achieved with his current course.

"Willow, my intentions with you should be clear. I have already discussed my plans with the captain, and he agrees our match would be a well aligned one."

"As romantic as all that sounds..." I said sarcastically, "I don't think my father has any say in who I date or what type of alignment I choose to enter."

"There's time for all of that, Willow. You can't tell me we don't have chemistry— I can feel it and so can you. That will grow with time, but I needed to make my intentions known and ensure your family's support. I apologize if it seems callous, but every well-built plan needs an architect. I intend to build a life with you Willow."

"The last time I checked I intend to be the architect of my own life," I replied. "Thank you for your interest, but that position has already been filled." I turned and headed off to the house, reeling inside from his assumptive declaration.

"I'm not going anywhere!" he projected as I passed the azaleas and headed for the front steps. "Plenty of time!" I could hear him say as I slammed the front door.

God he was an infuriating man. To think, I would ever be ok with giving some man the helm in my own life! "This is the twenties anyways...What does he think I'm just going to let everyone else decide my fate?" I muttered as I brushed my hair and changed for the night. Rain drops started to splatter across the glass window and made a break for the sill as they gathered. I left the lamp burning as I laid in bed and watched the rain drops run down the pane. I had been awake for several hours and decided to take in some night air and sit by the sea. I knew I wouldn't risk running into Joseph tonight as he had been assigned to early duty. My father had recently instituted around the clock patrols, and he would be fast asleep in preparation.

I crept down the stairs in my afghan and winced at every board squeak underfoot. Once outside in the cool night air I took a deep breath and sank my toes into the dewy grass. The waves bounced off the rocks rhythmically below, keeping island time in the still of the night. I remembered what Margie had told me about the cold water, how it took her grief, and also how it calmed me earlier. I felt the pull to the water and decided to dip my feet in from the docks, just to see. I walked barefoot through the grass and down onto the dock stairs.

The pier was dark except for the slow passing beam of light with every rotation of the lighthouse beacon overhead. I walked to the end of the dock and sat on the outermost edge. The tide was high, and the water splashed over the rocks next to me. The rhythmic sway of the dock and the lapping of the water created a soothing melody in my head as I thought through the events of the evening. The night was thick with fog that lay suspended over the water. It was heavy and cold with every breath, yet calming and grounding. I felt my life headed in a direction I didn't want it to take and felt trapped by my situation yet again. I wanted to be free to live my own life and be me, not a Captain's daughter, or now a trophy wife for someone else to parade around. I felt like a commodity to be traded lately, but outside in the blanket of fog and the mist of the evening I began to feel protected and hidden. The giant beam of light shot out above me and all around in a perfect circle, but here on the dock I evaded its path of exposure, safely concealed near the water's edge, tucked into the fog and the darkness.

The slow rhythm of the waves created an undeniable pull to the sea and I dipped my feet into the black water. The cold stung my feet and instantly made me recoil from the frigid water. *How the heck did I swim in this?* I thought. I dried my feet with the edges of the afghan and heard a slight creak from the direction of the water. Through the mist a faint golden glow emanated from inside the fog. The light flashed and flickered faintly, and the hull of a boat came into view. It was incredibly close to the shoreline and paralleled the land like it had been tethered to a track and not floating on the surface. Tall black sails were raised and went almost unnoticed in the dense fog. The figure of a man appeared slowly as he leaned on the helm and doused the lantern to a low flicker. The soft yellow glow illuminated his face for a split second as he turned toward the dock and before the darkness enveloped him. It was such a brief encounter, I wondered if I had dreamed it, or he was a ghost or a mythical thing creeping out of the liminal opacity between dusk and dawn. As quickly as he had come into view, he vanished into the fog and disappeared back into the night.

I second guessed myself if I had even seen anyone at all, it happened so quickly. A soft drizzle formed as I peered for a closer look, but the ship had disappeared. The cold drops of water on my face spurned whatever magic the night air previously held, and I headed back up to the main house to get some sleep. True night on the island smelled absolutely intoxicating during a rain. I breathed the surrounding forest in deeply as I walked back to the house. I had never smelled anything like it living as many places as we had. The salt air and the huge forest intermixed in the misty darkness, and I tried to commit it to memory as I walked back up the path and out of the cold. Oliver was waiting for me on the steps, and I hurried to greet him before he decided to sing. I gave his head a gentle pat and opened the door and he sauntered in. I guess we both couldn't sleep that night, I thought, as he stealthily climbed the steps without so much as a creak. I was jealous of his footwork and hoped I could do half as good a job.

Morning came, and with it the fatigue of being up half the night. I lingered cozied up to Oliver who had curled up in the crook of my legs. He yawned and stretched as I stirred and then flopped over on his back, also unwilling to extricate himself from the warmth of the bed. Exams were in two days, and the island social was later that week. What were supposed to be joyous occasions, now carried the weight of my father's expectation with them. I knew these summer milestones meant decisions and potentially disappointing either my father or myself. I just wished I was out from under his thumb, and college was one way, the only way, I knew to do that. I wasn't particularly excited about attending college, other than the fact that it would bring me the independence I had yearned for. Most of the things I had been excited to learn were from my own reading and time spent with others who were passionate about something. I didn't anticipate college providing the kind of knowledge I was craving, but ultimately, there was escape in the escaping after all.

The weekend had arrived, and everyone was independently busy with projects or play. Marjorie's father and brothers had just returned from a successful fishing trip. She would be busy until the day of the island social helping repair nets, cleaning, and prepping the boat for the next trip. I decided to take the day and explore Reid Harbor and the more Southern parts of the island alone. I brought a satchel and a book to collect wildflowers and press them. I wanted to make Marjorie something special for her hideaway and I needed local flora of the island to put it together.

I set out down the road and into the filtered light of the forest canopy. The air was warm and smelled sweetly of summer for the first time. I meandered up the hill, in no hurry, stopping to admire the island's bounty. Clumps of sea thrift had sprung up in some of the wind-swept exposures on the coast side of the road. Tall stalks of fireweed were also beginning to emerge along the road on the forest side. Color was starting to reveal itself everywhere on the island and the forest was filled with the sounds of birds and new life in general.

I walked along the road for a time and decided to turn onto a small path that led to a collection of large rock formations several hundred yards off the main road. Daisies peppered the tall grass and the leaves softly rustled overhead, both swaying in the rhythmic breeze of the island. The island was incredibly beautiful and peaceful this time of year. The madrone trees interspersed with the fir and the comparison made an interesting contrast in both size and form. The fir was pin straight, tall, and massive, each one almost identical to the next in trajectory. The madrone trees seemed to laugh in the face of conformity, with no two trees ascribing to the same rules. They twisted and hung precariously off rocks and cliffs. Some grew close to the ground, while others grew predominantly upward. Even the color of the bark varied wildly from a black and brown, to a deep orange, or to green. Many of the trees had peeling bark that revealed layers of colors, as they shed the old and entered a new season of their life.

The footpath meandered around the base of the giant boulders and made its way behind them. A small grove of Garry oak surrounded the boulders along the far side of the rock. The two largest rocks had round faces and more gently sloped to the back like ice cream cones laying on their sides. Along the sloped rear an indentation had been formed over time by erosion and the elements that loosely resembled a seat. It appeared that someone else had had the same idea as I had, as evidenced by the small piles of wood shavings to the right of the makeshift seat. Strewn on the ground a few feet in front of the seat were two half-finished wood carvings the artist had given up on mid carve. I walked over to the pile and picked one up for closer inspection. The detail was impressive, with multiple curves and turns in the wood. The carving was made of madrone and was fashioned in the shape of a horse coming out of the waves. The other was much smaller and was in the shape of a seal but was missing a flipper. The wood knot appeared to have torn out mid carve and the artist had cast it aside and abandoned the project. I took a seat on the rock indentation and ran the small seal carving around in my hand. It was beautiful and intricate and made me marvel at the fine detail the artist captured, suspended in the wood.

There were no other clues as to the identity of the mystery artist as I scanned the rockface, aside from a small feeder and a wooden box that had been nailed into one of the fir trees. As I approached the box the sweet sounds of young songbirds calling for their mother could be heard. I stood on a small rock near the tree to get a look inside the box and was greeted by four young wrens with mouths open gently calling. I smiled at the sight of them, and for the obvious care that someone had taken for them. Tufts of sheep wool and strips of old cloth had been gently woven together to line the box. The birds sat sweetly nestled together, waiting on the return of their mother and the promise of nourishment. The mother's call echoed from a nearby tree, and I retreated at the sound, not wanting to frighten her.

I leaned back on the rocky hardscape and rested in the dappled light. The oak trees overhead interlocked together creating channel like gaps between the branches, without ever touching. I admired how each tree maximized their own living space while careful not to encroach on the other's light path. This natural phenomenon was in stark contrast to the forest floor where everything was in a race for space, water, and light. The grasses and flowers, intermingling, sprawling, and choking each other out in their fight for existence. It was a first to the top race, and the winner took all. The forest floor reminded me of people sometimes as I yearned for the space I needed to grow into my own path. I tucked the discarded seal carving into my pocket and headed back toward the harbor in search of more wildflowers for Margie's gift.

Reid Harbor was much more secluded and had more of an intimate feeling that Prevost. There wasn't really any beach, save for a small stretch at the most interior web of the finger cove. Steep jagged cliffs lined the narrow cove, and the water was the most beautiful jade green I had ever seen. A narrow hill separated the two harbors, making each one invisible to the other by only a small stretch of land. The two harbors lay in parallel to each other but geographically were vastly different.

Reid Harbor was narrow, deep, and mostly inaccessible for foot traffic from the island due to the steep cliffs and large timbered hills. Prevost Harbor was more shallow, exposed, and open in two parts to the massive Strait. It was also more precarious as large shoals formed at the far shallow entrance. The massive jutting rocks that appeared on the island landscape were also present under the harbor as well. The area had been formed by massive shifts in the earth's crust and reflected in the topography of both island and seafloor. The seafloor was jagged, broken, and unforgiving and then suddenly sandy, deep, and calm. It was beautiful but treacherous if you weren't careful. Most of the locals knew the harbors and surrounding coastline like the back of their hand and knew where navigable channels were and where to avoid.

I decided to follow the Prevost coastline as it seemed better suited for avoiding inadvertently falling off a cliff into the cold green water below. Clumps of foxglove lined the trail that wound around the small coves of the surrounding harbor. It really was a majestic setting. As much as I had resisted liking my situation, the island was full of surprises, and it was growing more familiar and comforting with each passing moment. I had collected more than enough flowers for my project and now just found myself wandering and exploring in the afternoon shade. The water lapped softly at the shoreline, and I weaved back and forth from beach to the trail marveling at all the island offered.

A small homestead could be seen just across the bay at the far end of Prevost. Whisps of smoke streamed out of the tall chimney of the home that sat on the edge of the tree line and the shore, effectively straddling both worlds. As I drew closer to the small home's facade, I noticed the intricate stone patterns that were built into the structure. They looked Celtic in nature and had been partially covered in lichen and moss for many years. A low stone wall separated the small yard from being consumed by the awaiting forest. A soft glow emanated out from the low windows and a sweet tortoiseshell cat sat like a loaf of bread on the sill inside. It softly blinked in my direction, and I smiled back unconsciously.

The trail wound past the end of the harbor into the woods to the South, but I decided this was far enough for today and turned back along the path. The tide was coming up now and the water was covering where I had once walked on the beach below. A low grumble echoed down the path ahead, perhaps a herd of deer, and my heart quickened. I didn't think there were large predators on the island, but whatever it was had definite size to it. As I approached the bend, I could hear soft bleating and the thud of hooves on the stone and dirt path. Several wooly sheep emerged meandering on and off the trail foraging as they walked. A small bell around one sheep's neck softly clanged as it jumped from a craggy hillside of the path. They were thick with wool and in need of shearing as the season progressed.

As I was admiring the beautiful animals as they passed, I hadn't noticed a small form bringing up the rear of the flock until she as very near to me. She was a small elderly woman, with frizzy white hair and sparkling eyes that conveyed wisdom and a life story that would probably be fascinating to hear. She was wrapped in a long green cloak and carried a large worn shepherd's hook. She appeared kind, but also cautious and kept on her path directly towards me in a matter-of-fact way.

"Good afternoon, ma'am," I said politely.

"Ma'am she says, aye," she said in a thick Irish accent that ended in a chuckle. "I don't be knowin' anyting about that, but it is indeed a grand afternoon at that," she said as her blue eyes twinkled.

"My name is Willow, ma'am. Pleased to meet you."

"Like the tree, Oh I know who yar. Best be sure. And does this Willow have an affinity for our island and the sea? Does the island tell you its secrets and hold yours?" she said as she passed by, following her sheep along the path, clicking her tongue as she walked.

I didn't know what to say to that, so I ended up just staring at her as she passed. She turned and winked at me and said, "Go on and keep your island secrets now Willow." and she chuckled and shooed a straggling sheep as she walked. She ambled back down the path and out of sight around a bend. I laughed to myself in amusement over the oddity of our encounter. I wondered if she had been the inhabitant of the small stone house at the edge of the forest and I was determined to learn more about her and what was behind those sparkling blue eyes and leathery skin.

I walked home along the path as the sun dipped lower over the island. The breeze above rustled the stiff madrone leaves, and it sounded like a deck of cards being shuffled overhead when it blew. Sea birds called out to one another as they passed, suspended midair by gusts of wind. I felt like one of those birds now, momentarily stalled by life circumstance and awaiting the inevitable ascent or fall depending on which way

I adjusted my wings. The birds seemed unbothered by the change in wind and bobbed and weaved with the invisible currents, some even seemed to enjoy them if you watched for long enough.

6

One Thread of Gold

Exams were over and the school year had officially come to a close. Miss Katie had given each pupil a gift on the last day of school, and they were as uniquely thoughtful as she was. For Margie, she had a beautiful ukelele that she had picked up from a cannery worker in Friday Harbor, who had emigrated from the Hawaiian Islands. The instrument was hand carved and intricately painted and Marjorie couldn't put it down. For Charlie, she had given him a magnifying glass and he had been lost to his newfound world for the entire morning. He would only look up from the ground long enough to yell at anyone who would listen about what he had found. For me, she had given a small leatherbound notebook that had been pulled and shaped to form a willow tree on the cover. The inside was blank except for the first page, which had the following inscribed, "The pages are yours to fill, a world of possibility awaits…" I smiled at the beautifully lettered sentiment and the thought behind it.

Kyle had received a beautifully carved toy sailboat and was holding it over his head as he created imaginary waves for the boat to ride through the air. The sailboat looked oddly familiar, and I couldn't immediately place why I had that feeling. My mind raced back to the seal carving, and I remembered the familiar lines and matching wood grain of the seal. Both carvings were done from madrone wood and were nearly identical in style and technique. "Where did you get that Miss Katie?" I asked.

"There's a local here on island who likes to carve, and I had asked him to make a small sailboat for our resident boat enthusiast," she said as she tousled his hair as he walked past, still engrossed in his imaginary squall as the boat heeled over in his small hand.

"Well, I think I found his carving spot." I pulled the small seal from my skirt pocket and held it out for her to see.

"How wonderfully serendipitous." Miss Katie took the small seal carving from my hand, examined it, chuckled, and handed it back to me.

I thought about my gift to Margie and wondered if the carver could help me with my project as well.

"Miss Katie, do you know where I could find him?"

"His farm is on the corner before you turn onto Lighthouse Road, it's the MacDara farm. You could stop in on your way home from school," she said.

That afternoon I walked home with Margie and we said our usual goodbye at the turn off. I walked a short way up the road in the direction of the lighthouse, and then back tracked the road toward Prevost Harbor and the main house of the

MacDara farm. The gift needed to be a surprise, and I couldn't risk having to explain my visit to the farm had I been seen.

The pasture ran parallel to the road and the house was set back toward the water. A split rail fence ran the length of the road, and the rail sections were attached to large natural posts made of intricately stacked rock. I admired the craftsmanship of the stacked stone and how beautiful the simple fence was. Clumps of hollyhock, foxglove, and thistle grew along the fence line and provided a beautiful foreground for the picturesque farm that was revealed as the main house came into view.

The house was large and beautiful, but at the same time charming and welcoming. It was constructed of wood and stone and whomever had built the house must have had an artist eye as well as been a skilled craftsman. Large carved shutters framed each of the main windows, which revealed glimpses of the harbor view behind the home. Black trim framed the house, and a large porch anchored the front of the home to the landscape. The porch housed beautiful hand carved rockers and benches. Ferns and island wildflowers rested in carved wooden vessels. Their pops of color speckled the porch area and breathed life into the beautiful hardscape. A few small outbuildings and a barn lay to the right of the farmhouse.

Just as I approached the house steps, a black and white dog came around the side of the barn to greet me. It scampered up to me quickly and circled me while panting and wagging its tail. I crouched down to welcome the enthusiastic greeting, and the dog eagerly accepted the invitation of friendship. The playful pup quickly ran into my arms and started licking my face and squirming like a fish on a hook. The fervent greeting almost knocked me off my feet when I heard a man whistle. The dog immediately retreated a few feet and laid down on the ground motionless. I turned in the direction of the whistle to see an older gentleman with white hair in faded coveralls and muck boots wiping his hands on a handkerchief and walking towards me. As he approached, I could see kindness in his steel blue eyes and the rosy cheeks that highlighted them. He softly called to the pup and the dog quickly sprang up and sprinted to the old man and sat at his feet. The gentleman started walking toward me and the dog kept in stride with him expectantly watching his face for cues.

"Well now what do I owe the pleasure?" he welcomed. "Good afternoon Miss, how are ya on this fine day lass?" the gentleman said in a very thick Scottish brogue. His eyes twinkled as he spoke, and his voice was whisper soft as he lilted. He offered an outstretched hand as the dog looked up at him adoringly and back to me while he panted.

"Good afternoon Mr. MacDara, I presume? What a pleasure to meet you, I'm Willow Donovan," I chimed in as I took his outstretched hand. "I was referred to you by the schoolteacher, Miss Katie. I'm also an admirer of your work. I was wondering if you might be able to help me with a gift I'm making for my dearest friend Marjorie Borcher."

He stopped me with a gentle hand on my back and began guiding me to the front porch as he said, "Well lass, that's all you had to say, anything for Marjorie, why I'd give her my last bag of flour or the shirt off my own back, for that one. Ach, any friend of Marjorie's is a friend of mine, I'm as good as yours, and at your service."

He bowed to me playfully and asked if I'd like to have some tea and discuss the project and get to know one another. He ushered me to the far bench and excused himself into the house to prepare the tea. The door to the house was a massive wooden slab that was arched and looked Old World in design. The door was fastened with huge iron hinges that were rusted from the salt air of the islands. They groaned slightly as he swung them open to go inside.

The dog laid down next to me and kept a watch on the road and surrounding pasture. It was clearly a working dog and seemed very capable at their post. My new friend also kept one ear to Mr. MacDara, its ears swiveling at each sound coming from inside the house. "How do you take your tea, love?" he called.

"Oh, however you do will be lovely, Sir."

He told me that just wouldn't do, and a few moments later he came around the corner with a tray loaded with fresh milk, lemon, sugar, and honey.

"Everyone has a preference now, don't be afraid to speak up and let the world know what ya think about it." He took a seat in the carved rocker and set the tray down between us. He took a cup of tea in his hand and spooned a glob of thick amber honey into his tea and said, "Now ya see here, this is how I prefer it, but don't you let that influence yourself. Ya, ya... see there how it sinks to the bottom. One quick stir and let it be. Now that's a cup of tea." He clinked the teaspoon on the side of the cup. "Now then, you go," he said to me as he gestured toward the tea station between us.

I focused my attention on the tray in front of me and began, "Well now I am a woman of strong opinion, and also humble enough to recognize a true tea connoisseur when I see one… so I suppose I will see your honey glob…and raise you a small squeeze of lemon," I said playfully as I squeezed the fresh lemon into the cup.

"Well now I know when I've been beat," he said, "It's time to hang up my hat and recognize a genius when I've seen one." He whistled softly under his breath and chuckled. His eyes twinkled and he tucked his hands into the bib of his overall. We chatted for over an hour on the porch like old friends who had been reunited. He was the most endearing old fellow and I thoroughly enjoyed hearing his stories of island life and his early years in Scotland. He had lost his wife a few years back and the pain of her loss was still evident in his eyes as he spoke of her. He gestured toward the house as he told me,

"I built this house for her, you know. She painted it in watercolor before it was here… when this was just woodlands and meadow. She was a magnificent artist." He inhaled deeply and grabbed the buckles of his overalls like a lifeline in his turbulent sea of memories and continued. "She had the vision, I couldn't see it, but I brought that painting to life for her. She had the most wonderful eye you see— she could make anything beautiful. She brought life to the house. She made it a home."

His eyes grew misty as he introduced me to the history of his farm and the most special parts of his life. Mr. MacDara had come to the States from Scotland with his wife and son, who was nearly five when they arrived. He told me his son was out sailing today and was surprised I hadn't run into him yet. We chatted into the soft light of evening, discussing the specifications for the project, and I told him I would be back with the wood branch for the project once I located it. His smile emanated out of the creases of his eyes as he said goodbye and he saw me to the road.

The morning of the island social was buzzing with energy around the lighthouse. The men had been given liberal leave for the day, save one keeper per shift. The entire island would be in attendance, and it was probably the most exciting thing to happen since our arrival on island; everyone was talking about it. As much as Joseph's calculated proposal had left a bad taste in my mouth, the idea of a social gathering with people my own age overrode my annoyance.

Marjorie had been working on a new dress for weeks after finding inspiration in one of my mother's magazine hand-me-downs, and my closet. She insisted on making me wait for the big reveal until today. I could hear the front door swing open and her heels pounding up the steps long before my mother's announcement made its way up the stairs that Marjorie had arrived.

"Are you ready for it?" she said excitedly as she closed the bedroom door and laid her garment bag on the bed as she looked over at me with glee.

"I have never been more ready!" I told her as she hurriedly unbuckled the bag.

As the tan bag unfurled it revealed a fold of fabric so scarlet it was nearly maroon in appearance. Margie gently removed the dress from the bag, cradling it like a new baby and admiring it in the same manner. Pride beamed from her entire body as she held the dress out for me to size up. The neckline was exquisite, and I knew before she even tried it on that it would suit her entirely.

"Oh Margie, it's divine!" I declared. "Sam is the luckiest man in the world tonight; I can tell you that!"

She batted her eyes playfully and beamed at my response and then twirled with the dress draped over the front of her. The deep scarlet fabric accentuated her deep red lips and milky white skin. Marjorie could really make magic, and I marveled at how beautiful she was, and how joy seemed to radiate from her. Her ethereal movements around the room highlighted the satisfaction and happiness I felt in watching her joy. Her happiness was contagious, and I started to feel the excitement well up inside of me, joyful for the hope and beauty of it all.

We spent the afternoon in a sort of idle luxury, stretching out small tasks of preparation to savor the feeling that came with anticipation. My mother had called up to us as she made her way up the stairs that the boys would be around with the car in twenty minutes. Sam would be escorting Marjorie on foot up the road to the new barn and would be up the walk shortly. Marjorie and I came onto the landing to gasps of awe only a mother can make. She gushed over us both, Marjorie in red and I in a midnight blue.

"You ladies are the picture of stunning!" she exclaimed as her hands reached out to each of us, "I think… no, I know, I have never seen two more beautiful young women in all my life." We giggled as we descended the wooden stairs and hugged her as she beamed with pride for both of us.

"Mrs. Donovan, if I may, you are the picture of a Greek goddess, and it is my solemn vow to worship and admire you for evermore." Marjorie gestured dramatically as she threw her hands over her head and back down together simulating worship.

My mother laughed and said, "This is why you're my favorite Margie." and they both giggled as we walked into the kitchen to gather the potluck dishes for the picnic. Marjorie was softly humming in the kitchen when the thud of Sam's knuckles met the big wood door. I turned to Margie and flashed the widest grin. I scurried to the door to let him in.

Sam was standing in his dress uniform, beard trimmed, shoes polished and holding a bouquet of wildflowers for Marjorie. He looked nervously past me, and I melted when I saw his first glimpse of Margie. His boyish uneasiness rapidly faded into a certainty, a purpose even, as she walked toward him. I am entirely certain a pack of wild wolves could have run across the front porch at that precise moment and Sam would never have seen them. He rushed to her with eyes locked on her like an invisible string pulling him into her atmosphere. He offered her the flowers and apologized for not having words suitable to match the level of her beauty.

"Every word I know doesn't do ya justice Miss Borcher," he stammered.

Marjorie slowly descended the front steps and looked over her shoulder coyly at him. "That'll do," she said playfully as he quickened his step to offer his arm to her.

"You kids have fun, be careful, and we'll be right up as well!" my mother called to her. Sam was still locked in on Marjorie and I fully think the two of them forgot that we existed. My mother and I watched as Sam and Marjorie disappeared up the road, her arm in his.

We retreated through the large front door and into the parlor to wait for our gentleman escorts. I first caught sight of Joseph as he glided past the front window facing out to the porch. He had a confident stride to his gait, and he looked incredibly striking in his dress blues. He was clean shaven and held something small in his hand as he approached the door. I faintly heard my father start the car out back as he arrived at the door. My mother rose to answer, and I stood as well, suddenly unsure where to put my hands or how normal people stand. I quickly elected to clasp my hands together and look toward the window. He walked in and I attempted to turn nonchalantly to meet his gaze. My mother grinned and excused herself to the kitchen.

"You're the picture of perfection; you know that don't you?" he said to me as he walked over grinning. He swiftly picked up my hand and kissed it gently before I even knew he had done it. "I'd like you to wear this tonight," he said. "It was my mothers, and it would be an honor to see it on such a stunning creature." He circled behind me and laid out a gold chain and clasped it behind my neck. The chain fell softly on my skin, suspending a citrine pendant that was held in place by two delicate birds made of gold. The stone caught the light and gave off a fiery glint as I shifted to see it. I felt his breath on the back of my neck and my head tilted as he moved.

I looked up into the mirror above the fireplace and watched as his hands rested on my shoulders as he admired the necklace. His gaze rose to meet mine and I could feel his breath again on my skin. His chest pressed into my back for a slight moment, and my skin tingled where his hands and breath had fallen. He really was incredibly handsome, and maybe I had judged him too harshly. My eyes traced the ridge of his jawline and the depth of his shoulders, erasing my earlier annoyance at his callousness, drawing me in like an angler. He was a man after all, and men seldom said the right thing at the right time.

I was jolted back to reality with the sudden swing of the front door and my father calling to the kitchen for my mother. "Emily, I've pulled the car around, are you ready dear?" he bellowed as he walked toward the sound of my mother collecting the final items for the social. She bustled through the hallway carrying a basket and blankets and right past the two of us, off to greet my father as he kissed her cheek mechanically. "You look lovely dear," he offered without even looking at her as he grabbed the items and turned about face to head to the car. Joseph looked over at me and offered his arm with a confident smile. I softly placed my hand on his bicep and felt the round muscle harden as he bent his arm to meet my grasp.

The car was sparkling, as usual, as my father opened the doors for us all. We loaded inside and I caught my mother stealing side glances of us, thoroughly enjoying the idea of getting to be present on my first official date on the island. I shot her a playful glare and she knew she had been caught and quickly averted her gaze elsewhere.

The festivities were being held just up the road at the new MacDara/Ericksen barn located on the edge of their properties. The two families had jointly raised the barn together and had generously allowed the island families a place to gather before it would be filled with hay and grain from their upcoming harvest. The barn was a beautiful vibrant red with white trim and it had been decorated by the Ericksen family special for the social. Long wood tables were set up outside the barn with gorgeous wildflower arrangements in the center. Families were starting to gather and congregate around the tables for food. Each family had brought an item to share, and the tables were filling fast with their family specialties. The barn doors were propped open and revealed a small stage and beverage station. Candles were clustered together in large hurricane glasses along the floor and the walls of the barn, waiting to be lit. The sun was just sinking below the tree line to the west as the sky cast orange and maroon streaks of light against the purple glow of sunset.

We settled in around a long wooden table toward the barn as Marjorie and Sam reunited with the group. We quickly embraced and sorted ourselves for the evening. Mr. MacDara approached the barn entrance with another gentleman, whom would later be introduced as Mr. Ericksen, and welcomed everyone to the social. A special introduction was given welcoming my father to the island, and he stood and waved to everyone ceremoniously. The beautiful black and white dog had also decided to come and lay a few yards off, just inside the barn on the cool ground. As the two gentlemen wrapped up the welcomes and the crowd proceeded to the food tables, I headed for the dog, eager to say hello again. As soon as I neared the door her head popped up and she started panting heavily while her tail thumped the ground rhythmically. "Hello beautiful!" I said to her as she laid her chin in my hand and low crawled around me. She curled up at my feet and wrapped herself around my legs and whined excitedly. In her excitement, she entangled herself in my legs and leaned into me with full force. I momentarily lost my balance and started a slow fall toward the barn floor.

In a blur, an outstretched hand gathered me up and righted me almost as if the fall had never happened. The dog excitedly hurried to the gentleman, and he looked down at her and ruffled her ears and softly scolded her. "Ach Lola, look what you've done to the poor lass. Here she was giving you praises, and you try and run her into the ground. Where are your manners?" he said as his hands gently cupped her face. Lola looked up at him adoringly as she sat on his feet and her tail thumped devotedly.

"Are you alright, she hasn't caused you too much grief I hope?" he said as he turned toward me. His full face had come into view, and we were suddenly standing inches from one and other. His eyes sparkled familiarly and were filled with genuine concern and kindness. My face softened and I felt the corners of my mouth turn up in an easy smile.

"None whatsoever. It was I who lost my balance, thank you for your quick action and steady hand," I said as I smoothed the folds of my dress and Lola panted happily below us.

"Well, dinnae fash about your dress, it's just as lovely as it was the first time I saw you walk in." The corners of his mouth turned up playfully as he spoke the kind words. I could feel myself blush and tucked a strand of my hair behind my ear nervously. His broad shoulders rippled with trim muscle as his full frame came into view. He was very tall but had a naturally disarming quality about him. There was a calmness to him that struck me, juxtapositioned by his tall, visually imposing frame. He had sandy brown hair that curled ever so slightly around his ears and a light stubble on his face that glinted red in the light. His eyes were a sparkling blue grey, and soft creases outlined the corners of his eyes when he smiled. He had a strong jaw and soft dimples that I couldn't help but notice as he spoke.

"I'm Mack," he said as he looked over to me expectantly.

"I'm Willow," I replied with a genuine smile.

Just then Joseph had come around the corner and immediately made his way to my side. He told me the family was waiting for everyone to be seated before eating. "Please excuse us." He offered a stiff arm and an almost unnoticed backward glare to Mack. They seemed to have a history, and no love was lost between the two of them in their brief exchange.

"It was so very nice to meet you and thank you again!' I said over my shoulder as we headed toward the tables.

Joseph pulled me in tighter and whispered, "Have I told you that you look exceptionally beautiful tonight?" He smiled and held his head high as my family came into view and my mother waved over to us to sit.

"Aren't you two the picture of youth!" she said as we approached. My father nodded and smiled back to us and said "come, sit, sit. Let's eat."

The food was delicious and plentiful. The islanders had all prepared their best dishes showcasing their farms' specialty produce. There were sheep's milk cheeses and ham, apple and berry tarts, sourdough boules, and fresh cider. The table was filled with smoked salmon and fish, fresh clams and mussels, as well as an assortment of scones and preserves. The spread was a lovely introduction to the island's bounty and the generosity of the people who lived there. Even the island hermit Willis Maxfield was in attendance and had donated a venison roast for the festivities. We ate and talked as the sun fell behind the trees and the islanders prepared the barn for music and dancing. The large hurricane votives had been lit and the barn glowed with soft yellow light. A collective cheer from the crowd could be heard when the band struck up a few chords and the islanders migrated toward the music. Joseph grabbed my hand and gestured to the dance floor.

The barn was buzzing with music and energy as the islanders began to pair up and move to the lively music. Joseph spun me around and I laughed at his suddenly playful mood. He was charming and attentive as we danced around the barn. Margie and Sam were paired up and were the hit of the dancefloor. They both had a flair for drama and enjoyed the eyes of the crowd as they maneuvered and spun intricate extra movements into the dance steps. Their eyes were locked on each other, and they were having the time of their lives as the crowd cheered them on. Even my father was letting loose and laughed with my mother at their attempts to mimic the more complicated moves. We all clapped for the band as they played nonstop, elevating the energy and mood.

"Joseph, I need a break!" I panted as the song wrapped up and I ended a twirl into his arms.

"As you wish my dear, I'll get us some cider and find a seat outside to cool off. I think your parents just settled outside at a table anyhow."

I broke away to the dessert table and left Joseph to fetch beverages. The assortment of cakes, pies, and tarts were a testament to the islanders' diverse backgrounds and creativity. A warm blackberry cobbler caught my eye, and I served myself a heaping scoop. I scoured the table for silverware and couldn't find a single set. I searched again, moving pies out of the way and cursed my bad luck at their absence. To my right a shining silver fork appeared over my shoulder, and I turned to see Mack walking past as he placed it on my plate of cobbler.

"I can't keep saving your life like this," he teased.

I laughed and thanked him as he winked and walked past me with Lola in tow. She happily pranced past me, panting and smiling as some dogs do.

I started making my way to the outdoor tables as Sam and Marjorie came into view. Sam was dripping with sweat and as red as Marjorie's dress, while Marjorie was beaming from ear to ear. They were both laughing and pawing each other as they walked, completely engrossed in one another. Their joy was contagious, and I smiled as I watched them walk across the lawn to the waiting table. She had experienced so much loss in her life; it made my heart happy to see her filled with love on this early summer night. Marjorie clung tight to Sam's arm as they walked together, and she leaned into him. He beamed with pride and admiration for her, and his feelings were written all over his face.

My father and mother were sitting just outside the big barn doors and my mother was wrapped snugly in her shawl. She had a look of satisfaction to her as the soft light fell onto her face and she turned to me. Joseph had just come out of the barn with cider in hand and walked toward our table. My father stood and Joseph set the cups down and modeled my father's posture.

"Well, I suppose we ought to leave the rest of the evening to the younger generation. Your mother and I are going to walk home," he said as he turned to Joseph, "And I trust ensign, that both my daughter and my automobile will be in good hands in my absence," he asserted as he flipped him the car keys.

"Without a doubt, Sir," Joseph quickly replied.

I resented being lumped in with a possession, and my own well-being delegated to a man. *I was fully capable of taking good care of myself, thank you...* I thought to myself. I unconsciously made a face that only my mother noticed, and she quickly compensated.

"Now Willow, you look after Ensign Cail and make sure he behaves himself," she teased. My father frowned and wrapped his arm around my mother as we said our goodbyes and they started toward home.

Sam and Margie walked up just as my parents were leaving and we all looked at each other excitedly to finally be free of the formality of the evening and to be left to our own devices. Marjorie grabbed my hand, and we all raced back to the barn for more dancing. The band was gearing up and began playing a reel that got a few of the islanders on their feet and center stage. They began clapping with Sam, who charged to the middle leading the chant. The man on the bass gestured to the back of the room, and I turned to see Mack make his way through the crowd and get hoisted up on the makeshift stage. One of the band members placed a fiddle in his hands and the whole crowd cheered. He tipped his hat and nodded to the crowd and the lively music started like clockwork.

The drummer was beaming as Mack expertly plucked the strings and ran the bow across the instrument in time to the beat. A cloud of white powder flew from the bow as it flew across the strings as he played. The crowd was clapping and lining up for a dance and Marjorie grabbed my hand and said, "Follow me!" as we fell into line.

Sam was the volunteer official caller and began loudly yelling out the next moves of the group dance. "All the fellas in!" he roared as the men sauntered into the center of the barn forming a circle and then quickly retreating. "Now the ladies!" Marjorie grabbed my hand as we skipped to the beat into the center circle in step with the lively tune. I could see Mr. MacDara at the front of the line swinging his arms and tapping his feet to the music gayly. Mack looked down on him as he played and threw his head back in laughter and joy.

Mack's hat slid from his head and landed squarely in my hands as I do-si-doed past him. I laughed as it happened and gestured for him to bend down. He dropped to his knee, and I placed it on his head gently. He winked and smiled mischievously back to me, still keeping time to the music.

I called up to him, "I suppose now we're even!"

He rose to his feet, unable to contain the huge grin as he looked down at me, his dimples on full display.

"Twirl your partner!" Sam bellowed and Joseph quickly whisked me toward the right side of the barn as we danced, away from the band, and away from Mack.

I didn't want the night to end. It felt like home for the first time in a long time and I tried to soak it in for as long as I could. Eventually, like all good things, it had to come to an end, and we gathered our things and made our way to the car. We had promised to drive Margie home, and Joe, Sam, and I would return to the lighthouse together. Margie and Sam filed into the back seat, and she slid back across the bench seat next to him. He looked ecstatic and both Joe and I averted our gaze simultaneously. Joseph started the car, and we set out down the road toward Prevost Harbor and the Borcher house. Margie was humming softly as her head leaned onto Sam's shoulder and the moonlight streamed into the car as we drove. Sam slid out of the car as soon as we pulled into the carriageway of Margie's house and opened the door for her. He whispered something to her, and I could see Margie grin even through the darkness. He kissed her on the cheek and they disappeared in the cover of night as he walked her to the door. He returned moments later obviously lovestruck and floating through the night air back into the car.

"You better tie yourself off tonight Sam, or you might float away," Joseph teased as Sam returned.

Sam grinned and said, "Tease me all ya like lad, find what I found, and you'd be in the clouds as well." Joseph just sneered and shook his head as he pulled out to the road toward home.

7

Free Flowing Sails

The excitement of the last week's festivities had died down and we all settled back into the slower pace of island life. The lighthouse men were busy making repairs to the oil room and my father was making plans and readying the small fleet for his new patrol around Haro Strait. He had found a loyal following in a few of the young ensigns, particularly in Joseph. They saw eye to eye on prohibition rum running and they had been busy the last few weeks discussing a system of patrols around the area.

My mother had fully settled the family into our new post and was just now enjoying the fruits of her labor. She sat contently on the front porch watching Kyle play along the rocks and on the dock most afternoons. He was loving life at the lighthouse and could usually be found along the shoreline hunting for shells and crabs or collecting driftwood for his fort along the tree line. Life had slowed down and I too felt a certain peace settling in, a kind of insulation from the rest of the world. I suppose that made sense given the massive moat of Salish Sea surrounding our remote island fortress.

When Joe wasn't with my father, he was making frequent visits to wherever I happened to be at Turn Point. He was really making an effort to connect with me, but it all seemed so forced on some level. Logically speaking, a relationship with him just made sense. Afterall, he was incredibly handsome, driven, and my family seemed to really like him as well. Despite his efforts to spend time with me, I wondered if he ever actually saw me. If his affections grew for my spirit, or merely for what I represented— the idea of me. Afterall, I made sense as well for him. He had made that clear from the start. I wanted love though... genuine affection. I wanted someone who wanted my company, not money, or position, or social status. Perhaps I was overthinking things, but I had yet to feel a connection to him beyond the physical. Fortunately, I wasn't pressed to figure everything out today. Neither of us were going anywhere and time was a luxury I had a lot of these days. I didn't have a lot going on at the current moment, and the distraction of the possibility of a love interest was a good problem to have.

Meanwhile, Margie was full steam ahead plowing through her brand-new romance at full throttle. She spent her days writing songs, no doubt inspired by her newfound love, and living her best life. She was so full of joy, I'm not sure who enjoyed seeing it more, Sam or myself. He was her biggest fan, aside from me, and gleefully encouraged her creative side that summer. Perhaps my blossoming relationship with Joe, set against that kind of standard, was the reason for my hesitation. The way they cared for each other and supported each other was not the default for most relationships I had witnessed. There was a genuineness to their mutual adoration, and it went much deeper than what the other person afforded them by being by their side. He saw Margie's spirit, and she his, and they both genuinely liked the person underneath the exterior facade. It was rare, and I felt so fortunate to be there to witness it. It was the kind of thing you couldn't unsee, and I'm sure it fed the seeds of doubt I was beginning to feel about Joe.

After feeling restless all morning, I decided to set out and source the madrone wood I would need for Mr. MacDara and our secret project. My first trip out to Satellite Island with Margie had been weighing on me ever since. Margie was happy, but I also knew a part of her was missing after her mother's passing. I knew that old driftwood shack, and the lookout point all held deep family memories and I wanted to help her keep those memories alive and honor her relationship with her mother. It would have been hard losing a mother, but the other hit was being alone on her journey into womanhood. There were some things brothers and a father just couldn't understand, and I was so grateful I had come to the island when I had. We both needed a sister, and the island had brought us together at just the right time.

It didn't take me too long to find the right piece of wood for the project, surprisingly. I needed a semi straight piece of the dense wood to support the glass case that would be perched on top. Most of the branches were beautifully twisted, but I had found a relatively obedient branch that forked perfectly about six feet in. I must have been a sight to behold dragging a six-foot branch down Lighthouse Road, but I reached the

MacDara farm with relatively no issue aside from a small blister on my hand from carrying it.

Once inside the farm gate I heard Lola bark and race toward me. She had seen me coming and apparently thought I had come to play the biggest game of tug o' war ever. She grabbed the end of my stick and began to playfully pull and low growl. For such a small dog she was tenacious and very strong in the jaw. She tugged and jerked on the stick and threw me around as I tried to battle her for the stick and continue toward the house. I heard a chuckle from the top of the porch and looked up to see Mack grinning that grin and thoroughly enjoying the spectacle of it all.

He came hopping down the stairs to help extricate Lola, who was having the time of her life. I stumbled and laughed as she pulled and lurched backward, still locked onto the branch like a shark. He reached out to steady me and said, "We have to stop meeting like this you know."

I laughed as he gently pried Lola from the branch and gave her light pats on her head for her effort. "I have to assume you didn't drag that branch all the way down the lane to play with the dog; what on earth are you planning?" he asked playfully.

I told him I had made plans with Mr. MacDara, and I needed the branch shaped to hold the glass orb and add some carvings.

"Aye, that's a fine idea you've got. How did you know my father was a woodworker?" he asked.

I removed the small seal I carried with me most days and held it up for him to examine. "I may have stumbled onto his carving spot and made some inquiries at the schoolhouse," I proudly revealed.

His eyes crinkled and his dimples flashed as he stuffed his hands into his pockets and shook his head. "I'm afraid you've got the wrong man for the job," he replied seriously. "Aye, my father dinnae carve that, I would bet my life on it," he said as he looked up at me solemnly.

"But Miss Katie said Mr. MacDara was a carver, and he had made similar pieces for her only a few months back?" I questioned.

"Oh Aye, he's a carver, to be sure," he said as he kicked the ground softly. His eyes were twinkling with mischief at this point, and I couldn't help but smile.

"Well, can you tell me who made this?' I said as I held the wooden seal up.

He took the seal from my hand and studied it intently. "Well, I can tell ya just lookin' at it, this is sloppy work to be sure, look at this missing flipper, look at the wee groove along the back. It's like the bloke wasn't even tryin'," he asserted.

"Well do you know who made it?" I asked again as he studied the seal.

"Of course I do. You're lookin' at him... you had the wrong MacDara," he said as his grin returned and his eyes crinkled at the corners.

I laughed at our situation and continued the playful banter. "Well, the Mack is obviously short for the MacDara, do you have a real first name, wrong MacDara?"

"My name's actually Dylan, but everyone calls me Mack," he replied and handed me back the seal. I felt his hand linger a second longer as our fingers brushed. He picked up the branch and turned to me over his shoulder and said, "Are ya comin'?"as he headed toward the barn. Lola ran to the branch and began to tug on it as he walked toward the barn. We both laughed as he tried to maneuver through the door as Lola clung onto the branch and low growled in delight at the restart of the game.

Once inside the barn Mack hoisted the heavy branch onto a workbench and Lola stared expectantly in anticipation between the two of us. The front of the barn had been turned into a woodworking shop of sorts and was filled with scraps of wood and boat parts. A stained-glass window depicting a thistle hung high in the peak of the barn. The soft filtered light illuminated the rafters and revealed decades of sailing accessories and nautical living. Bits of colored light were cast around the room, refracting off the colored glass and landed haphazardly around the room. Coils of line hung from the rafters, along with wooden pulleys, and hoards of netting. Several sails were folded over the top of the rafters as well, in both black and white, suspended in the low light.

"In the spirit of not making any other incorrect assumptions, are you the sailor or is your father?" I asked as I looked around the room in admiration of the nautical curation.

"Actually both," he said as he watched me wandering around the workshop still grinning.

"I used to sail quite a bit when we lived back East," I told him. "My father is very into boats, if you hadn't guessed."

"I'm sure in his line of work, he'd have to be. It's funny I had you pegged as a train lady through and through," he teased.

We spent the next hour talking about our families and island life, Margie and Sam, and the madrone branch project. The conversation was light and sustaining. He had the same easy way of talking that his father had. He felt like an old friend...

someone my soul recognized in my core. I wanted to know him and felt drawn toward him like a rip current, not that I was fighting it. He talked about his mother and the past few years on the farm. She had become very ill, and his father had done everything in his power to make her well. Despite his best efforts, she had died at home two springs ago, surrounded by her favorite things, and fell asleep peacefully on a rainy morning.

His love for his family was evident as he spoke. His eyes were windows to his heart, an exposed passage revealing the sorrow reflected in the blue grey depths. I remembered how they twinkled when he laughed and how matte they appeared as he spoke about his mother. His vulnerability was special with me, and I was intentional with the delicate strands of memories he wove around me as I listened.

The light began to fade outside, and the rest of the world started seeping back into our space like slow water after a slack tide. I didn't want to leave that soft glow and my new friend.

"When can I see you again?" he questioned.

I grinned up at him as I hopped down from the haystack and dusted myself off. "I was wondering the same thing," I admitted coyly.

"Meet me at the dock at sunrise?" he asked.

"I wouldn't miss it," I answered, delighted at the thought of seeing him again so soon, unable to contain my grin as I exited the barn.

Lola and Mack both jumped up and followed me to the end of the lane as the soft afterglow of the evening ascended. As we said our goodbyes, I caught him stealing glances and wondered if he had noticed my enamored looks as well. I brushed the hair away from my face as the wind picked up. He stopped and tilted his head, looking contentedly back at me as he spoke. "I'll see you tomorrow then, Willow."

As I walked up the road toward the lighthouse the warmth of the evening enveloped me. A soft salt breeze wafted up from the harbor and I felt light and happy. The rustle of the trees in the wind kept me company as I relished in the sanctity of the island and the events of the afternoon. I felt seen in a way I hadn't experienced, and a sense of harmony with the island and with myself.

My mother was on the porch as I approached and Oliver was purring in her lap, flexing like an acrobat perched on a highwire. He looked ridiculous, and also perfectly content, and I laughed at him as I ascended the porch steps.

She threw her hands up in the air in surrender, "I tried to move him, but he just keeps coming back unbothered by my need to check on dinner." Oliver looked up and slow blinked at me as I shook my head.

"Well of course we can't move him, look at him," I said as I pointed to his Highness. "I suppose we just have to wait him out... a King demands his court." I curtsied in his general direction and my mother laughed.

The next morning sunrise came early, and with it, my excitement as I left the house. The cool rush of island air and the soft rustle of the trees invigorated me as I walked up the hill. I could hear gulls playing in the currents below and then as they flew overhead. My shoes crunched on the gravel as my cadence kept time with the symphony of nature that enveloped me.

As I approached the dock the sky was glowing with oranges and pinks. The light bounced off the water below and gave a fiery illumination to the sailboat that was tied off to the end of the low pier. Mack was busy readying the boat and hadn't noticed my approach. I admired his strong frame as he nimbly perched on the mast footing and untied the sails. He turned to greet me as I stepped on the dock and it creaked underfoot. He quickly jumped down and offered his hand.

"Are you ready to get off this island?" he asked as he hoisted me aboard in one gentle motion.

"I thought you'd never ask," I retorted as he pulled me in very near to him unexpectedly as our weight shifted. I suddenly found myself cradled into his strong shoulder and pressed against his chest. It took us both by surprise and we both instinctively leaned into each other like it was familiar.

His touch was both strong and soft and I melted into him for a brief second. He smiled down at me and I felt a calmness wash over me.

"Are you hungry?" he asked gently as he led me down the companionway.

As the interior of the ship came into view and my eyes adjusted to the dim light, the splendor and detail of the sailboat was revealed. Warm wood paneling covered the walls which were adorned with small brass finishes. Two small oil lamps sat on a gimble perched above the main table, which was set with a plate of fruits and breads and a kettle and mugs. A small tartan blanket was folded delicately over the bench seat midship. A doorway led forward and revealed a cozy berth adorned with woolen blankets and large pillows. A small galley lay forward of the companionway on the starboard side of the ship. A small copper pot and a kettle hung securely from hooks above the wooden table.

"Mack, it's perfect," I complimented as I took in my surroundings.

"It's one of my favorite places to be these days," he said proudly.

"I'm going to get us underway, make yourself comfortable and come up when you're ready," he offered sweetly as he squeezed my hand and turned up the stairs to the helm.

I walked over to the table and noticed how meticulously he had arranged the table and set out the small breakfast items. A small glass bottle held a branched thistle in bloom next to the plate. I smiled to myself and celebrated the obvious care and attention that had gone into it. I snacked on the fruit and breads as the boat slowly pulled away from the dock, smiling at the discarded burnt toast that had been abandoned in the sink. I poured two cups of coffee and turned to head up the stairs. I paused on the first step, intrigued by a small brass-framed picture of him as a child with his mother and father, in front of the house. The sailboat just visible off in the distance of the frame. He had his mother's smile, even as a child.

As we left the calm waters of the harbor I sipped on the coffee and felt safe and excited as the sails were raised and the boat leaned with the weight of the wind. We turned the corner into the strait and the boat picked up speed and water began to splash rhythmically on the bow. The wind threw Mack's hair around haphazardly and he grinned a boyish grin as the boat cut through the water. The sun was still low in the sky, and I felt a chill as we ventured out farther from land. Mack propped the wheel on a set course and popped below briefly. He came up the companionway holding a thick wool blanket and a piece of apple in his mouth.

"You're about to have the best seat in the house," he announced as he grabbed my hand and took a bite of the apple slice, and then led me carefully forward toward the bow. A small rowboat sat upturned on the forward deck. He unfolded the blanket and gently wrapped it around me. He leaned up against the boat and invited me to sit. I leaned into him and the warmth of his body surrounded me. The boat heaved rhythmically in the deep water and slowly rose and fell with a soft spray from the bow as the boat cut through the water. I could feel Mack's chest rise and fall, almost in time with the boat. My own breathing aligned with the water and the boat, and with him behind me. I leaned into the magic and melted into the moment.

We stayed out on the bow with only open water and a distant glimpse of Pender Island in view. We sat in silence for some time, just breathing and feeling. Our bodies magnetic as we watched the waves and listened to the ruffles of sail in the wind as it blew. I rested my head on his shoulder and felt him breathe deeply and envelop me with his strong frame. A small group of sea birds flew over the mast and gently cawed as they played in the sails. The sun rose fully out over the strait as we bobbed in the water with the gentle current and soft morning breeze. A gust of wind blew in, and the blanket slowly slipped from my shoulders. His fingers grazed, then slowly traced, the back of my hand. I instinctively upturned my hand and intertwined his fingers with mine. Cheeks pink from the cold, I leaned into him, and he pulled me in tighter until I was fully covered in his warmth.

The winds inevitably shifted, and the captain was called back to the helm by the luffing of the sails. We begrudgingly left the bow of the boat and returned to the cockpit to adjust sail. I grabbed the line and made ready as he turned through the wind and the boom shifted port side as the boat moved with the wind. He laughed as he realized I had already started the maneuver, and the boat came through the wind and the sails filled.

"Looks like I'm not the only sailor on this boat," he said proudly, admiring my work. My hair swirled in the wind, and I laughed out of joy for the moment and the company. I was invigorated that day and felt the color returning to my face. I could almost feel the life pour back into me as I explored my newfound freedom away from expectation and reputation at the lighthouse. The weight of those burdens couldn't follow me out to sea it turned out.

We arrived back in Prevost Harbor as the sun was at its highest point. The glare off the water hid his form, sitting just off the dock laying patiently in wait for our return. Joe leaned gently up against the car hood, casually smoking one of his cigarettes. He rose to his full height as the boat came to a halt on the pier. He exhaled a cloud of smoke and squinted in Mack's direction as he tied the boat off. Joe slowly walked down the pier and flicked his cigarette in the water forcefully as he walked.

"Your mother asked me to fetch you at the MacDara house." Joseph looked up at me still onboard, staring down at him. "Your father told me you had left on the boat." He squinted at Mack and made a sour face at the wooden sailboat in front of him.

"I'm not sure she would approve of you being out on this thing, it doesn't look seaworthy if you ask me," he said in Mack's general direction. "True North, eh?" he enunciated the words slowly and mocked a terrible Canadian accent. He knocked on the hull as he sauntered along the dock. "What type of boat name is that?"

Mack looked at him with a confident grin and without missing a beat said, "It's in reference to finding your internal compass. You should try it."

I quickly intervened on everyone's behalf and cut off Joseph before he could reply. "My mother trusts my judgement in all matters, Ensign Cail, which is none of your concern...may I politely remind you," I answered quickly.

Joseph swiftly realized he had overplayed his hand and began to try a different tactic to stop what everyone present knew, but hadn't said already.

"Of course, Willow, I am only concerned for your safety, I hope I haven't offended you," he stated solemnly as he reached up to help me down from the boat.

Mack visibly stiffened as he watched my demeanor change and felt my uneasiness in the situation. I wanted to jump back on the boat and sail off again into the carefree. I hastily said goodbye to Mack, much more formally than I would have liked to, truth be told. Joe ushered me with his arm, formally up the pier and to the awaiting car like a ward. I resented his presence, primarily for the interruption, but also for the callowness insinuated in his interactions. We drove up the lane in silence until Joseph callously asked, "Are you involved with him?'

I didn't answer and he continued. "There are things about him you don't know Willow; he is not the man for you. I have a career, and station, I can provide for you and keep you safe," he went on. I stared directly ahead, unwilling to engage in his line of questioning.

"Damn it Willow, be reasonable!" he yelled as he slammed his hand on the steering wheel, and I jumped at the sound. He grabbed the wheel aggressively, his knuckles white from his exaggerated grip. I was frozen to the seat, immobilized by the aggressiveness of his sudden outburst. His eyes widened and he saw the fear in my posture and the panic in my eyes. He knew I had seen the temper behind his normally calm exterior and quickly shifted gears. His persona changed instantly and he shrunk in stature and tone. "Willow, dear, I care for you so much. You're young and impressionable and I don't want you to throw your life away on a simple islander with a questionable reputation," he explained as we pulled up to the house. I opened the door as the car came to a halt and I slammed the door behind me. I had an unshakable, almost eerie feeling that I had seen the real Joseph just now, and I hurried back toward the safety of the house.

I found my mother in the kitchen and asked her what had been so pressing as to send an escort to retrieve me. She countered, "I never said such a thing, Willow, really, it wasn't like that. He simply inquired where you were, and I told him you'd gone to the MacDara farm, and you might need a ride home. It was innocent, for both of us. I asked him if he'd like to fetch you as it was the time you said you'd be home."

I fumed at the naivety of my mother and felt like she had been manipulated in some sort of unprovable way.

She continued around the kitchen putting dishes away and unreasonably refusing to see my side of the story.

I was quick on her heels as she flitted around the kitchen, hoping to make her understand the seriousness of my request. "I saw something tonight mother, he scared me, I don't trust him, and you shouldn't either."

"Honestly Willow, he's not like that. I would be shocked if you told me he could be cross, especially with you." My mother was only half listening now as she folded a tea towel and clearly wasn't taking my situation seriously.

I slowed my pursuit in futility, switching my strategy to defense until I could prove to her what I had started to see, and that which she was apparently blind too. "From now on I will walk home from everywhere I go. Mother please, don't send him for me again."

"As you wish Willow, but I think you're making a bigger deal out of it than it needs to be," she trailed off down the hall.

That night I lay quietly in my bed wondering if I had read too much into it. If I had somehow provoked him or encouraged his pursuit of me. I thought about Mack and the boat ride and how perfect it had all been. Oliver purred contentedly next to me as I ran through the events of the day and drifted off to sleep. That night I dreamt of clear blue water and high tides which quickly progressed to dark skies and rough seas. In my dream I sat perched in the lighthouse lantern room keeping watch out over the strait. I sat helplessly watching small boats tossing and turning as the current swept them out away from shore. With each pulse of light their silhouettes grew smaller and smaller until they were specks on the horizon and disappeared.

I woke to a soft thud on my window and Oliver alert with ears pricked. Another thud landed squarely on the glass pane. Oliver turned and stared at the window preparing to pounce. I cautiously lifted the bed covers and placed my feet on the floor. Oliver was one step ahead of me, already in motion to the window, ready to investigate. I crept slowly toward the hazy window and gently pushed open the sill. The cold night air wafted into the room and made me shiver as it glided over my skin.

"Are you ok?" I heard from a dark form crouched next to the stone cellar just outside my window. The cellar was built into the hillside and was shorter at the far end, where it met the earth. The door faced the rear of the house where the structure stood at full height. Mack slowly rose to his feet and whispered again, "Willow, are you ok?"

"What are you doing Mack?" I eeked back. "Yes, I'm fine! If my parents catch you, we're both dead," I reminded him.

"I had to make sure. I'm sorry, I couldn't sleep."

I worried the sound of our voices would carry to unintended places. I instantly knew what I wanted to do, and I tucked my head out and said, "Into the cellar, and wait there."

Oliver looked up at me with his tail swishing as I hastily grabbed a jacket and made my way to the stairwell as quiet as a mouse. It felt like an eternity carefully lowering myself down each individual stair, but I was soon out the kitchen door and into the cool night air. I slipped down the steps and into the shadow of the raised stone cellar and straight into Mack. Our arms instinctively reached for each other, and I nestled into his warm embrace.

"I was worried about you," he whispered as he squeezed me tighter. "I couldn't stop thinking about you, I'm sorry I woke you," he continued.

"I missed you too," I admitted as I pulled away to meet his gaze. He looked down on me as he held me with such tenderness, and I leaned up to meet his mouth with mine. His hand gently moved up the back of my neck and rested in my hair cradling my head. His warm body drew me in as my hands made their way up his strong back and I pressed his body into mine. I had never had this level of attraction with anyone before. It was more than physical; it felt like coming home when he touched me. I was drawn to him, and I know he felt it too.

I remembered where we were and the hour of the night. "What do we do now?"

"Go back to sleep and go get warm, I just had to see you and know you were ok," he whispered as he wrapped me up in my jacket and kissed the top of my head. "I'll dream of you," he said.

"See me tomorrow?" I asked.

"I've got business on Pender Island, and I'll be gone by first light, but I'll be back in a couple days. You'll be on my mind and my first steps off the boat will be in your direction." His hand trailed off mine and I walked out of the shadow of the cellar toward the door.

"Sweet dreams and be safe." I tip toed back toward the house.

"The sweetest," he promised as I crept back up the stairs and into the warmth of the house. Oliver was waiting for me at the top of the steps with a slow blink and a swishing tail.

We hopped back into bed together and I drifted back to sleep most assuredly with a smile on my face. There were no storm dreams the rest of that night, only the soft purr of Oliver and the warmth of the house around me.

8

Even If You Aren't One

Margie and I had made plans this week to help Miss Katie with something. Miss Katie had been purposefully vague in her request for help, only that we should meet at the schoolhouse and keep an open mind. We spent the walk to the schoolhouse catching up and reveling in the new love we both had found that summer. Margie told me about the long walks Sam and her were keen to taking these days, and most importantly, the way he supported her singing. He told her he was going to follow her anywhere — 'wherever the music led her'. They spent hours now down at the water's edge playing music and killing time in the slow days of summer. Margie was going to set up a double date, naturally, now that Mack and I were getting so close, she said.

"Oh, it can be a picnic!" she exclaimed as she walked with my hand in hers. "And after we can go for a swim?" she added playfully. We spent the rest of the walk just enjoying each other's company and the slow pace of the morning.

We arrived at the schoolhouse just as Miss Katie was dragging old buckets and brushes from the lean-to shed adjoining the small porch.

"Good morning, ladies!" she waved as she put her hands on her hips and smiled mischievously. Margie and I both groaned at the sight of the cleaning supplies laid out in front of us.

"But Miss Katie, the school is sparking clean already!" Margie objected.

"You are absolutely correct Margie, the schoolhouse is pristine...that's not where we're going," she said as she turned and winked at me and handed me a rake. "Let's be on our way now ladies...the widow Clare is expecting us."

"The witch?!" Marjorie exclaimed. "Are you out of your mind Miss Katie?!" She hurriedly collected the remaining supplies as she followed Miss Katie, broom in hand toward the road.

"'What a person believes may be ascertained, not from their creed, but from the assumptions on which they habitually act.' George Bernard Shaw said that ladies, and you'll do well to heed that bit of knowledge, and never stop challenging your own assumptions. They are the windows to your true self."

Margie sighed and caught up a few paces. "Alright Miss Katie, but if we all get warts or go down in flames, don't say I didn't warn you."

Miss Katie shook her head at Margie and took a long deep breath. "You may find spending time with someone and getting to know their story has the oddest way of transforming the scariest of monsters, the larger-than-life characters, into people just like you and me," she offered. "Give her a chance, you might be surprised with what you come to know."

We arrived at the small stone cottage just as the light had crested the top of the trees and streamed steadily over the tree line. The cottage had seen better days, but its charming character shined through the layers of grime that the years had deposited. The door flung open as we crossed the small stone fence into the inner yard and the old widow stood in the doorway smiling and gesturing a welcome with her hands. She was wearing a long tan frock with a dark brown apron drawn across her waist. Her hair was haphazardly drawn up in a bun, as taming the wild strands had appeared to be a fruitless endeavor.

"Come in come in, failte failte," she greeted as she ushered us through the heavy wooden door. The house was dimly lit as we walked inside the stone frame. The tortoiseshell cat I had seen before wove in and out of the furniture craning to get a better view of us. Miss Katie was the first to speak and introduced us to the old widow.

"The pearl and the water, why of course you are," the old woman muttered as she walked to the hearth to fetch the tea. Marjorie and I giggled at her seemingly nonsensical mutterings. She was surprisingly agile for her age and plopped down on the chair next to the table and began pouring tea. She grabbed our hands and looked sweetly back and forth between us. Miss Katie smiled warmly and said, "Marjorie means pearl in Old English doesn't it, but isn't Willow connected to the tree? Clare you aren't slipping up in your old age, are you?"

Mrs. Malby just clicked her tongue and shook her head. "Oh Katie child, the Willow is a tree of enchantment, a tree of secrets, you see," she gestured with her fingers as she spoke, "but the Willow only grows where the water flows. The Willow knows the water, like a child knows the mother." Mrs. Malby looked over at Marjorie and declared, "My Pearl."

"You've found your Anam Cara have ya? Aye, Aye she has," answering her own question as she patted both of our hands and smiled. She sat back with a knowing look and began to sip her tea.

"What is an Anam Cara?" I asked and leaned further into the conversation at hand.

The old woman smiled and pointed to Marjorie and said, "You're looking at it, to be sure says I," and cackled to herself knowingly. "An Anam Cara is the soul friend. The one who knows you, deep down. Someone you don't have to hide from. It's the person you can reveal your true self to, the juicy bits you keep hidden from the rest of the world." She nodded approvingly at her own description and took a slow drink of tea. "The Anam Cara comes when the soul cries out to another, usually a lost soul, an alone soul, and the Anam Cara answers, able to hear the other's need."

Marjorie looked over at me knowingly and smiled a soft smile. The widow Clare winked at me as she sipped her tea.

"Now then," she exclaimed as she jumped up from her chair decidedly, "we have business to attend to." The widow grabbed her crook and made for the door.

We meandered down a small path for a short while and came to a small clearing not far from the water's edge but tucked into the tree line far enough to go unnoticed from shore. The clearing was directly behind the widow's home, but only accessible from the meandering trail around the front of the garden due to large boulders and rock outcroppings that cragged out of the mossy ground. The clearing contained a small stone bench and table, and a large stone marker that had been weathered by the years. Vines had crept into the clearing and had started to creep up the old stone marker. The widow's eyes shone as I happened upon her gaze in the soft light. A well-worn foot path to the small stone seat and table was visible as it wound to the foot of the stone monument and back to the seating area.

"The old widow comes to this stone every day," Miss Katie whispered to Marjorie and me, as we watched her take her place of honor on the low stone bench next to the marker.

"Now Mr. Malby, these fine young ladies have come to get you cleaned up says I," the widow Clare patted the stone marker and nodded her agreement. She rose up from the bench and thanked us and set off back up the path toward the house.

"The poor thing never misses a day, rain or shine, she comes to his grave," Miss Katie started, "It's tragic really..." she paused as she glanced back toward the trail, ensuring the widow was out of earshot. "Mr. Malby's first love was always the sea; he was always leaving for another adventure, and she was always here waiting for him to return. The woman loved him no doubt, but it always seemed an unrequited love from his end, or so I'm told. He's been dead a long time now, or he just never came back for her. He was presumed dead at sea after a ship went missing in a storm up the Inside Passage... but she's just as faithful in her grief as she was in her love," Miss Katie explained as she pulled the ivy away from the stone and cleared out the ground around the old memorial.

We spent the early afternoon scrubbing the stone monument and clearing weeds and debris from the small clearing. When the sun was directly overhead Miss Katie decided to run up to the main house to ready refreshments as we finished up. Margie and I plopped down on the stone outcroppings just outside of the main clearing to survey our hard work.

"I wonder if that old cad knew how faithful she was, and still is?" Margie asked rhetorically.

"I'm sure he wouldn't visit her grave every day," I surmised as I leaned back on the rock to stretch my back. As I turned my head, I noticed a small cavern in the rock that was hidden by the larger outer stones. There appeared to be some type of canvas heaped in the far corner of the cavern and I nudged Margie when I saw it. She peered over the edge and her eyes widened in interest at the discovery.

"Well, isn't that a nifty little treasure trove," her voice trailing as she climbed up the rock face and into the empty cavern below. She walked to the back of the stone hollow and lifted the canvas sheet as I peered over the ledge above. Under the canvas was a crate of old empty whiskey bottles and an old tin of tobacco.

"Who knew the old hag likes to hit the hooch?" Margie mimed overindulgence with her hand and laughed wildly. "Oh, I bet it was Mr. Malby's stash! The cad!"

"Come on and get out of there!" I shouted as I laughed at her one woman act below. She ignored my directive and pretended to stumble around and be a drunken sailor with the empty whisky bottle and the canvas as a makeshift robe.

Margie clambered up the stone sidewall still in character, pretending to be inebriated and slurred, "Damn it woman, the sea she calls me!" doing her best impression of the late Mr. Malby.

We walked back up to the stone house and found Miss Katie and the widow Malby having tea by the fire. There were several jars of herbs laid out on the table and the widow was gathering up a small assortment of the contents in a piece of cloth.

"Now there, dear," she said kindly, "this should do the trick, and you let the old lady know if the troubles continue." She patted Miss Katie's arm knowingly as she spoke.

"Thank you again Clare, you have been most kind, as always," Miss Katie affirmed as she clasped her hand over the widows.

"And with that, I think we will say our goodbyes," she said as she looked over at us.

As we walked home that evening, I asked Miss Katie what the herbs were for. She told us that she had been ill for a few years, but not to worry, and that the widow had made a special tea for her to help ease her symptoms.

"She's really the kindest woman. She has the most caring heart, and it's sad that some of the islanders have treated her as an outcast."

Margie grabbed Miss Katie's hand and told her thank you for taking her along today.

"She'll always have a friend in me Miss Katie, I swear. If I hear anyone call her a witch again, I'll set them straight."

"I knew I could count on you two," she said proudly as she squeezed Margie's arm and offered her other arm to me. We walked together, arm in arm, down the wooded path back toward home.

Things were abuzz back at the lighthouse when I returned. The men were down at the docks and there was a bit of commotion as they pulled a small steamer into the dock. Sam walked briskly up to me as I made my way down to the dock to see what was going on.

"I'm afraid you can't go down there Willow," he said as he lowered his voice as he neared. "There's been a bit of a situation out on the water and we're tryin to sort it now. There's been some type of foul play, and the captain is alerting the authorities as we speak."

The men shouted as they tied off the last of the lines to the dock and my father exited the main house and headed back toward the docks with Joseph close on his heels.

"Willow go inside and stay there for now," he barked as he walked past me briskly.

"What do you mean foul play?" I asked Sam as they blew past.

"I don't know much yet, but a boat was spotted that was potentially adrift out in Haro. The captain sent out a patrol boat to investigate and found no one on board but did find signs of a struggle. There was blood in the main cabin. It appears to be a bootlegger's boat," he shared in a low voice.

"I can't talk right now, but I'll let you know what I find out." He departed with a nod and turned back toward the dock and the gang of men that surrounded the small vessel.

I walked back up to the main house and sat in the kitchen with my mother as we waited for the authorities to come from the mainland. Kyle was glued to the living room window intent on having a front row seat to the day's events. My mind raced to Margie's family, and all the other islanders who lived off the sea and worked the surrounding waters. The Salish Sea could be a dangerous place, which the island community knew all too well. I thought about Mack, still out on the water, and Mr.

Malby lost at sea. I hoped that the unfolding events wouldn't touch our small island community, and everyone I had grown to love remained out of harm's way.

My mother decided to do what she does best in crisis; keep busy and feed everyone. She had already begun making coffee and preparing sandwiches for the steady train of people who were inevitably going to come. Word spread quickly of the bloodied boat and the locals were quick to try and get a glimpse of it first-hand. A few came by road, and were quickly turned around by the men, but others came by boat, coming dangerously close to the rocky shore to get up close to the mystery vessel. My father, who had been glued to the dock for hours, periodically yelled to the approaching spectators in an increasingly agitated tone.

It was after one of these outbursts I heard the front door fling open and his booming voice fill the hallway corridor. "This is precisely the type of activity we've been reporting!"

Joseph replied, "Exactly Sir. We've got to increase our presence in these waters and ensure that law is upheld. Our borders are increasingly compromised, and this riff raff is just undermining our own authority over the strait. We've got to shut these operations down!" He slammed his hand down on the big wooden table for effect.

My father looked out the front window pensively and stroked his chin as he began to speak. "I will not have my legacy tarnished as the outpost that allowed this type of activity to permeate and fester. These bootleggers bring a dangerous game to these islands and I for one will not stand for it."

Joseph had caught sight of me in the hallway and without taking his eyes off me mirrored my father's sentiments and announced, "I'm glad you feel as I do Sir, I also will do anything necessary to protect the good people of this community from such depravity."

I turned and walked back into the kitchen feeling disoriented to my thoughts, wondering why that had felt so threatening when it hadn't been directed toward me. Or had it? He had said the same thing my father had, but somehow it felt ominous in its intent. The two continued plotting in the front room while my mother and I readied the sandwiches for the men who were on their way from the mainland.

I walked out of the kitchen later that evening and ran straight into Sam near the cellar.

"What have you heard Sam? My father and Joseph are all up in arms about bootleggers in there," I said pointing back to the house.

"It's most definitely rum runners, Willow. There's a bullet hole in the foc'sle door and there's a bloodied cap with a bullet hole through it. The anchor is missing a well. I don't want to think about what's happened to the people aboard that boat, and where they might be now," he hesitated.

My eyes widened at the new information. "Do they know who the boat belonged to?"

"Not yet. The boat's called the Beryl-G, so they'll track down the owners, but they aren't local to Stuart or the surrounding islands from what we've gathered."

"That's at least good news," I said again thinking about Margie and Mack selfishly, hoping they hadn't been caught in the crossfire of whatever happened out there. Sam read my mind and tapped me on the shoulder softly. "Dinnae ya fash Willow, it's not his boat and I'm sure he's just fine."

"I'm sure you're right," I agreed. "At least I hope you are."

I sat up with my mother in the kitchen while she waited for my father for as long as I could. Eventually the low light and the previous excitement of the day caught up with me and I retreated up the stairs to bed. Kyle had long since lost the battle to sleep and had been ushered up earlier after falling asleep at the window. I laid down and my thoughts drifted to Mack. I wondered where he was and when he would return. I hoped he was safe. I drifted off dreaming of him and I on the water, peaceful and calm, like that day on the bow.

A gentle thud pulled me back from my watery dreams, followed by another. It was the sound of a pinecone or a small pebble gently hitting the glass paned window. I leapt up from my bed knowing what that sound meant and who it brought with it. I lit the lamp and signaled two flashes and stoked it. I grabbed my night coat and made my way painstakingly down the stairs, hoping my father had ceased his investigative activities for the night. I rushed out the kitchen door, once I had made certain the coast was clear, and straight to the shadow of the root cellar wall. He was waiting there in the dewy grass, and I ran to him and straight into his arms. His warmth again surrounded me, and I buried my face in his neck and breathed him in.

"I was so worried," I cried. "Did you hear about the boat?"

"Aye, I had. My father told me when I came in tonight." He pulled me in closer for another hug, kissed my forehead firmly, and I felt his chest exhale with a deep breath.

"You can't stay long. This place is on high alert tonight. I'm not entirely certain my father has gone to bed yet," I said in a whispered voice.

"Then I won't keep you, meet me at the house tomorrow when you can?" he asked.

I leaned up and kissed his lips gently in reply.

Mack's eyes twinkled, "I'll take that as a yes."

I walked back toward the house, and felt compelled to set eyes on him, one last time tonight. I glanced back as I opened the door and saw him standing there grinning and I couldn't help but do the same. He winked at me and disappeared into the night air. I closed the door softly and crept back up the stairs feeling lighter knowing he was safe. I made my way back into my room and as soon as my head hit the pillow, I could feel him sneaking into my dreams again. We walked along the rocks, high atop the island and nothing could touch us there.

The next morning the house was buzzing bright and early. My father was already on the dock with the crew, and they were pulling away in the few boats that had lined the docks. The Beryl-G still sat tied up to the inside of the pier, awaiting its tow to Friday Harbor. The police were on the dock as well, interviewing a few of my father's men. I made my way up the road toward the MacDara place happy to have some alone time away from all the excitement.

9

On the Way Home

Summer was in full swing now and the air was heavy with the smell of grass and earth. Small orange and yellow wildflowers dotted the roadside and patches of thistle were blooming to reveal soft bursts of purple. The grass was fading to a soft yellow in the summer heat along with the exposed moss along the road. The mornings on the island were still crisp and cool however, bringing the salt air in from the sea with the midsummer breezes. I drew in long deep breaths as I walked, partly due to contentment, and partly because the air smelled so sweetly it was almost intoxicating.

I was greeted at the property line by Lola and Mr. MacDara who were both out in the field. Mr. MacDara was mending fence and they both seemed to be enjoying the cooler morning air. Lola squeezed through the fence rails to greet me, and Mr. MacDara laughed and stood from his crouched position.

"Well now I see you've got a friend for life in that one." He pointed to Lola who was now circling me and whining out of excitement. I reached down to pet her, and she sat squarely on her haunches on top of my feet. "Something tells me you haven't come to see this old man now, have ya?" he teased as his eyes twinkled, and he gave me a wink. "My boy has been going on about ya, nigh on a month now. Reminds me of the first time I laid eyes on my Leannan."

"Was that her name?" I asked. "I would have loved to meet her, I bet she was absolutely wonderful."

"Ach, no," he chuckled. "Leannan means sweetheart or dear one in Gaelic. It's just something I've called her since we were young. Her name was Catriona."

Lola's ear perked up as she spotted Mack coming up the fence line. She whined and looked up at me and then raced to meet him. I don't think either of us could contain our smiles as the other came into view. Mr. MacDara looked tickled to see his son that happy and his eyes twinkled as he watched us. He muttered something in Gaelic and chuckled to himself and waved to Mack as Lola ran back to us ahead of him.

Mack approached slightly formal in stature, "Hello Willow." He tipped his hat as he drew near to the two of us, stopping short of his father and I.

"Oh Jesus, Mary, and Joseph, I know that's not how you greet the woman you've been talkin' about non-stop now is it Mack," his father scolded as he turned his head slyly to Mack.

Mack grinned that grin and lifted his downturned head up to meet his father, and then to me as he laughed at the old man taking so much joy out of teasing him.

"Come on Willow, I think the sun is getting to the old man," he said as he smirked at his father. They clearly had a very playful relationship, and it was even more endearing to see it unfolding in front of me. "Don't be mindin' me now," his father lilted and winked again.

"You know, I think your father is on to something here…" I said as I placed my hand to my chin in gest.

"Oh come now, not you too!" Mack laughed and took his hands out of his pockets and walked toward me with intent.

"Be careful what you wish for!" He picked me up and held me high over his head and brought me down with a kiss on the forehead.

His father and I erupted in laughter as my feet returned to the ground and Lola barked and pranced happily underfoot.

"I've got a surprise for you," Mack revealed. "Are you ready?"

I nodded and he started off toward the house and reached back with outstretched hand and a grin.

"Goodbye Mr. MacDara!" I called as I grabbed his hand and waved back.

As soon as we were out of earshot, he squeezed my hand and said gently, "I missed you." The sentiment spoken in an almost whisper of a voice, almost as if the words frightened him, they were so full of conviction. I knew just how he felt.

We stopped by the house briefly and Mack grabbed a basket off the porch that was brimming with picnic items. We headed for the dock, and I asked him where we were going.

"Way out there." He pointed playfully out of the harbor off into the distance.

I made a face at him and squeezed his arm as we walked onto the dock. He lifted me onto the boat with one motion and I bent down and met his upturned gaze with my lips on his. He kissed me hungrily as I kept just in reach of his soft lips.

"You're gonna be the death of me if you kiss me like that again," he teased. "I might just up and die right here, dead from a burst heart." he continued as he reached for me with his mouth, and I met his lips with a firm deep kiss. I stood up and turned to walk away and smiled back at him playfully as I did. He jumped on board after me and soon after we were pulling away from the dock and out into Boundary Pass. A warm breeze was cutting across the island to the East and we were under full sail as soon as we were free from the harbor.

Mack leaned back against the transom and motioned for me to sit against him. I leaned back into his chest and felt his arm wrap around me tightly. We spent the sail talking and laughing, and just enjoying each other and the stunning scenery laid out before us. Our course was set for Pender Island, just across Boundary Pass to the North, and well into Canadian waters.

We entered Bedwell Harbour in the early afternoon; the tides and the wind had been with us for the entire crossing. Large logs dotted the entrance to the harbor and swirled in counter current pockets around us. Mack was entirely at ease at the helm and maneuvered through the maze of debris effortlessly. Basking seals raised their sleepy heads as we sailed past their resting place on the floating logs, the creatures surprised to see us so close. Some of them slipped quickly into the water, and some paid no mind to our presence and closed their eyes and drifted back to sleep, sprawled out on the floating logs.

We anchored the boat at the far end of the harbor and pulled the dinghy down from the bow. Mack loaded up the picnic supplies and lowered me into the boat and headed for shore.

The spot he had chosen was a small cove with a sandy beach which was surrounded by steep rock outcroppings on the sides. The water was a beautiful turquoise green and crystal clear to the rocky bottom below. The sea floor was covered with starfish, shellfish, and anemones. The rocky floor was popping with color in purples, whites, oranges, and pinks, set against the grey and green hues of the rocks below. I had taken up a seat at the bow of the rowboat and had been hunched over in absolute fascination at the spectacular world below me. I yelled to Mack every few feet, excited with each discovery. He laughed as he rowed and said he had hoped I liked it as much as he did.

We slid onto the sandy beach and the rowboat lurched to a stop. Mack pulled the boat up well away from the waterline and we set up a blanket and ate lunch. We spent the afternoon playing in the water and beachcombing, just enjoying each other and the island itself. We sat on the blanket and talked as we looked out over the water and the slow rhythmic whoosh of the waves played in the background.

It was so peaceful, just the two of us and I told him about how I had been feeling lately. "The days are so long now, once the hustle and bustle of the mainland is cut out. I feel as though I can see myself more clearly and understand what's really important."

"Aye there's loads of nothing out here in the islands, but there's so much in that nothing," he said thoughtfully as he looked out over the water and back at me. "What fills that void is who we really are Leannan." He reached over and brushed the hair back from my face as he spoke.

I kissed him softly and touched his face knowing the significance of that word and wondering if it was intentional or unconsciously said. We sat quietly together listening to the waves as we rested on the sandy blanket, leaned up against the overturned rowboat. I thought about Mack's words and how much the island had changed me since I'd arrived. I had never really had the luxury of a time when the pressures and expectations of others hadn't clouded up the idea of who I wanted to be. These past few months at the outpost had given me reprieve from the clutter of modern mainland life. Although the strained relationship with my father was not resolved, it was not looming over me like some unshakable, ever-present force.

After a while we walked along the water's edge and up onto the rock outcroppings that surrounded the cove. The sun was just beginning to set, and we sat next to each other in the warm glow of evening to enjoy the scene that was unfolding. The sky was rapidly turning orange and red, with streaks of dark purple and blues running through the colors like a ribbon.

"Tell me about the first time that you saw me," I asked playfully to him.

Mack smiled and cleared his throat, "I won't soon forget that." He looked pensively down at our intertwined hands and started to speak.

"The first time I saw you, you hadn't seen me yet. You were with Margie for most of the night, and I'll never forget watching you, as you watched her. Aye, we both know that Margie has had a rough go, and we both know she's one of the best people on God's green earth as well. Ach, when I saw you so full of love and pride watching Margie in love and happy, well it made me want to know you Willow... and I do, you know. I know you... and I love you." He looked up at me earnestly as he said it. "I probably have from that first time I saw you, but not even I could have predicted how deeply I would care for you. Sometimes I can't believe it."

He twisted a piece of seaweed in his hands as he considered his words and carefully crafted them.

"I'd do anything for you, ach, I'd gladly die for you... but mostly I want to live for you, for us." His eyes met mine as he said the words and they were filled with resolve and strength, and genuine love. "I want to be the person you think of when you see something beautiful, and you just have to tell someone. And I want to be the man you run to when life is cruel, because you know you'll always find comfort. What I mean is, I want to make a life with you Willow... and be the man you always need me to be."

The sun was just sinking below the horizon and the sky was now aglow with orange and red streaks. I placed my hand on Mack's cheek, so deeply moved I was unable to say anything other than, "I love you too." I leaned into him and felt our lips move together with magnetic force as the sun dipped below the tree line. The moment was perfection and the love he felt for me radiated like the sky that was unfolding in front of us, both equally beautiful. The waves crashed rhythmically into the shoreline as the last orange rays faded into the horizon. It felt like we were the only people in the world right then.

"Tonight was wonderful, it was the symphony of us. I can almost hear the wee melody," he said, breaking the silence. "Perhaps we can ask God to play it again?" His eyes settled on the sun sinking below the treelined horizon, mourning the moment as it faded.

I grabbed his hand and told him to follow me. I climbed up the rocks, about fifteen feet or so, and turned around toward where the sun had set, verifying I had climbed high enough for what I needed him to see. I reached my hand down to Mack below. He hoisted himself up the rocky cliffside and laughed as he turned around to see the bright orange ball still hanging over the horizon from our new vantage point. Mack shook his head playfully. "You're a mastermind."

"Ok, tell me about the first time that you saw me," he requested as he pulled me into his arms.

"My god, I can't top yours!" I shoved him playfully and we both laughed. I scooted closer to him as I spoke.

"The first time I saw you, you hadn't seen me yet," I started with a grin.

"No... No way, he said, now you're stealing my story!"

I grabbed his arm playfully and promised, "I swear it on my grave! Now let me tell the story!"

He made a button gesture to his lips and crossed his hands in anticipation.

"It was a night in early summer, very late, when I went out to the docks at the lighthouse. I hadn't been able to sleep, and I was feeling lost and hopeless about moving to the island. You appeared out of nowhere, alone at the helm, with only a lantern to light your face for a passing second. I caught sight of you for just a brief second, but your face has always stuck with me. It was almost as if time had frozen, and my mind took a perfect picture of that moment to capture it. I can still see every detail of it like you were right in front of me. Had I known who you would end up being to me, I might have swum out in that frigid water to meet you."

Mack laughed and smiled that smile with eyes that were brimming with love. The sun began to dip below the horizon again and the light slowly faded.

"Quick, or we'll miss it," I whispered as I leaned in to kiss him.

"I love you Leannan." His lips brushing mine as he spoke.

"I love you right back Dylan MacDara." I kissed him again intently.

After our replayed kiss, the sun lowered behind the land again, and Mack looked up at the remaining sea wall and then back toward me. We both laughed and shook our heads no, as the top of the cliff became extremely narrow and precarious. We made our way back to the beach and decided we should probably make for the boat to be out of the harbor before dark. We loaded up the remains of the picnic and shoved off in the small wooden boat for True North.

We headed out of the harbor after loading the dinghy and ourselves and made for the small speck of Stuart Island that was barely visible from Pender. The wind had shifted, and we had to point the boat toward the Eastern tip of Stuart Island to catch it. The last shades of light dimmed as the moon rose in the sky. Its reflection shimmered in the water below as we glided across the water for home. I hadn't meant to be this late, and hoped my parents wouldn't be wondering where I was. Mack saw the worry on my face and put his arm around me and said, "I'm sorry Leannan, we cannot control the time or the tide."

The sky began to grow dark as we neared the Eastern part of the island and changed course, intending to use the new wind current to fill the sails and push us up the coast. Small drops of rain started falling and Mack asked if I'd like to go below to stay warm and dry. I grabbed a woolen sweater from the hook by the chart rack and brought it up along with a small blanket. I wrapped it around myself as he slipped the sweater overhead and I burrowed into him for warmth as he steered.

A small passage into the far end of Prevost Harbor appeared to the port side of the boat and I asked Mack why we couldn't turn in there to avoid the growing wind pushing from the channel.

"We can't go in there, it's absolutely riddled with exposed reef and rocks, if we'd like to keep the hull intact, we'll have to go the long way. There is a very narrow channel that zig zags through, but it's really only deep enough for a skiff. We'll be there in no time now; the wind is giving us a nice push," he said reassuringly.

I leaned into him and watched as Satellite Island passed under the sails. I could just make out Margie's outpost in the pale moonlight sitting up on the bluff overlooking the Strait. I thought about her father and brothers out for days on end, and how Mack would be out in this at times as well. It was humbling to be on the water during a storm, to be cradled in a small wooden safety net on the sea as it tossed and churned. This was not even a storm, more of a quick sprinkling, and I had already grown mildly uneasy at the rapid transformation the surrounding waters had taken. Mack was more attentive to the sails and the way the boat moved now, and his brow was slightly furrowed in concentration as his eyes went from the horizon to the sails and back again. The rain had made his hair clump together in loose curls at the nape of his neck. He smiled back at me as he caught me watching him.

We pulled into Prevost Harbor under full moonlight as the clouds were just starting to clear again. Mr. MacDara was waiting for us at the main house and came down the steps to meet us as we exited the dock.

"I was hoping you'd made it back in before the rain. You kids get caught up in any of it?" he asked. "Jesus, Mary, and Joseph, you're soaked through to the bone lass. Mack, go in and grab your mother's cover and bring it out here to the wee miss," he instructed.

Mack tilted his head at his father's request and smiled and nodded. He came down the front steps holding a blue wool flowing cape with a deep hood. He wrapped the garment around me and gently fastened the buttons on the coat. They both took a step back and stared at me sweetly.

"You look lovely dear. She would have loved to see you in it." Mr. MacDara beamed. "Now you best be off, both of ya. Get her home before her parents start to worry Mack. There's a smirr about tonight," he warned.

We set off down the road toward the lighthouse, hand in hand, walking in silence. He looked deep in thought about something, and I caught him peering over at me as if he was checking to make sure I was still there, or some figment of his imagination. I felt him gently caress my hand and again get lost in his thoughts. Finally, he spoke. "That coat has been hanging by the door since my mother died. She wore it every day. He's never allowed anyone to move it, not until today."

I placed my hand against the breast of the jacket and looked over at him knowingly. We stopped and I squeezed his hand and pulled him close to me. I kissed his cheek gently and whispered that I was honored to wear it. His eyes shone so brightly and reflected his honorable intentions in the moonlight. They were filled with love and tenderness, and he said, "You're my best friend you know." He took his arm and wrapped it around my shoulder, and we walked up the road together happy and light. I leaned into his body and felt perfectly content.

"Look up," he suddenly announced and stopped in the middle of the road. The clouds had parted perfectly to reveal a crescent moon overhead framed perfectly by soft whisps of clouds. "It looks like the Cheshire cat smile from Carroll's book."

"Perhaps we've found Wonderland," I joked, "Let's just hope the Queen of Hearts isn't waiting up for us."

"Indeed." He nodded knowingly.

We came down the long hill to the lighthouse, engrossed in each other and the magic of the night. We had just made the turn to the front of the house when Joseph came out from behind the smokehouse, sitting squarely to the left of the main house.

Joseph sauntered over. "It's pretty late...isn't it." Mack stiffened as he approached.

"It's a good thing that time and my whereabouts have absolutely nothing to do with you," I said as we blew past him up the steps.

"Why don't you ask him about his late-night runs Willow, or where he gets his money." Joseph smirked. "Guess that's none of my business as well." He turned to walk back down to the lighthouse. He whistled softly as he walked off and left Mack and I on the porch facing each other. I looked confused and asked Mack what he was talking about.

"I'll tell ya everything Leannan, just not here, not now." He looked worriedly through the front window and back to me again. "Trust me, I'll never lie to you, and I should have told you sooner regrettably, but the time wasnae right." He turned to me through darting glances at the door and back to the window.

Just then the front door opened, and my father and mother were standing in the threshold, my father with his hands on his hips and my mother just slightly behind him.

"Have you any idea what time it is young lady?" my father said firmly. "Your mother and I have been worried sick about you since early this evening."

Mack stepped forward and outstretched his hand to my father, who took it reluctantly.

"Hello Sir, please accept my apologies, we were out sailing, and the winds changed, and it took us a little longer to get back..." he started.

My father cut him off abruptly and said, "Please don't make excuses for worrying her mother and I so."

He looked sharply at Mack then back at me. "Please get in the house, it's incredibly late." He took a puff from his pipe and turned back to go inside the house.

"You didn't even give us a chance to explain!" I snapped back.

"We will discuss this inside Willamina." He turned coldly to Mack, "Good evening to you, young man."

Mack tipped his hat to my mother and said good evening. He turned back to me defeated as they walked into the house and my father slammed the door. Mack lowered his head and his voice as he approached, "Dinnae fash, it will all work out. I'm sorry to get your father so cross with me. Meet me tomorrow at noon at the top of the hill if you can, I'll explain everything," he blurted quickly as he descended the stairs and slipped off into the night.

I turned back into the house with conviction, convinced to not let them cage me like that, even if they had raised me. I grabbed the handle and flung the door open ready to go to war against the injustice of my parents' treatment of us. My father was standing near the fireplace and my mother was seated on the sofa when I entered. They were clearly mid conversation about me, as they stopped talking abruptly the moment I entered the house.

"What was that?" I snapped at my father and pointed toward the door.

"You'll watch your tone with me young lady," he said firmly.

"Willow, we are only looking out for you, we want what's best for you," she interjected. "Your father heard he's involved in some unsavory business around here and it could impact your father's job, and not to mention your good name being seen with him."

"He's a good man, this I know," I snapped back.

"I don't like you seeing him, period," my father said as he emptied his pipe more forcefully than necessary. "That's the end of it."

He walked out of the parlor and into the kitchen, pushing past me without even looking at me. I looked over at my mother for some type of sign that she couldn't possibly support this. She walked over to me and gently held my arm, "I'll talk to him Willow, but I don't like this MacDara boy."

"You don't even know him," I snarled as I pulled my arm away from her and walked up the stairs.

10

Tossing Out Blame

The next morning was tense, to say the least. My father had vacated the house early and it was only my mother and I and Kyle for breakfast. Kyle was oblivious to any undertones in the niceties we exchanged and rambled on about the new game him and Charlie had invented.

"We call it hoops and we have to throw them high up into the tree. The first one to get the hoop over the branch to stay in the tree wins! We've found loads of old barrel rings near the MacDara farm. Charlie and I have gotten real good mom!"

My mother scowled at Kyle's declaration and then looked worriedly over at me. "That's nice dear. I bet you are a real tiger at that," she said and ruffled his hair. He scooted down out of his chair still holding half a piece of toast and ran down the hallway. "Bye mom, I'm going up the road again with Charlie!" he yelled as he flew out the door and down the front steps.

I grabbed an apple out of the fruit bowl and went out onto the porch to avoid the awkwardness with my mother. I sat down in the rocker and looked out over the point and out into the water. The skies were grey and so was the water as it churned passed Turn Point. The Beryl-G was gone now from her temporary holding at the end of the dock. She must have been towed sometime yesterday or earlier, before sunrise. I wondered what else would be found on the boat as the investigation continued in Friday Harbor. The lighthouse and the docks looked empty this morning and I was thankful to be alone with my thoughts. The men must be out on another early morning patrol, which was more and more frequent since the incident with the Beryl-G.

I went back upstairs and got dressed for the day. The house was still, and it was slightly unnerving to move about. Every creak felt as though it were a reminder to my mother that I was upstairs, and we had a rift that needed mending. I wasn't in the mood to discuss my love life with her, and hoped we could casually avoid one another for a bit longer. I had plans to see Margie today, and hopefully see Mack on the way. I walked down the stairs and into my mother who was standing in the hallway.

"I'm going to see Margie today," I said coldly, "unless you want to forbid me to see her as well." I pushed past her down the landing. "Not sure when I'll be back, before bed though. Please don't send the police looking for me."

My mother scowled at me, "Honestly Willow..." she uttered as she made a deep sigh.

I closed the door behind me and instantly felt remorse over how harshly I had talked to her. I was angry with her, but most of my resentment was reserved for my father who was conveniently absent as I left the house. I continued up the hill, resolved to speak with her later this evening about how she had hurt me. We were usually so close and I disliked the distance that had been created recently.

Mack was waiting at the top of the hill; he had seen me before I saw him. He jumped down from a moss-covered rock and led me down a small deer trail off the main road. We stopped near a large rock, and he took my hand.

"I wasnae certain if you would be allowed to see me again, or if you wanted to, so I figured we'd want to keep off the main road to talk," he said. He looked pensive, like he was unsure of how I felt and was waiting for me to tip him off.

"What did Joseph mean when he said those things about late night runs and money? My father also alluded to your 'unsavory' actions, as he put it."

Mack sat down on a small boulder, took a deep breath, and began solemnly:

"Remember how I told ya my mother was ill? Well, my father spent everything we had taking her to the doctor on the mainland. He didn't plant for two years; we sold off most of the sheep. We were in a bad way. When she finally died, we had nothing left and my father was so stricken with grief he couldn't get out of bed."

He hung his head and touched his fingers together nervously. He looked up at me and continued, "We couldn't even afford to light the lamp Willow, we had nothing but the house and the barn and the boat left," he admitted as he shook his head and looked back down at the ground.

"I couldn't let my father lose the house to his grief, not when there was so much of her in it. He just needed time, he needed to get back on his feet and everything would be ok," he told me, but it also sounded like he was still telling it to himself reassuringly.

"I've some friends on Pender that run a still there. They make and bottle whiskey and I bring it across in my boat to the island. From there it goes to the mainland, and it's sold to a Speak Easy or two in Seattle and Bellingham."

He looked up at me pale and with a slightly tormented look in his eyes. "There you have it," he said fatalistically. "Perhaps I'm not the man you thought I was after all."

"You should have told me Dylan." My eyes meeting his for the first time.

I walked over to him and cupped his face in my hands, "You're exactly the kind of man I thought you were...The kind of man who protects his father, who sacrifices his own safety to help others. I couldn't love you more Dylan MacDara, I couldn't love you more."

He sprang up from his seated position and wrapped his arms around me. He kissed my forehead and then took my face in his hands and kissed my lips. He looked like a thousand-pound weight had been lifted from his frame and the light returned to his eyes as he straightened his frame.

"I've got two more runs and then we've enough money to make an honest go of it again. I swear to ya, once I finish this job and we're out of the woods with the debt, I won't look back. I can't let him lose the farm Willow," he said earnestly.

"And *we* won't," I replied calmly. "We'll do this together."

"I cannae let you risk your safety, getting mixed up in this, it's my cross to bear, and I'll bear it, but I won't risk your safety or your good name," Mack insisted.

"My good name...? That's mine alone to disgrace Mack. And not helping you save the farm would be a sure-fire way to do it." I concluded sternly.

We left each other back at the main road. Mack had business at the Ericksen farm, and I had promised to meet Margie for the afternoon. I walked on down the road and came upon Charles and Kyle, on the side of the road opposite the MacDara farm. They were laughing and running around the base of a tall fir tree. The boys were fully engrossed in their new game, throwing rocks at a small metal hoop that had been flung onto a high branch. They were trying to push the hoop down the horizontal branch and have it rest next to the trunk of the tree. They waved to me as I passed them, but too wrapped up in the game to stop and come over.

The sky was covered in thick grey clouds, but not dark enough to be heavy with rain. The air smelled damp and salty as the breeze blew in over the road. Several sheep sat quietly near the fence watching me walk down the road. They had mown down a tiny strip of grass and clover just outside of the fence line, as far as their necks could stretch. Small areas of wear on the fences mirrored the mown patches in the clover. As I watched them, I thought about how agonizing it would be to have the thing you wanted just outside of your reach. They'd have to see it every day, to smell it on an afternoon breeze, and I wondered if it was worse to have it so close and get only a taste, or to never have it at all and be unbound by the knowing of something.

I walked to the fence and plucked handfuls of clover and wildflowers. The sheep had seen my harvest and were sticking their necks out from inside the fence, craning and contorting to be the first to be fed. I pulled several handfuls and listened to them baa softly as I fed them. Their soft velvet muzzles gently twisted around the stems and the sweet clover vanished into their mouths. They sat along the fence line that afternoon, content with their gifts, and unbothered when I left.

I arrived at Margie's place and was instantly flung into chaos. One of her brothers opened the door, as another one pulled at his shirt from behind the door to try and pull him down. They were laughing and wrestling and the older one yelled, "Margie, your friend's here!" just as he was pulled to the ground by a third brother. Mr. Borcher had come out from the kitchen and yelled at the boys to simmer down.

He was wearing a loose-fitting cotton shirt and dark pants tucked into his boots that were soiled with the day's activities as a fisherman, no doubt. He was carrying a frying pan and waved to me with it as I walked into the house. His beard hid a disarming smile, and his eyes looked weary from years of seafaring. A delectable aroma of fish, butter and bread filled the house. There were piles of garments littered around the house and the table was filled with nets awaiting mending. Mr. Borcher retreated to the kitchen and the sound of clanking pots and dishes rang out from behind the wall. Muttered cursing ensued and the boys went back to wrestling and teasing each other unbothered by the commotion in the kitchen.

Margie soon appeared in the hallway and motioned for me to come to her room. "Quick, it's not safe out here!" she joked. We hurried down the hall into her small room, which was covered from head to toe in pastels and jewel tones. The bed was covered with a rag quilt of every hue of pink and purple patchworked together. Golden frames of magazine cut out stars adorned the walls and bejeweled bottles of sea glass sparkled in the window light. It was a truly feminine and artistic space, a far cry from the male dominated space of the rest of the house.

"Welcome to the sanctuary," she announced and threw her arm out in a dramatic flair. "My brothers know they aren't even allowed to come in here." She shook her head and continued, "Destruction and chaos follow wherever they lead. I swear they could knock down the Woolworth building, if only they had a few hours of uninterrupted time." She smiled and flung herself on her bed. A small crash sounded off in the main room beyond the walls and Margie smirked and spread her arms to the sky and said, "Exactly my point."

She put on a record, it hummed in the background, and we sat down on her bed together. I told her about everything—the trip to Pender Island with Mack, the run in with Joe and my parents, but held back about the recent discovery with Mack and the illegal rum running. I don't know why I didn't tell her straight away. I trusted Margie with my deepest secrets, but this one felt like it wasn't mine to tell. The stakes were high with the farm and the illegal nature of what I knew.

Margie fiddled with her necklace while I recounted the last week of events. She walked back and forth from the bed to the window, then back to the record player as I replayed the sequence of events for her. She seemed pensive and as if she was just about ready to speak and then silently pacing again.

"It's not like you to not have anything to say Marjorie," I said to her on yet another lap to the record player.

Marjorie detoured back to the bed and sat across from me. She grabbed my hand. "I have something to tell you, and I don't know if I should...I only just found out two nights ago and I swore my secrecy to Sam." She grabbed her necklace and placed it between her lips as if the necklace itself would stop the words from pouring out. "I know why Joseph hates Mack, and I know why your parents don't want you to see him."

I stopped her outpouring of words as I grabbed her wrists and said, "Margie I know," I paused. "I know."

She sat upright and snapped out of her moral dilemma at my confession. "When?" she asked. "How?" she continued, eyes wide, searching my face for answers.

"I found out around the same time you did honestly. Joseph had made some ambiguous allegations when we returned to the house that night and Mack explained everything the next day when we met. Oh Margie, don't think him a bad person for what he's doing. It's for his father and the farm," I pleaded.

"Sam told me everything Willow. Mr. MacDara is kin to him as well, he knows first-hand what the farm means. He has been tipping off Mack about the patrols in order to ensure safe passage at night," she revealed.

My eyes widened at the implications as the full breadth of the situation started to settle in my mind. Sam could be imprisoned and at best relieved of his post. If Mack were caught it would be the ruin of him, and their blossoming relationship as well. My father and Joe were relentless these past few weeks, their fervor stoked by the incident on the Beryl-G. *What would they do if they found us out now?* My head and my heart swirled with emotion like a violent undercurrent.

This was so much bigger than I had first assumed, and more was at stake than just the family farm.

"Goodness gracious," I said still trying to process everything in my brain. I looked over at Margie and covered my mouth.

"Goodness gracious indeed," she said, shaking her head knowingly as she put her arm around me, hugging me tightly.

After we had talked a little more about Sam, the Beryl-G, and the other things happening in our lives her father had yelled down the hall that supper was ready. He knocked on the door and asked if I'd be joining the family for the meal. Margie wrapped her arm around me and said, "You can't miss my dad's salmon chowder." We walked down the hall together toward the growing sound of laughter and shouting.

The table had been cleared of the nets and a large ceramic pot sat in the center of the table. A plate of sourdough rolls sat off to the side with a crock of butter. The boys were seated on a long bench to one side of the table looking like wolves ready to devour a lamb. The opposite side of the table was set for two, and Mr. Borcher took a seat at the head of the table while the boys pushed each other and jostled for position. Mr. Borcher gestured for us to sit and shot the boys a look to settle themselves down. They sat upright immediately and smiled at their sister and me.

"What are you waiting for Margie, trumpets to play and a red carpet?" the oldest called out.

"Be thankful you only have one brother," she joked as she turned her head back to me before sitting.

The boys watched as we dished up our bowls with several ladles of the creamy chowder. As soon as we were served Margie's dad made a gesture and the boys attacked the rest of the food, in precisely the manner I had expected them to at first sight of them. In a flash the rolls were gone, and the soup was spooned up into each heaping bowl. Mr. Borcher watched in a mix of slight amusement and slight disdain.

"This is why we had you ladies serve yourself first," he chuckled and shook his head. "These boys would eat through the walls if they could get their teeth around them."

It was a wonderful dinner, although loud and chaotic, it was nice to see a father and his children so close. They all talked freely, sometimes over one another, and although a lot of teasing took place, it was all under-toned with love. Margie and her siblings cleared the table after the meal was finished and Mr. Borcher asked Margie to bring out her ukelele and play. The boys all started cheering and whooping and settled in on the benches and the chairs in the living area. Margie took up a seat near the hearth and started to sing a sea shanty and strum her ukulele to the tune. Her oldest brother kept time on his knee and the younger siblings all chimed in to the melody. Her father pulled a harmonica from his breast pocket and started to play along as well. The family was astonishingly musical, and I sat back in awe at the show that had unveiled before me.

Margie sang melody and strummed her ukulele, and the boys chimed in with the chorus and percussion at times. The youngest of the group tapped his feet and clicked his heels on the leg of the chair in time to the beat. Mr. Borcher's hands moved deftly over the shiny steel of the harmonica. His head swayed in time with the music and his eyes sparkled as he played for his children. I clapped along in awe of Margie's vocals and the musical storytelling that ensued. The night wrapped up with everyone out of breath, full bellies, and copious laughter. I said my goodbyes to the family and started for home.

I had just come upon the MacDara farm and hoped I would be able to say a quick goodnight to Mack. The main house and barn were dark and quiet as I walked past. Lola came down off the porch when she saw me and ran out to the road to say hello. She whined and circled me as I stroked her ears and gave her a quick pat. I told her to go home as I continued up the lane, but she refused to listen to me. She always stayed a few feet in front of me as we walked up the road. I pleaded with her to turn around, knowing now was not the time to be late again.

Headlights appeared down the hill from Lighthouse Road and continued towards us. I assumed it was my father and became visibly annoyed, and also slightly fearful, being seen with the MacDara dog and hoping it wouldn't spark more conflict. The car did not slow as it approached. As it passed by, I saw Joseph behind the wheel and young Charles riding in the front seat waving out to me. Joseph stared straight ahead as if I did not exist, which was eerie and unsettling. Lola moved to the side of me as the car passed and watched it until it trailed off along the bay.

I was at a loss as to what I should do, as I knew he would be coming back this way shortly. I didn't want to see him, but I also didn't want to be enemies either, especially given the new information I had regarding the bootlegging activity on the island. Perhaps he would just drive past again, I argued with myself, hoping to rationalize the uneasy feeling I had in my stomach. I had to give him his mother's necklace, so I undid the clasp from my neck and held it balled up in my hand in case the opportunity presented itself. I hadn't wanted to lose it and had been afraid to take it off for fear of something happening to it. As much as I disliked Joe currently, it was a family heirloom, and I wanted to treat it with care. However, I couldn't let him see me wearing it and think I carried any affection for him, or he had any claim to me; the latter being the gift's true intention I presumed.

I saw the headlights on the horizon before I heard the car come up the road. The brakes squeaked as the car started slowing and I felt a lump rise in my throat. The car crept slowly forward and came to a soft rest directly to my left. Joseph leaned across the car and cranked the window down. "Would you like a ride?" he said seemingly disinterested in me, and oddly uninvested in the outcome of the offer. Lola whined and circled my feet making sure to keep herself between the car and myself.

"I'd love one, however I'm worried that the poor dear might chase the car, and I don't want her to get lost," I said, hoping my excuse wasn't too thinly vailed as I looked to Lola.

He opened the car door unprompted and made a shoo noise to Lola and clapped his hands. Lola leapt toward him, ensuring I was behind her and growled and barked at Joe. The hair on her back stood straight up at the nape of her neck and her head was low and unwavering.

"Damn dog," he said as he clapped at her and tried to run her off.

"Stop it Joe!" I yelled as he advanced toward the dog. Lola let out a loud growl and stood her ground.

Joe stopped his advance and turned to me and said, "Is that what I get for trying to help?" his voice was low and menacing. Lola continued to growl as he stared at me. "Why must you be so difficult?" he asserted as he looked up to the sky dramatically.

I took a step toward him and Lola barked in protest. I put my hand on her back to calm her and then walked up to Joe. Lola didn't like it, but she allowed it watchfully from my side, eyes glued onto Joe, teeth slightly barred.

"I don't want this anymore," I said as I emptied the contents of my hand into his. "It's honestly doubtful I ever did."

He smirked as he saw the necklace cascade into his hands and his fist closed tightly over the chain. His grasp became tighter and tighter as his fist turned red and white and trembled slightly.

"Are you giving this back to me because of that degenerate bootlegger you've been hanging out with?" he asked coldly. "Don't think I haven't heard the rumors about him, like everyone else on this island Willow...including your father." He lowered his hand and still clutched the necklace but not as tightly now. "Do you honestly think your family will allow that? Do you honestly think you could have a future with him?" he questioned as he spoke with his head turned to one side not breaking eye contact.

"You know nothing about Mack, or my father for that matter," I contended, meeting his icy stare with one of fire. "Know your place ensign," I said. "and for the record your place is not with me."

I saw Joseph's fist ball instinctually in the headlight and I backed away out of his reach. He unclenched his fist purposely at my retreat. "Don't paint me a fool Willow, I assure you I am not one," he hissed as I stepped back in retreat.

I turned to walk up the road and Lola stood frozen in her tracks, eyes still locked on Joseph, until he returned to the vehicle. The head lights began to move, and I shuffled to the side of the road, afraid to turn around, but also afraid not to. Lola ran to my side just as Joseph sped past and left us in a cloud of dust along the now dark road. I sat down on a nearby stump and Lola put her head in my lap.

Tears slowly fell from my face as the adrenaline of the moment started to fade and the worry and grief for what was to come was laid out. If they knew about Mack, it was only a matter of time before they caught him. Joseph was never going to give up his personal vendetta for Mack, that much was clear after tonight. If anything, the events of the evening had probably strengthened his resolve on the matter. Lola licked my hand and panted as she pressed her body against my leg in the dark. I stroked her soft head and wept a little more at the recounting of her bravery and protection. I kissed her forehead, and she licked my cheek in response.

I heard a low whistle come from down the road at the MacDara farm and Lola's ears perked up at the sound of it. Mr. MacDara's voice could be heard off in the distance calling for Lola. She looked back at me and whined and then back down the road. "Go on, go," I said. And she gave my hand a soft lick and sprinted off down the road toward home. I walked the rest of the way home, happy to come through the front door to the warm glow of the house, the instant feeling of safety, and the smell of something sweet baking in the oven.

My mother was tidying up in the kitchen when I entered. She smiled at me by pursing her lips together and tapped the table for me to sit. She slid over a still warm piece of blackberry pie and a cup of lemonade and came up behind me and hugged me. I put my arm on her arm and we both stood there motionless until we both started to speak at the same time. We laughed and she told me she was sorry. She talked about how she trusted me, but worried as a mother. She admitted solemnly how she knew I was a grown woman, but it was hard to let go. "You have always been the careful daughter, Willow," she started with her hands on my shoulders. "My precocious child, my first born. You of anyone I know has the best read of people. You're kind and smart, and just."

I got misty eyed as she said these things about me, and I felt my emotions welling up. My mother began gently tending to my hair as she spoke, tucking tendrils into the woven braid as she went. She continued, "and because I know these things to be true about you, I have to trust the woman that I know you to be to use the gifts you've been given to create a life for yourself that makes sense."

"Mom, I..." I started to speak, and she gently placed her hand on my shoulder again. "Please let me finish Willow," she continued.

"I have life experience Willow. I have experienced heartache that thankfully you know nothing of. When I see you making choices that could potentially cause you the same kind of pain, my instinct as a mother is to protect you." Her fingers wrapped nimbly around the last whisps of hair, and she slid a small rubber band from her pocket around the nub of braid.

"I know I cannot protect you from everything, and I know that your life path is, and hopefully will be, very different from mine," she paused and lifted her head matter-of-factly. "Island life will be unforgiving Willow, especially for a woman."

The fear in her eyes made my heart ache. She mustered a trembling smile and squeezed my hand. "I don't want to create a rift between us because I can't see your vision Willow— or understand it. What I will say is that I trust you, even when, and most importantly, when I don't understand.

She knelt next to me and looked me in the eye, her own eyes misty. "Do you trust him dear?"

"I do mom, I really do," I promised.

"Do you understand the severity of what is at stake?" she asked. "I won't, and can't, ask you anymore, for good reason, but I trust you to make the right decisions. Just promise me you won't be so kind, that you forget you need to be clever." She smiled at me with pain in her eyes.

"I know everything I need to mother, and in time I can explain. I can promise you this...he is a good and honorable man."

A tear slid down her face and she hugged me in relief. "Be safe my precious daughter," she said as she hugged me tightly. "Don't ever forget that I'm on your side." She kissed my forehead and brushed both of our tears away and laughed. "Now then, where were we with this pie?"

We spent the rest of the evening laughing and catching up like old times. It was late before I headed up the stairs, my feet and eyelids heavy with the events of the past few days. Oliver was sprawled out on my bed and turned his head slowly as I crawled in next to him. He didn't give an inch as I tried to jockey for position and moved his long body across the bed. I wrapped my hands around him, and he went limp in protest as I slid him down to the foot of the bed. His hind feet curled up in a stretch as he raised his front paws out in front of him and flipped over with a yawn. My head hit the pillow and I didn't wake again until well into the morning.

11

Long Live

A week had passed since Mack had met my parents, and thankfully, emotions had slowly quelled around the lighthouse. Everyone seemed to be enjoying the lull, especially me. My mother and I had come to an understanding a few days ago, and my father had taken the complete opposite approach, deciding physical distance was best for everyone. He would leave for the dock before sunup and return after I had gone to bed. If he did make it up to the house for dinner, he was cold and too preoccupied with his Coast Guard correspondence to entertain a meaningful conversation with me.

To be fair, I wasn't exactly making myself approachable either. Something about this summer had really pushed me past the point of caring anymore what he thought of me or my friends. For the first time, I was solid in who I was and I stood proudly in defiance of his disappointment, rather than running to fix it. If he wanted to have my respect, he was going to have to earn it, as he was so fond of saying to others. I snickered to myself as I sat lazily on the front porch that afternoon daydreaming about the imaginary battles I was fighting with him, and winning, in my head. He didn't know it, but I had entertained no less than five arguments with him in my head since the actual argument, and verbally destroyed him each time.

My mother had come out the front door on one of these occasions, just as I was delivering the Magnum Opus of closing statements in one of my imaginary altercations. Apparently, my face displayed a compelling tell and my mother mistook my savage grin for one of a softer nature.

"What, or should I say *who*, has got you grinning like that?" she teased as she walked past me with the laundry for the line. I most definitely could not tell her I was daydreaming about making my father crumble with my logical and verbal prowess.

"Come on and help me," she added, arms full holding a large basket.

I followed her down to the clothesline and began stringing up the clothes and fastening them with the pins from the basket. Once all the clothes were on, I decided to walk the dock, emboldened by my imaginary battles and most decidedly not interested in skulking around the yard of my own home. Luckily the only seaman I ran into was Sam as he popped up from the engine hold of one of the small crafts.

"Willow!" he called enthusiastically, "How are ya now?" he continued without letting me answer. "Margie and I were just talking about you, we were. Ran into Mack as well." He looked around cautiously and lowered his voice. "We're all meeting at the beach down in Reid Harbor after supper and I was supposed to find ya and see if you'd go?"

"I would love to!" I declared, feeling excited at the chance for all of us to be together.

"I'll gather ya as soon as I'm released here after supper, and we can walk to meet up with the others. Plan on six o'clock, or roughly thereafter," he said. "Oh… and bring some of yer ma's biscuits if you've got any lying about." he suggested as he winked and disappeared back to the engine compartment.

I headed back to the main house to finish my chores for the day and ready myself for an evening with friends. Sam came around shortly after six and we were off to join the others where Lighthouse Road met the MacDara farm.

Mack and Margie were sitting on the fence when they finally came into view, laughing about something and acting like siblings of sort. In truth they had grown up together, being part of such a small island community meant many of them were essentially kin to one another, although not blood related. They hopped down when they saw us and made their way over, Margie running full steam ahead to hug me and then into Sam's arms. He promptly swooped her up and spun her around after kissing her unabashedly. Mack was a few steps behind, not needing to run to match Sam's stride, but grinning that grin as he briskly walked toward me.

He too picked me up with a one-handed swoop and then lifted me above his head and lowered me down to meet his lips. "I missed you," he said still smiling. I took his hand in mine and leaned into him unconsciously as we started walking down the road together.

"What about me?" Sam said as he came up behind Mack, set his feet, and lifted him in the air. "Dinnae tell me you don't have a kiss for your wee cousin?" he said as Mack squirmed in the air laughing at Sam's playfulness. Sam set him down squarely with a thud and Mack and Sam began to playfully wrestle and pretend fight each other as they ran around us.

Margie and I both laughed uncontrollably, and Margie quipped, "You see…I just can't get away from it. Thank God for you Willow!"

We spent the walk to the cove engrossed in idle chat and just doing what good friends do together. The beach was set at the end of the road obscured by the dense forest that came right to the tideline. The tide was out and most of the rocky shore was exposed where the ferry would beach itself when it came through. We walked to the left of the landing and found a small clearing amongst the rocks and trees where we could all sit. The dark ash of a previous fire stained the ground in the center of the area. The guys began collecting firewood and tinder and then reassembled a bygone stone ring for the makeshift firepit. Margie and I began unwrapping some small morsels we had both gathered from home to share.

Sam saw me uncover a tin of biscuits and instantly dropped what he was doing to grab one. Margie laughed and looked at me and silently mouthed, "Why are boys so hungry?" to me. Mack had taken out a knife and was running the blade down a fallen fir limb creating wooden curls that were paper thin. He collected them in a small pile and began to construct a small stick frame around them. Mack pulled out a small tin of matches and carefully lit the fire. The fire slowly climbed the tower of sticks and soon engulfed the contents of the small firepit. Crackles and pops sounded off from the fire as smoke billowed up to the sky.

"That should do it," Mack announced proudly as he walked over to the tin of biscuits himself. He got a rather mischievous look on his face as he produced a small bottle from inside his bag. "I don't know about you lads and lasses, but I don't think I'd be a proper bootlegger, if I didn't bring a bottle of Canada's finest to Stuart Island's finest," he said as he bowed to the rest of us.

Sam and Margie clapped, and I reached for the bottle and smelled it. Mack looked at me intrigued, and I took a long pull from the bottle. It was harsh on my throat as the warm liquid made its way down, but I managed to keep my composure while it settled. Mack laughed at my stoicism and took a pull himself from the bottle. He winced as it went down, and added, "It's definitely not Scottish, but it will do in a pinch." The glass bottle was cast with the words Early Times, creating a raised lettering to the bottle. A shoddy label that read 'Canadian whisky' was affixed just below the embossment. The golden liquid glowed in the firelight as it sloshed in the bottle and was passed around amongst us.

Margie brought out her Ukulele and we sat by the fire idly passing time and the amber bottle. We talked into the evening, laughing and joking about nothing and everything. As I sat on the rocks, I drank in the beauty of the people around me, Margie's effortless confidence, Sam's wild joy, and Mack's thoughtful exemplar. We were the embodiment of youth, hopeful and resilient as we laughed under the stars that night. I couldn't help but marvel at how unwavering and evergreen our little group of friends was, considering all that encircled us that summer. We stood tall in the face of everything, our friendship growing steadily despite the circumstances that threatened our collective futures. This night felt special to me, like a part of me knew the delicate beauty of our position, and the fragile nature of the magic that surrounded us. The sky was turning a deep purple now against the dark green island, and I vowed to take in every detail and remember it as we sat around that evening. I leaned my head on Mack's shoulder and breathed in the night. We sat around the fire and I told him about some of the things I had been thinking, mostly about how much love I had for everyone there on that beach.

Mack brought out a penny and started flipping it towards a small tide pool near the fire. Sam got in on the game and soon they were betting on who could get it closest to the ledge without actually going in. The glow from the fire lit up their faces and Margie and I sat back together watching them, laughing at their boyish charm.

"Here we are, the grand roaring twenties, and we're tossing pennies in a tide pool," Mack said as he shook his head laughing. "It's hard to believe there's a whole world out there tonight, away from this island." He looked out into the harbor and the stillness of the water as he spoke. "Truth be told, there's no place I'd rather be, this night is kind of perfect," he said as he looked back at us, the glow from the fire highlighting his face.

"Here, here!" Margie chanted as she raised the bottle of bootleg whisky and took a swig.

"To Stuart Island's finest!" she called out and handed the bottle to Sam, who tilted it back and raised the bottle.

Mack took the bottle and softly said, "To the Evergreens," as he kissed the top of my head and took a long pull.

We talked and laughed around the fire well into the night, savoring the last bits of the evening together. We reluctantly decided to end things before it got too late and we unintentionally sparked any additional controversy. Sam had said they had early morning patrols and needed to be back at a reasonable hour anyway. We begrudgingly snuffed the fire and made our way back up the hill toward home. We walked together until the MacDara farm and Lighthouse Road met, still basking in the energy of the night and each other. Mack and Margie made their way down towards Prevost Harbor and the farm, while Sam and I turned up Lighthouse Road toward Turn Point.

Sam told me about his plans after his military service, and how Margie was central to them. We chatted the rest of the way home, the lightness of the evening still present, as the two of us walked together. We descended the final large hill to the lighthouse as a form appeared from the rocks near the dock. A trail of white smoke followed the shadowy shape as it came into view.

"Evening," he offered as his profile came into the light. It was Joseph, and he looked ominous as he aggressively blew smoke as he leaned up against a tall fir tree.

"Evening Joe," Sam replied as he tried to walk past Joseph. Joseph rose up at the last minute and bumped shoulders with Sam.

"You'd better be more careful," he said as he inhaled a drag from his cigarette. "Phew, is that whisky I smell on you?" he questioned as he turned to Sam.

"Tsk Tsk tsk, that wouldn't be conduct befitting a seaman now would it Samuel MacDara," he intonated, with careful enunciation on the MacDara as he spoke.

Sam had raised to his full height and his eyes flashed, despite the darkness. Joe met his stare, pretending not to notice Sam's demeanor.

"You folks have a good evening," Joe's voice trailed off as he sauntered back toward the lighthouse with his hands in his pockets.

I walked toward the main house and Sam watched me make it safely inside before leaving to follow Joe back to the bunks. The family had gone to bed, and I was thankful not to have to run that gauntlet of sanctimony tonight. As I brushed my hair I hiccupped and tasted the bootleg whisky on my breath. I smiled to myself as I recounted the evening and how much fun we had had. I crawled into bed, hoping Oliver was lurking somewhere under the bed, but he was nowhere to be found. I guess I wasn't the only one to have exciting plans this evening, I thought to myself, and drifted off to sleep.

12

Watch What Will Become

I awoke much later in the day than I had planned, but my late night out had meant I slept more soundly than normal. I walked down the stairs to my mother and brother playing a game of cards at the kitchen table. My mother raised her eyebrows at me as I shuffled past her to the ice box. "Someone had a late night." she said in a playful tone.

"You smell like campfire," Kyle announced and made a face as I walked past.

I grabbed my braided hair and brought it to my nose. I did smell like campfire, I thought.

"A group of friends and I had a small campfire down by the water last night, if you must know," I commented as I spun around my brother with a glass pitcher of apple juice and set it on the table.

"No fair Willow, I want to have a campfire!" he responded in a whiny voice. "Mom, can Charlie and I have a fire tonight?"

177

"Only if you want to burn down the whole island," I interjected. "Giving you two matches would be a grave error," I teased as I tousled his hair.

He scowled at me and pushed my hand away. My mother and I laughed at his annoyance with me.

"Perhaps another time dear," my mother answered. "Tonight, we are hosting all the men for a dinner in the main house."

"Your father thought it would be a good idea to reward everyone for all the hours they've put in with these new patrols," she added as she played her hand with Kyle.

"Willow, I'm going to need your help today with all the preparations. I thought we'd pull the big tables out of the houses and join them together on the front porch tonight. The boys caught a few salmon off the dock yesterday and we can cook those up for everyone."

I didn't want to see Joe, let alone have dinner with him, but I also knew my mother had a job to do as the captain's wife, and I didn't want to make waves for her and protest. I agreed happily, for her sake, and hoped that everyone would be on their best behavior.

The men were all out on patrols that morning and we took the opportunity to go into the officers' quarters and commandeer the large wooden table from their lodging. We had to clear away several piles of papers, rubbish, and ashtrays— primarily the signs of gentleman, being not so gentle. Long standing stains of food and grime speckled the table, and the entire room for that matter. My mother made a deep sigh as she made a mental note of the additional time it would take for her to clean the table this afternoon.

"Men," she uttered as she shook her head.

It took some serious muscle to move the table from the bunkhouse to the porch, but my mother and I had everything set up and washed before noon. We took a break after the heavy lifting had been done and enjoyed iced tea and small sandwiches we had thrown together with the leftovers from last night's meal. Our rest was short lived as the afternoon swiftly dwindled and there was still so much to do. My mother had tasked me with collecting vegetables from the garden and flowers for the table. The garden was in full swing as we were well into August. Patches of bright yellow flowers and large green zucchinis decorated the far row. Small red tomatoes hung full on the vine and draped over the wooden supports. There were rows of beans and peas, carrots, and onions interspersed with radish, lettuce, and beets.

My mother had an incredibly green thumb, and I admired the vegetable bounty she had nursed to life that summer. Surprisingly the garden had lain undiscovered by the resident deer on the island, and the small white fence had kept out rabbits and other small creatures successfully. I tied the low strings of my apron around my waist and created a makeshift pouch for my harvest. It was overflowing the confines of the apron as I left, and the garden was still brimming with produce left unpicked.

I heaped the offering onto the counter and wiped the sweat and dirt from my brow. "The cherry tree is positively weighed down with fruit. I'll go pick a bag and we can make pies if you'd like?" I suggested to my mother.

"That's a wonderful idea!" She whirled around me in the kitchen, whisk in hand, singing an unrecognizable tune. A closeness enveloped us again, after our talk, and I wanted her to know she could rely on me as well. I too was always on her side, and if felt nice to work side by side with her in the warmth of that afternoon.

As the heat of the day subsided, the table had been set with the fancy China. Collections of flowers in small crystal vases dotted the center of the table, cut from my mother's best colors and varieties that season. Small votives peppered the place settings and the house smelled heavenly. Three cherry pies sat cooling on the buffet as the salmon went into the oven. My mother and I took the small reprieve from the active preparations while the salmon cooked and went to get cleaned up before the men arrived back to the lighthouse from the boats.

We were both finishing up when we heard the boats come back from patrol. We met on the landing, and I told my mother how beautiful she looked and what a great job she had done today. "They're going to love it!" I assured as we hurried down the stairs. My mother went to the kitchen to check the salmon, and I welcomed everyone as they came up the steps.

Sam immediately removed his hat and commented on the elaborate set up. "I don't think I've ever been at such a fine table," he offered. "My compliments to the host."

"Thank you," my father returned, assuming the compliment had been directed to him. He sat down and motioned to the others to find a seat, pushing the carefully lain silverware from its position to set down his pipe. Joe found a seat next to my father and began talking about the events of the day. He whispered something to my father, who nodded and said, "Absolutely my boy, these types of situations call for exceptions. It's really the vagrants those laws are put in place to protect." Joseph disappeared back into the bunk house and re-emerged holding a bottle of wine.

"My family is renowned for their cherry wine back home and I happen to have a bottle if there is no objection," Joseph proposed as he approached the head of the table and stood behind my father.

"Indeed, no objection Ensign Cail," the captain declared.

"Wine is one of the more noble beverages. It's not like that rot gut whisky that plagues our waters and clouds the mind," Joe asserted.

"Willow, may I pour you a glass?" he quipped, "or perhaps you have a moral objection to imbibing anything of this nature."

"Of course not Ensign Cail, although I do believe that people should use the good sense they've been given and abstain from vile things that mean them harm," I snapped back and smiled.

Sam chuckled under his breath, sporting an entertained smirk and Joe shot him a foul look.

"To good sense," I said as I raised my glass of wine and smiled sweetly at the table.

At this moment my mother had come through the door carrying a beautiful platter of salmon. "What are we drinking to?" she inquired enthusiastically as she raised her water glass unaware of what had transpired.

"To the ensign's family wine," my father declared, not understanding the nuance of the conversation, but being astute enough to try and change the subject.

"Let me help you mother," I offered as I excused myself from the table before he could escalate the situation. My mother had gone all out for this meal, and I didn't want the tension to take center stage. As I walked into the kitchen, I saw platters of beautifully dished sides on the counters ready for us to parade in for the meal.

"This looks amazing!" I told her as we walked down the hall, dishes in hand. She beamed with pride as she approached the table.

The table was quickly brimming with food and my father stood from his chair and began a sanctimonious soliloquy about the important nature of their work. He went on about safeguarding the foundation of morality and protecting the country from essentially itself. He did all this with the ensign's wine in hand and his conviction resolved. I wondered if anyone else at the table saw the irony in the situation and for my mother's sake, I ate my salmon and made polite small talk like a dutiful daughter. At the end of the meal, I left a full glass of wine on the table, minus one sip from my toast.

My father had asked the men to come into the parlor for coffee, pie, and a smoke. My mother and I walked the long train of dishes and food back to the kitchen invisibly as they smoked and talked of engines, current events, and the upcoming elections. We divided and conquered, and I made sure every last dish was cleaned, dried, and put away so my mother wouldn't have to be up all night. My father walked into the kitchen just as we were finishing up and said, "Thank you, ladies, that was a wonderful meal." He kissed my mother on the lips and me on the cheek and went back to the parlor to read the paper.

"It really was perfection, mom," I said knowingly. "The food was divine, and the presentation was gorgeous. The way you cut the tomatoes into small roses," I gushed. "and the flowers... the Queen of England herself can't grow roses like that!" I exclaimed.

My mother smiled and leaned in close to me, almost afraid to speak it. "It really was something, wasn't it?" she smiled at me. "Thank you for your help; this is just as much your victory as it is mine," she declared as she squeezed my shoulders in solidarity. We finished up putting the leftover salmon in the ice box and drug ourselves up the stairs and into bed.

13

Willow's Version

I had plans to see Mack that afternoon as I wanted to see how the project for Margie's gift was coming. I made my way up the hill for what seemed like the millionth time that summer. I realized I had committed to memory each turn and bend in the road, and I could now predict each rock outcropping, special tree, or deer trail visible from the road. I couldn't pinpoint the exact day it happened, but it had started to feel like home to me, casually comfortable, in a familiar way.

The forest floor was turning yellow now, a scorched carpet transformed by the hottest days of the year. The grass had also yellowed, the last holdout in the late summer heat. It seemed everything had succumbed to the inevitable period of dryness that came every year at this time to the San Juans. All signs that the cold weather and rain would soon come to the island again and renew the cycle.

The road was littered with the first fallen leaves, and they crunched under my feet as I walked. I heard a flock of geese high overhead signaling to their group as they flew. It seemed remarkable that they just knew where they were supposed to be and when. That one day they would be eating grass in a field and then suddenly understand it was time to go. I pondered what kind of internal mechanism they had that told them it was time, and which direction they should go. I wondered if it felt more like a calling to answer or a compulsion they had to obey.

I arrived on the farm to a hearty welcome. Lola had met me at the property line and escorted me personally down to the house. Mr. MacDara had been resting on the porch and nearly tripped down the stairs to come and greet me. Mack had heard the commotion and popped his head out of the barn to investigate. He dropped his chisel into his tool belt when he saw me and met me with a big grin. He waved me into the barn and brought me over to the workbench.

"I'm not finished with it yet, but nearly," he said as he propped the large wooden staff up in front of me. The wood was hand carved from the top to the bottom with interconnected intricate symbols. Wildflowers crisscrossed around the symbols and rose to the top of the staff where it branched out three ways. I knelt to get a closer look and saw the silhouette of the Borcher family boat, a ukulele, and an outline of Stuart Island. He twisted the staff sideways and ran my fingers over the initials of her family that were carved into Ivy. My eyes moved to the fork at the top and noticed each branch off the main stem had an evergreen tree with our initials, DM, SM, WD.

"It's us! The Evergreens!" I exclaimed.

"It's perfect Mack, it's so much more than I ever dreamed it could be." I smiled and rose to hug him.

He stood back proudly as I admired every detail of the beautifully carved piece, running it through my hands as I examined it. He was a master craftsman, but this piece was something more for good reason. He had grown up with the Borchers and he also knew firsthand what it was like to lose a parent. He had a personal connection to the carving and the love he felt for his friend was evident in every detail.

"Now we've got to talk about the top. Have you worked out what you're going to use for that?" he asked. I told him about the large glass float I had seen in the root cellar back at the lighthouse, but I didn't know how I could vent the top without it cracking.

"That should be easy enough if you bring it by, I'll have a look," he answered.

I kissed his cheek and told him he was my favorite Dylan.

"How many Dylan's do you know?" he asked grinning.

"Just one," I teased and smiled devilishly. He took off toward me laughing and I ran for the back of the barn. I darted around one of the stalls and pushed a small stool in front of him. He faked to the right and I faked to the left. We ran into each other and nearly fell as we intertangled, both of us breathing heavy from the chase. He stood holding me as we righted ourselves, laughing together. Our breathing started to slow and sync as our bodies pressed against one another. We stood motionless for a few moments, the mood shifting as our proximity sparked a more primal emotion. He moved my arms up around his shoulders and moved one hand to my lower back while placing his other hand under my chin and gently tilting my mouth onto his. He kissed me slowly and gently as his hand ran down my neck and onto my chest. The back of his hand traced the curve of my breast and gently followed the outline of my body as it descended. He placed his hand under my sweater and kissed me tenderly as his hand gently caressed me. I leaned into his kiss and felt his arm tighten around me as we embraced.

Just then Lola came trotting into the barn and we heard Mr. MacDara call out to Mack.

"Where are ya now?" he questioned from the front of the workshop. Mack sighed deeply and delivered a short kiss to my forehead before answering his father.

"We're back here Da," he said as we untangled, and I straightened my shirt and giggled. "Just showing Willow the rest of the barn."

His father appeared from around the corner and gave us a sly grin. "To be sure...well you're a gracious host now boy." Mr. MacDara sighed and winked at Mack as he took my hand and asked if I'd like to join him for tea. We walked up the steps to the porch together, with Mack and Lola a few paces behind. Mack looking slightly defeated and flushed and Lola grinned and pranced along happily next to him.

We spent the rest of the early afternoon talking on the porch together. Mr. MacDara brought out a plum cake after we were seated to accompany the afternoon tea. It was evident the love the two had for each other, as Mack jumped up every time his father needed anything, and Mr. MacDara told stories of Mack as a young boy with pride in his eyes. He talked about teaching him to sail and how he had once become stuck in a tree and refused to climb down. His mother had spent the afternoon trying to coax him down unsuccessfully and the Borcher boys had to climb up and get him.

He talked about the widow Malby and the run-in's he'd had with the late Mr. Malby in Friday Harbor.

"She was such a devoted woman, I will never understand her loyalty to him, truth be told," he confessed as he sipped his tea.

"He never stayed on land very long, always out chasing the wind, and leaving her to wait." He shook his head and let out a deep sigh.

"She nearly starved one winter, had it not been for the good people on the island to aid her after he was gone for nigh eight months with no word and no money sent home. She could be seen most days standing out on the rocks, looking out at the sea for his return. It was pitiful to watch."

"Most of the old folks remember her as she was, when she was young and vibrant. After Mr. Malby died or deserted her, she became a shut in. A few locals took to calling her the Mal after she took up her post keeping watch out on the rocks. It's an inside reference with some of the Scots and Irish folk on the island, it's with respect to Hag's Head and the Legend of the Mal.

Mack chimed in and continued, "The story goes that a sea witch fell in love with a great warrior, who did not return her affections. She chased him all over Ireland and he leapt out over the water to nearby sea stacks to evade her magic. She followed him to the great stacks and leapt as well. He saw her give chase and leapt back to the mainland. She fell short in her leap back to Ireland and fell to her death. The legend goes her head washed up three days later at a headland just North of Kilkee, which became known as the Hag's Head."

"That's a tragic story," I whispered, feeling a new level of empathy for her situation.

"There's a lot of those stories out here in the islands," Mr. MacDara commented. "This place can be unforgiving, but also full of redemption...Just like the sea I suppose," he chuckled. "Now enough of that talk," he said as he patted my knee and rose to go into the house.

He announced his intention to nap in the heat of the day and left the two of us on the porch alone. Mack took the opportunity of our newfound privacy to tell me he planned to complete a run in two days' time. He told me Sam had assured him of the patrol schedule and he had a window of time at night to make it across Boundary Pass undetected.

The man he was meeting, Mr. Olmstead, was making several runs a week now in his speed boat. He could not keep up with the demand back in Seattle, although he needed to lay low for a bit after a near run in with a rival operation. The plan was for Mr. Olmstead to keep the Coast Guard busy on the other side of the island in his speed boat, while Mack slipped past the border undetected under sail. He was to dock back at the farm and hide the whisky in the barn until Mr. Olmstead sent the ferry for his monthly grain purchase from the MacDara farm. The whisky would be hidden in burlap sacks, in bags of grain, and be offloaded in Seattle without having to pass through customs. I had to admit it was a good plan, but I knew what he was up against seeing my father ready his resources in the "Noble experiment" of Prohibition. I asked him if I should go with him, and he told me there was no need; he could make the run and be back before anyone even knew he was gone.

He seemed confident in the task at hand, and I wished some of it would rub off on me. My father had just received a fleet of boats a few weeks prior that nearly doubled their speed on the water, and their presence. Radio devices had been installed on the new boats and they would now be able to send real time intelligence out on the water. The boats had also been equipped with small one-pound cannons and the men had been recently authorized to carry small arms. I didn't want to think about Joseph with a gun, and what would happen if he ran into Mack on the water. His disdain for Mack seemed to grow as I distanced myself from him, more and more as the summer went on, and more of his character was revealed.

We walked back to the barn and he showed me the secret door where the whisky was kept. There were already crates of whisky stacked up and ready to be sealed in the grain. The door was hidden conveniently behind a pile of old sails, concealed in the grooved paneling, it had no handle or visible pull. To open the paneling, he pushed where the wood seams met, and the door sprung open slowly. I had to admit the whole operation was pretty impressive.

"You've really thought of everything, haven't you?" I complimented as I tucked my head inside the small door and surveyed the tiny room. There were several rows of crates, totaling over a hundred bottles of whisky easily. I marveled at the amount of money that must have been sitting in front of us.

"With this, and the bottles of the next two runs, I'll have enough to pay off the house loan, buy back the sheep we sold off, and plant seed next year. My entire future is in this room," he told me.

He moved his hand into mine and whispered, "And hopefully your future as well." He kissed me gently on the top of my head. We closed the door to the secret whisky cache and left the barn hand in hand. Mack would need to be down at the boat over the next two days, making ready for his run, and I didn't want to distract him from the task at hand. I kissed him goodbye and headed back to the lighthouse with a heavy mind, knowing the risk he would take in just a short time.

14

Unforeseen Circumstances

The next run was imminent, and I decided I couldn't just sit around all day and do nothing. I made my way down to the docks as a form of reconnaissance, thinking maybe I could hear some bits of information, or see something that would help Mack evade capture or harm. The new boats were lined up closest to the shore, their hulls barely below the water line. They were designed to not only go fast, but to cruise over shallow shoals and reefs in pursuit of the smugglers who used these landmarks to hide. The San Juan Archipelago was riddled with small coves, inlets, and famously inaccessible coastline for larger keeled boats. The rum runners seem to always be one step ahead of the law, each year bringing faster and more agile boats to the island chain. The elevation of operations was much to the dismay of the Coast Guard, which never seemed to be able to keep up with the ingenuity of the bootleggers.

These boats looked promising, however, in their capability. The small cannons had been affixed to the front of the bow and gave the impression of long forgotten war ships of centuries past. *Who uses cannons anyway?* I thought to myself… but would never speak that aloud in front of my father. He took great pride in his new fleet of boats, and he spent most of his time these days, either on patrol or down at the docks ensuring their care and maintenance.

The boats had large outboard motors attached to the transom. These engines were much larger than the other patrol boats and I wondered just how fast they could go. My father had just come down the docks and greeted me with a slight hug. "Taking an interest in my work finally?" he asked.

"They are very impressive dad," I said as I walked alongside one of the boats and ran my finger against the rail.

"Those engines have 12 cylinders Willow; they were once in an airplane if you can believe that. We can hit speeds of 15 knots, even fully loaded," he spouted proudly as he loaded his pipe.

"Why, we've stopped at least four shipments just last week. Business is good, haha! Business is good." He took a few long pulls from his pipe, and he patted me on the back. It was perhaps the most joy I had seen on the man's face that I could remember.

I left my father still out on the docks with his precious boats and went back up to the main house to help my mother. She was running around the kitchen like normal, making bread and shelling peas for dinner. I grabbed the peas and sat down at the table mulling over what I had heard and knowing Mack's old sailboat could never hit 15 knots, or anywhere close to that even under full sail. I hoped the patrol boats would be far away from Mack when he finally made his crossing.

Dinner was uneventful and felt normal for a change. My father and brother left the table after dinner to listen to the radio. Kyle had been hooked on the Uncle Arthur segment of the Radio Times and had been glued to the radio after dinner for the past few weeks. Oliver was sprawled out on the landing of the stairs. His body stretched across the entirety of the landing, and he seemed most pleased with the level of inconvenience this would no doubt cause for anyone wishing to ascend the stairs.

I stepped over him as I hugged the banister for leverage, and he looked mildly annoyed as I deftly outmaneuvered his blockade. He trotted after me, perhaps hoping for another chance at inconveniencing someone for fun. He jumped up on the bed and settled in, apparently too sleepy for any more mischief. I settled in for the evening and tried to read to keep my thoughts off tomorrow night, but my mind wouldn't hold space for anything other than the looming danger. I would read a bit and find I hadn't any clue what was said on the page. I put the book down in futility and watched the wind blow the branches of the trees outside until I drifted off to sleep.

The next morning, I told my mother I was going to visit Mack, and then Margie. I wanted to tell Mack what I had learned about the fleet and make sure he had everything he needed before tonight. I had packed a small satchel of food, so at the very least, he wouldn't be hungry as he navigated Boundary Pass alone in the dark. I filled the satchel with biscuits, ham slices, and an assortment of fruit, and wrapped it up tightly.

I opened the front door to darker skies than I would have liked given what the night held. A brisk breeze was coming in off the water and I reassured myself that the wind would play in Mack's favor and facilitate a speedier crossing. I went back inside for Mack's mother's coat and admired the deep blue wool in the hall mirror. It really was a beautiful covering, and I smiled as I recalled how sweetly it had been offered to me.

I made my way up the hill, watching the sky at every open clearing that revealed the changing horizon. The breeze had picked up slightly and my hair was being blown in nearly every direction. I pulled up the deep hood and tucked my hair into the back of my shirt and quickened my pace. The rain started just as I hit Southside Road and the edge of the MacDara property. Mack was down on the boat and must have been somewhere below when I arrived, as he didn't answer my call when I neared the boat. I climbed onboard and found him sleeping in the aft berth. He must have been sleeping very soundly as he didn't wake as I approached. He looked exhausted and must have been up half the night attaching the black head sail and rigging. I slid off the jacket and my shoes and climbed gently into the bunk next to him. He woke as I laid down and he smiled and wrapped his warm arms around me.

"I must have dozed off," he said sleepily.

"Go back to sleep," I told him, "You're going to need your rest for tonight."

He dreamily agreed and I took a deep breath as I felt his chest rise and fall next to me. I hadn't slept well the night before and I quickly fell fast asleep with him safely next to me. We woke to the sound of water lapping at the hull and rain on the top deck. Mack nuzzled into my neck and kissed behind my ear gently. We both lay in silence, holding on to the last moments of stillness together until it was time. I was afraid to go above deck, fearing a massive storm on the horizon and not wanting to know.

Mack popped his head up through the companionway and looked out towards the water and back over the island. His eyes traveled up the mast, to the windvane, and back out to the water again. He came back down below and wiped the rain from his arms. "It'll be fine Leannan, nothing I can't handle." His eyes made me believe him, but the sound of the rain above made me leery of the assuredness.

I remembered the conversation I had earlier with my father and told him everything I knew. I described the boats and their number and relayed my father's zeal in putting them to use.

"I'll make sure to let Mr. Olmstead know; he'll likely have fun outfoxing them in his boat." Mack chuckled as he dug through the satchel and bit into an apple I had packed.

"That was supposed to be for later." I shook my head at him and kissed him on the cheek.

We went over timelines together and he promised to tap at my window when it was done, no matter the hour. He had to have the boat back to the dock by sunup before the main morning patrol ran. He planned on leaving at sundown and arriving in Canadian waters under the cover of darkness. Given he would make the journey completely under sail with no power, the only tell he offered to awaiting patrols was a visual one. He had attached a new head sail last night and it was as black as a winter's midnight rain. With the sail fully hoisted it obscured most of the rigging and mast and True North would blend seamlessly into the night sky.

"You're a genius Mack. I hope you're as good a farmer as you are a bootlegger," I said as I admired the new sail.

The sun had started to set, and I knew it was time to go. If I couldn't be with Mack, I wanted to be home, with eyes on the men as reassurance. I kissed him gently and then left him to make his last-minute preparations. Margie was spending the night with me, and I set off for her house so we could make the walk back to the lighthouse together. It would be nice to have someone with me who shared in the knowledge of our secret, and who also loved Mack and feared for his safety like I did.

Margie had come prepared for best friend duty. She had packed her magazines and made snacks; she had the whole evening planned to the minute to take our minds off what was happening out on the water. She recently read somewhere about a kelp facial that was all the rage in Hollywood and she told me all about it on our walk. "Your skin will be positively glowing when this is all over, by tomorrow morning we will be dazzling. It's my personal guarantee." Margie made her best attempts to distract me as we walked, but my mind stayed with Mack as we made the trek down to the lighthouse.

We made my bedroom our home base for the evening and brought up tea and blankets for comfort. Margie made me stop going to the window every five minutes to check the weather and did her best to distract me. Every sound or creak of the house made me whip my head around to the window in hopes that it was him.

"I may have to strap you to that chair," Margie said as she looked up from her magazine. "He's the best sailor I know...aside from me. He's going to be fine, it's not even time for him to be back yet," she reminded me.

"I've never wanted my father to fail so miserably in my life."

"I'm proud to say we've really made a rebel out of a careful daughter," she joked.

The storm outside seemed to worsen, and the night drug on, despite our best attempts to pass the time. Margie fell asleep on the bed around two in the morning, mumbling about a quick nap and I let her sleep. I stood next to the window and watched the rain drops hit the windowpane hoping they would stop unsuccessfully.

A gentle rumble started coming from the front of the house and grew in intensity. It sounded like a boat! I strained my ears; the sound became louder and even Margie awoke from her deep sleep. "It's a boat!" I whispered as I threw on my robe and made for the bedroom door.

"Where are you going?" Margie whispered as she automatically got her robe on as well and followed me out the door and down the stairs. We made it onto the front porch just in time to see and hear a small, very loud boat speed past. The crescent moon shed little light on the passing vessel, and I couldn't make out if it was a Coast Guard boat or perhaps Mr. Olmstead in the decoy boat. The sound of several engines could be heard out in Haro Strait, but we couldn't make out anything, even with the occasional beam of light from the lighthouse.

"It sounds like a regatta out there," Margie whispered as she clung to my arm.

"The more noise in Haro, the better. That's one less patrol boat in Boundary Pass that he has to contend with." I strained to hear the boats as they must have been far off now or turned East around the corner of the island. In any case, it was the opposite direction from Mack, and I breathed a small sigh of relief as the night became still again.

"He should be back in an hour or two now at the latest," I affirmed. "I'll make the tea, and you go on upstairs and get another hour's rest. I'll wake you when he comes."

We snuck back into the house and Margie went upstairs while I quietly lit the stove and boiled water for the tea. I sat in the kitchen for a few minutes drinking in the warm liquid, not wanting to disturb Margie as she fell asleep. The light was just starting to filter through the kitchen window as I sipped the last bit from my cup. I poured a second cup and started to feel sick in my stomach. He should be here by now. I looked up at the clock and back out the window expectantly hoping it to stay dark for a little longer.

My parents would be up soon, and I cleared away any evidence of my late-night doings and headed upstairs out of sight. Margie was already up, looking the most worried I had seen her look since this ordeal began. She was sitting by the window and her gaze shifted from me to the window, and back again. "What do we do?" she asked in barely a whisper.

"We can't sit here," I decided. "Get dressed."

We snuck down the stairs and back out again into the cool dawn air. The good news was the rain had stopped and the winds had mostly died down. The air smelled clean and crisp in our lungs as we ran up the hill toward the MacDara farm. We cautiously stayed out of sight as we came into view of the farm and my heart sank into my chest as the dock came into view. True North sat tied up to the dock, safe and well, but so were two patrol boats. The men had boarded Mack's boat, and he stood at the end of the dock with two other men, one of them being my father. He must have left the house sometime in the night or never gone to bed. I cursed my carelessness and assumptions seeing him standing there with Mack.

We quickly took to the woods to continue our descent toward the dock to remain out of sight. Margie and I crouched down as we approached the clearing near the entrance to the dock and tried to listen to what they were saying. Margie slipped her hand in mind and squeezed it three times. I squeezed it back unable to think I was so sick with worry.

"You're a god damn liar!" I heard Joseph's voice first as he ascended from below deck and shouted.

We both jumped at the intensity in his voice and volume. We watched as he kicked a small stool on deck out of his way and jumped down from the boat and approached Mack. My father had said something to Joseph, but it was too muffled to make out.

"Well, I know he didn't have time to leave the farm. It has to be here!" we heard Joseph avow.

"If it is here, the authorities will find it. You know we can search the boat, but we have no jurisdiction on land, Cail. I will remind you of our obligation to uphold the law, and not your personal vendetta."

"Mr. MacDara, I'm sure you'll give us full cooperation and come with us while we radio for further guidance from the authorities in Friday Harbor?" I heard my father say calmly.

"Mr. Olmstead, given your long-standing relationship with the law enforcement community, I'm sure you have no objection either?"

"None, Sir," he said cooly. "I'm certain once we involve the mainland authorities, we will all realize this was just a big misunderstanding."

My father instructed Joseph to take one of the boats with Mr. Olmstead and another seaman and he would follow in the second boat with Mack. Joseph turned on his heels at once and followed the instructions of the captain. He looked incredibly pleased with himself as he sped off, even from as far away as we were.

Once it was just my father and Mack, I jumped up and told Margie to follow my lead. "What are you crazy?" she said as she peered around the large clump of trees that obscured us from view. My father had been busy readying the boats and had his back turned to the road and the entrance to the dock.

I called out to him, pretending to just notice him as we made the turn toward Margie's house. "Hey Dad!" I said cheerfully, pretending to be totally ignorant to the situation around me.

"Willow, I'm in the middle of something here, and you can't be here," he said sternly.

"Ok, I'll see you later then. We were just on our way to Margie's house to send the boys off for another week of fishing, an early breakfast before they shove off."

Mack's eyes were huge as he followed me wondering what I was doing.

"That's wonderful dear, now please run along," he said mildly annoyed at my continued talking. He went back to adjusting the lines and I flashed a look to Mack as I spoke.

"Ok, just wanted to tell you that after the early time breakfast with the boys we've got to meet behind the Mal, to help Miss Katie clean up again. See you later!" I made sure I made direct eye contact with Mack as I uttered the phrase.

If you wouldn't have been looking for it, you would have missed it, but I saw it and it was the tiniest quick grin from Mack, and I knew he understood.

My father grew more impatient with me and threw down one of the lines, "Fine, I don't care where you go right now. Tell your mother, honestly, just leave me be."

I walked off the dock with Margie and as soon as we were out of ear shot, she asked me "What is going on?" in a sharp whisper.

"Just keep walking until they are out of sight," I said looking straight ahead. With the sound of the engine firing up and the boat speeding away I was able to speak. "We haven't much time. I need you to get the MacDara mule harnessed in the cart as quickly as you can. Take the cart to the back of the barn and do not let anyone see you, for the love of God."

I ran to the barn as quickly as I could, thankful that Mr. MacDara didn't seem to be anywhere in sight. I fumbled through the passageway leading to the back of the barn and ran my hands along the wall to access the door. I pushed on the paneling and the door popped open, revealing several more crates of whisky lined up in rows. I worked quickly as I cleared the back barn door of hay bales and piles of sails. I ran to the door and threw the heavy wood crossbeam lock into the pile of sail and pushed the doors open. Margie was just coming around the side of the barn with Jacob, the MacDara's mule, hitched to the cart.

"In here!" I yelled and guided the mule into the barn. Margie came around to the small door as I approached, and I revealed the hidden cache. "

The police will be back with a warrant, and we have to get this out of here quickly."

"Where will we take it?" she asked and just as quickly said, "Oh my God the Mal…behind the widow's stones!" as she realized the secret code I had relayed to Mack.

She instantly sprang into action, and we wasted no time loading the near 300 bottles of whisky into the back of the cart. Once the cart was loaded, we grabbed the old sail and tucked it neatly around the cargo, ensuring no part of it was visible to anyone who may pass by. We loaded ourselves into the cart and I snapped the reins for the donkey to move. Jacob brayed and put his ears back. I snapped the reins again and said "Heeyaw!" with conviction. Jacob pranced his feet back and forth, but refused to move forward. He bared his teeth and shook his head in defiance.

"I think the damned thing only understands Gaelic!" I cried as I tried to remember the word for forward. Margie got out and tried to lead the animal with the reins, but he stood obstinately as she tried to move him.

"Move damn it!" I cried in desperation as the stubborn animal stood his ground.

Just then, we heard movement coming from the front of the barn and listened as someone was fast approaching. We looked at each other in terror as the footsteps grew closer. Mr. MacDara appeared, with a look of bewilderment at the scene he had stumbled on. Quickly he walked over to the beast and grabbed the reins, calming the donkey. He steadied the creature with a gentle hand on his brow, softly stroking the frightened animal.

Mr. MacDara looked up at me and Margie and without hesitation leaned in gently to Jacob and softly said, "Coisich" and the donkey started to move. Margie let out a deep sigh of relief and quickly jumped in the cart. No explanation was given, and none was asked for. He just pointed the donkey toward the road and whispered "Coisich" again to Jacob and closed the big barn door behind us as we left.

Thankfully the road into the far side of the harbor had been empty. We made it almost to the edge of Mrs. Malby's property when she came bounding down the narrow lane from her house.

"Quickly, quickly!" she directed, "We haven't much time." She looked past the rear of the cart and then took the reins and led Jacob onto the property. "I saw the boats come into Prevost," she explained as she walked abreast of the cart. "The MacDaras have always been good folks, whatever bad luck was swept in with the tide, well we'll just see about righting it." She winked at us and smiled assuredly.

"We need a place to hide this, for a short while," I explained. "It's not exactly on the up and up…"

"Oh child, enough said, I know places we can hide." She cackled and clicked her tongue at Jacob who picked up his pace at the sound of her voice. She led us to the clearing behind her house and stopped us directly in front of the stone outcroppings that Margie and I had discovered earlier. We wasted no time in unloading the cases of whisky into the hidden crevice and covered them neatly with the large sail and canvas remnants. The whisky was entirely concealed inside the stones, visible only from above, but only if one knew where to look.

"Waste no time in getting that cart back to the farm," Mrs. Malby insisted as we finished concealing the cache. "Now off with ya, and don't come here for a few days," she added. "They may be looking for how and where you gave 'em the slip." She pulled some grain from somewhere inside her long cloak and held her hand out to Jacob while she whispered in his ear. Margie and I got back into the cart, and she straightened Jacob's bridle and handed us the reins.

"Coisich Jacob," she coaxed, and Jacob trotted off down the road toward home.

We pulled into the farm and there were still no signs of activity at the MacDara place, thankfully. Mack and the others must have still been back at the lighthouse undergoing questioning and waiting for the authorities from the mainland. We quickly unhitched Jacob and sent him into the pasture to graze. We crept back into the barn to make sure everything was as it should be before heading out. I posted Margie at the main door as a lookout in case anyone came down the road or by boat back to the farm. I opened the concealed door and surveyed the area one last time. There was nothing in the room but stray whisps of hay and some old tack in the corner. I closed the door and took a deep breath when I heard Margie shout, "They're coming!" We quickly dashed out the back door of the barn where we had come in and made our way down the far fence line, unseen, back onto Over the Hill Road near Margie's place.

Once we were on the road we stopped to take a breath. I dropped my hands down onto my knees and hunched over, elated we made it out of the woods undetected. Margie threw her hands up and interlaced them behind her head as she looked up and down the road. We both panted and caught our breath. Margie started grinning and I covered my mouth, in shock about what we had just accomplished.

She reached her hand out to shake mine and said, "If there's no body, there's no crime my friend." We shook hands and laughed as we straighten up and the initial panic had worn off. "Now what?" she asked as we stood in the clearing looking warily up and down the road. "Back to my place or back up the road toward the farm?"

"Let's see it through" I decided, "we'll just be headed back to the lighthouse like we said we would be." Margie nodded and we set off back toward the farm, by way of the main road this time. As the farm came into view, we could see the entire group that had first been present on the docks that morning, add Mr. MacDara. The gentlemen were all outside of the barn talking and I saw my father shake Mr. MacDara's hand. We walked as slow as we could muster without being obvious, hoping to get a better read on the situation than we had from our current vantage point down the road. I also wanted Mack to see us, as confirmation that the job was finished.

As we passed the entrance to the estate, Mack briefly caught my eye and resumed the conversation with the group. The men were too far off the road to glean any real information about what was being said, but it did let Mack know where I was headed and that the barn was clear. I saw him gesture to my father with his arm and step back toward the barn. Joseph threw his cigarette on the ground and entered the barn first. At this point we couldn't risk gawking, and our last glances were of all the men entering the barn as they disappeared from sight.

We made our way up the hill and then back down again toward home. We went straight up to my room and waited by the window for someone, anyone, to come down the hill with news. My father's blue Buick was the first to arrive back at the lighthouse. I watched as Joseph and my father exited the vehicle on opposite sides. Joseph looked in a foul mood, which made me slightly hopeful that our plan had worked. Joseph walked off toward his quarters and my father lit his pipe and stood by the car for a few moments alone. After he entered the back kitchen door I could hear a muffled conversation with my mother, none of which I could make out.

I waited for my father to leave the kitchen before I ventured downstairs. My mother was at the sink, and I causally asked, "What was that all about?" as I went to the ice box for a glass of juice. My mother looked toward the parlor and then back to the dish she was scrubbing.

"Nothing too serious, it turns out it was all a misunderstanding. Your father had some bad information from one of the officers, and it turned out the lead they had led nowhere," she said smiling. "The good news is your father has less of a bad taste in his mouth for the MacDara family. They let your father and his men search the property, even so the law never sent an agent out. I guess they didn't want to wait for the authorities, and they wanted to clear their good name. Your father said they were very cooperative, and he felt a little embarrassed by Joseph's tenacity during the investigation." she continued.

I tried to act unsurprised and slightly disinterested, but inside I was screaming into that glass of juice. I poured another and almost fell over myself up the stairs to tell Margie what had happened. We both collapsed on the bed, able to breathe normally for the first time in over twenty-four hours. Now that everything had been sorted, Margie decided it was time for her to actually go home and check in. I asked her to deliver a message to Mack on her way home to meet me after dark, around ten, at the bluff just up from the lighthouse. It felt like an eternity until the sun started to set and the dinner plates had been cleared.

My parents had thankfully turned in early that night, and I was certain they were both fast asleep this time as I crept out of the house. I made my way up the hill and smiled as a dark shadow appeared out of the tree line and started walking closer to me. Mack's familiar shape began to take form, and we ran to each other and embraced. He wrapped his arms around me and stroked my hair with his hand. He leaned down and kissed me and whispered, "You're remarkable, you know that…God what a mind." He hugged me again and kissed me on the forehead.

"Tell me everything," I said as we walked hand in hand down the small trail toward the high cliff. We tucked below a small rock ledge that anchored a singular madrone tree near the base. We sat down together and settled in as I nestled into the crook of his arm as he spoke.

"God, where to begin…" he said as he took a deep breath and made a slight laugh.

"The night started out fine, the sea was choppy but manageable. I made it to the rendezvous point on time, met

Mr. Olmstead and I loaded the whisky no problems. This is when the wind and the rain really started to pick up. I was fighting the current the whole way and the wind wasn't exactly cooperating either. It put me behind schedule, but nothing too drastic. Aye, Mr. Olmstead had taken off and headed West toward Moresby Island, to approach Turn Point from a different direction. He made first contact with the patrol boats shortly before sunup and had them in hot pursuit for over an hour. Apparently, he had been ripping up and down the West side of the island, playing cat and mouse between Canadian Waters and Stuart Island. He had just made several passes at Turn Point and as he was near the Northern end of the point his engine had died. He flooded the damn thing trying to get it going and that's how the patrol boats caught up with him. This was just about the time that I was making my approach into Prevost. The patrol boat was occupied with Mr. Olmstead, and thanks to his theatrics, he was able to keep them busy as I unloaded. Someone from the patrol boat must have spotted me as I came into the harbor and radioed for the captain, because just as I was returning from the barn your father was on the dock waiting for me."

"I had managed to offload all the whisky unseen, but he had arrived just as I was leaving the barn and was asking questions. Ensign Cail showed up shortly after, towing Mr. Olmstead's boat and demanding to search True North. I let them search the boat to no avail, and good God you should have seen Joseph's face, it was a thing of beauty. Beet red, and full of fire. He was absolutely enraged, Willow. If I hadnae been so damn scared myself, I woulda laughed."

"This must have been right as we showed up, we hid behind the rocks at the tree line near the dock when Joseph was screaming from the top deck of your boat," I chimed in.

"It's a miracle you showed up when you did. We were as good as caught at that point. Your father had jurisdiction over the boat in the water, but couldn't search the barn without a warrant, and the police. This bought us time, and you showed up just in the nick of it. I take it the widow Malby knows of your temporary stash? How did ya know to take it there?" he asked.

I told him about the rock formations we had found near Mr. Malby's stone monument and how there were remnants of possible bootlegging activity already there.

"Aye, she's the one who introduced me to Mr. Olmstead shortly after my mother passed. I never knew if it was intentional or if it was coincidence, but I guess now I know the answer."

He told me about Mr. Olmstead and how he had been a Seattle police officer, retired now. He had assured Mack that the authorities would not come from the mainland and would refuse the captain's request for a search. He knew that didn't solve the problem of dampening suspicions and stopping the unsanctioned search of his property, especially from Joseph. If he suspected the barn to be full of bootleg whisky, he'd never get it off the island, especially on the ferry in grain sacks. It would have been a matter of time before Joseph tracked it down, legally or otherwise.

Mack told me once he saw us pass the road, he knew all was well and decided to let them search the barn, find nothing, and think they were in error. He told me how Joseph had almost immediately found the secret door and if the stash had not been moved, the morning would have gone very differently. He said Joseph had looked positively beside himself when the room turned out to be empty.

I told him how we loaded up the cart and how his father had discovered them in the barn and asked no questions. He took a small stick and carved at the ground between his feet pensively. I could tell he had wanted to shelter his father from what he had been forced to do to keep the family farm. I put my arms around him and kissed his head as we sat on the ground together.

"It will all be alright in the end, I promise," I said gently. We sat in each other's company for a while that night. I could feel Mack's breathing slow as I laid on his chest. "Go home to your bed and get some rest," I whispered as I sweetly kissed his lips and got up to walk home.

"Let me walk you down the hill, I want to make sure you get in safe," he said softly as we started the short ways back down the hill to Turn Point. We walked silently down the hill, hand in hand, and were just about to say goodbye when Joseph's outline came into view. He had been sitting just off the side of the road away from the main house.

"You think you won, don't you?" he called as he looked up from his seat on a nearby stump. He wrung his wrists mechanically before standing to his full height. "I know who you are Dylan MacDara, but more importantly... I know what you are," he said menacingly as he approached the two of us.

Mack stared at him unwaveringly. "Not here, and not now, but I promise... you'll find out exactly who I am. I'd love to show you." Mack stiffened his frame, and his eyes flashed in the moonlight.

"I'm never going to stop Mack," he mouthed his name sarcastically, "everywhere you go, until the world knows the fraud you are, I'll be there…waiting. You won't make a fool of me twice… either of you." he enunciated the words as he walked off into the moonlit clearing. Joseph lit a cigarette as he made his way down to the lighthouse and disappeared inside the building. Mack stood in the middle of the road just staring at the door that Joseph had entered. He gripped my hand tightly and I was frightened by the resolve I saw in his eyes. I kissed him gently and brought him back from wherever he was mentally. I told him to go home and get some rest.

"I love you. We're still here, we're still together, and we're so close to saving the farm. We *are* winning Mack… We *are* winning," I reminded him.

He kissed me gently and saw me into the house. I watched him disappear up the hill towards home and kept an eye on the lighthouse door for a good ten minutes before heading up to bed. I don't think I have ever looked forward to my own bed as much as I did that night. Knowing Mack and the farm were safe for the immediate future meant my body could finally slow down. I think I was asleep before my head even hit the pillow.

15

Glowing In the Dark

For the most part we had settled back into our normal rhythm and re-embraced the slow island pace. Almost a week had passed since we narrowly avoided catastrophe and everyone was back to their usual lighthearted selves, at least on the outside. The next and final run was still on our minds, but was still thankfully several weeks away, and we all relished the luxury of time that this gap afforded. Margie and I had spent the last few days cooped up as the weather had taken a turn for the worse. The dreaded shift in weather patterns meant the start of the rainy season here on the islands. The nights were brisk now and the skies a continual grey. We spent our afternoons together nearly every day. Margie was teaching me how to play the Ukulele and I was reading her Chaucer's *Canterbury Tales*. It wasn't going well. I had no musical talent whatsoever, and Margie had no interest in anything Chaucer had to say.

"I don't understand anything this man is talking about! Honestly, what language is this written in?" she said as she flopped on the bed dramatically. "Give me Gatsby, give me Mrs. Dalloway, just get me out of this inn!" she bemoaned. I laughed and closed the book and decided to give up on her literary education for the time being. Hopefully she would offer me the same kindness and forget about my musical shortcomings as well.

My brother had also felt the confines of captivity while the rain lingered. He had grown increasingly restless, much to the dismay of my parents, and was creating chaos everywhere he went. The living room was cluttered with train sets scattered across the floor. A blanket fort had been created at the top of the landing and just as quickly, abandoned. His bed sheets were still tied to the spindles of the banister, even after several requests from my mother to remove it.

My father was the only one in the house whose motivation was unaffected by the change in weather. The Coast Guard operations in the Pacific Northwest had garnered notice from the highest echelon of leadership. Thanks to his efforts and another, Captain Dorr Tozier, commanding officer of the iron-hulled Grant, this year had been a successful one. Together they had dramatically decreased the flow of illegal items and human smuggling that had been a steady stream until recently. The advent of new radio communications meant more cooperative efforts from the Port Townsend outpost. My father was cooperative yet competitive in his quest with Torr in their mission.

I decided to walk Margie home and stop in at Mack's. He had told me the glass orb was finally ready and I could pick it up on the way back home. Mack was out in the workshop when I arrived, stitching up a sail tear that had happened the night of the run. The wind had gusted unpredictably and tore a small hole near a grommet at the top of the sail. His brow was furrowed as I arrived, deeply engrossed in the project at hand.

"A tailor and a sailor," I teased as I came in the door.

"Well now, here's the poet laureate of MacDara farm, Miss Willow Donovan."

He grabbed me and pulled me into his lap and kissed me hungrily. He reached up and gently cleared a lock of hair from my cheek, and effortlessly slid me up his thigh, all the while softly kissing my upper lip. His strong arm cradled my head under the soft sail. My body rose up to meet him as he held me. His mouth playfully grazed over mine, our lips brushing, searching for each other. He kissed my neck, and I ran my hands down his muscled chest and grabbed his thigh instinctually. He pushed the sail out from under us and sat me up on his lap in one motion as his hands ran down my waist and he pressed my hips into his firmly.

I'd never been this intimate with a man before or felt this much desire inside of me. I needed to be closer to Mack and reached out for him with my hands and my mouth exploring his body as I went. He reached hungrily for my mouth as my hands grabbed his chest and he pulled me in tighter, hands on my hips pulling himself into me. He lifted my blouse and softly kissed my bare chest, his hands caressing me as he moved. He wrapped one hand firmly around me and slowly lowered us onto the soft pile of sail. I could feel the power in his arms as he effortlessly laid me in the sail and his full body pressed into mine. He pushed to his knees and softly pulled my skirt up to my thighs. He leaned down and gently put my hand on the back of his head and began kissing my inner thigh. I wanted him with every fiber of my being, I was his. My hips rose with every caress of his mouth and touch of his hand.

He moved his hand onto my inner thigh and gently stroked the outline of my body working closer and closer inward. I leaned back in ecstasy, never feeling such intimacy in my life. My hands gently stroked the back of his head, running my fingers through his soft curls as he leaned in and buried his face under my skirt. I moaned when he touched me, and he started breathing heavily as he kissed and caressed me. I felt waves of intensity rising inside of me as his strong hands stroked me softly. I grabbed the back of his head and pushed his face into me as I erupted in pleasure, writhing under his strong grip and gentle touch. Every part of me reached out for him in those moments, fully exposed and his to pleasure. He kissed the inside of my thighs as I slowly sank into a deep contentment, fully sated from his touch. He took a deep breath, gently lowered my skirt, and laid himself next to me.

He wrapped his arms around me as I laid next to him in complete euphoria, stroking my hand as ours intertwined. He kissed me gently as he whispered sweet nothings in my ear, telling me I was the most bewitching woman he had ever known.

"My God, I can't get enough of you," he whispered and nuzzled into my neck as he spoke. We laid together in the barn that evening as the rain started to softly fall outside. The storm cast a lavender haze over the sky as it rolled in. A slight breeze began to creep into the barn and goosebumps appeared over my bare skin. He covered me with his body and said we should get inside, 'before you catch your death out here.' He lifted me gently from the sail and slid my shirt softly over my head, kissing my neck as it lowered onto my frame. He wrapped his arm around me tenderly and opened the barn door for me to walk through. The rain had started falling harder and we ran from the barn into the main house hand in hand.

The house was softly lit and a fire was going in the fireplace. He seated me in a chair near the fire and went to the kitchen to make tea. He returned with a few apples, scones, and a pot of tea that was steaming as it steeped. He took a large blanket from the back of the other chair and wrapped it around me tenderly. Just then, Mr. MacDara had come up the lane, hurried in his steps and holding his jacket against the rain and the wind. He entered the house in a great commotion, stomping his feet on the porch and shaking like a dog attempting to dislodge himself from his wet jacket.

"Miss Willow, it's grand to see ya," he said kindly as he noticed me sitting by the fire. "I see my boy has got the right end of things, ensuring you stay warm and dry in this nonsense," he lilted.

I smiled and looked at Mack, who had a sly grin on his face as well.

"He's taking excellent care of me," I replied, only the two of us knowing full well what that had actually meant. We spent the better part of an hour having tea and chatting with Mr. MacDara who had been at the Eriksen farm just next door talking about seed for the upcoming spring. He had grand plans to grow peas this season and bring them to sell to the cannery in Friday Harbor. It was nice to see him in such high spirits and hopeful for the farm's new beginnings, together with Mack.

The rain stopped just as we had finished the last morsels of afternoon tea, and the light was just beginning to fade. Mack went to the barn to pack up the glass orb in a burlap sack for me to carry back to the lighthouse. He walked me back up the road to Turn Point, close to the main house. He decided he didn't want to see my father until he was formally invited back on better terms, and after he made his final run and put bootlegging behind him. He kissed me softly on the cheek and whispered, "I love you" in my ear. I squeezed his hand and told him, "I love you Mack... always." He grinned and watched me walk inside.

I went upstairs and took a long hot bath, slowly erasing the cold of the long walk back to the lighthouse. My chin sinking into the water and with it, resolve for the heading I was setting in love. I went to bed that night love drunk for the life I was slowly creating here on the island. Oliver had heard me crawl into bed and slunk in purring as he levitated onto the bed and sank down next to me. The soft patter of new raindrops on the window and the slow purr of Oliver next to me lulled me to sleep in complete contentment.

The next morning the storm had fully broken, and the sun streamed through the window and onto my pillow. Today was the day that I would finally finish the glass signal for Margie. I woke up invigorated and excited for the task at hand. I had meant to complete it earlier in the season, but August had slipped away that summer and I could hardly believe the season was almost over. I reached for the burlap sack and pulled out the gently wrapped glass orb. Mack had once again proved what a skilled craftsman he was, not only with wood, but now also with glass.

The top of the large float had been seamlessly cut to create a small hole in the top. I couldn't wait to see it lit. I wanted it to glow a brilliant yellow in the night, like the moon itself, just for her. I had collected several bunches of Goldenrod around the island and dried them over the course of the summer. My plan was to grind them down to make a dye and apply a delicate decoupage to the interior of the glass wall. The grinding of the flowers proved to be more time consuming than I had previously anticipated, but I wanted the orb to glow a fantastic amber and didn't want to skimp on color.

Once the pigment was created, I pulled out several sheets of tissue paper I had saved from a hat purchase on our trip to New York last year. The hat had come in a fantastic box and was nested beautifully amongst large wafts of the billowy paper. It had been too beautiful and delicate to discard. The paper was thin and sheer, and I was careful not to tear it. I decided to mix the glue and water and the pigment together, given the fragile nature of the paper.

I divided the sheets of paper into workable segments and carefully dipped the sheets into the mixture. The paper immediately absorbed the golden hue, and I smiled as the paper slowly transformed into the perfect mirror ball of moonlight as I placed it inside the glass orb. Once the paper had been set, there was nothing to do but let it dry. I stood back admiring my work, hoping Margie would love the gift not only for its sentimentality, but also for its dramatic flair. Even as it sat unlit, the sunlight caught the orb as it lay drying in the window and created a radiant golden glow.

I was snapped out of my thorough inspection of the piece by a soft thud against the window. A small pinecone gently cascaded down the eave and fell to the unseen depths from the roof. I instantly smiled, knowing what this abrupt, yet welcomed distraction signified. I moved the orb to the vanity and lifted the window feeling the warm rays of the sun on my face. I looked out into the backyard and just past the cellar, but he was not in his usual place. Perhaps as he was not under the cover of darkness, he had to remain more hidden, I thought. I closed the window and ran down the stairs. I walked around the side of the house and scanned the area again. Nothing, only the sounds of chickadees and crows, and a soft rustle in the trees. I walked around the back of the stone structure and then slowly into the dark cellar as the door was slightly ajar. As my eyes adjusted, I saw Mack near the corner of the cellar, and he closed the door and drew me into his arms. He kissed me passionately and I stumbled back as he released me.

I giggled and said, "I like your enthusiasm."

He smiled that gorgeous smile, with those dimples that even a dark cellar couldn't erase. "I saw the orb; it was glowing in the window just by the sun's rays. I cannae wait to see it lit."

"I'm so happy with it! I hope she loves it!"

"Aye, I'm sure she will. That's part of the reason I came by, I was thinking the weather's turned for the better, Sam has a pass tomorrow, and hopefully you're free. What do you say we go for a sail, all of us, for the day?"

"That sounds perfect!"

"We can meet at my place together, and you can give her the gift before we head out."

"That's a fantastic idea! I'll make us a picnic lunch."

"It's settled then," he said and pulled me in for another kiss. "I suppose I best be on my way before yesterday happens again." He smiled coyly and winked at me. "Ya best fetch me the orb and I'll get it attached before tomorrow."

I ran back into the house, carefully placing the golden orb in the burlap for Mack and back down the stairs to the cellar. I handed him the sack and he kissed me on the cheek. He peered out from behind the door and took off like a flash for the woods.

16

Lantern Burning

Sam and I made the walk from Turn Point to the MacDara farm together for the day's sail. I gladly accepted his company, one because he was one of my best friends, and two because the picnic basket I packed was positively brimming with sandwiches, pie, cake, and salads. He laughed when he saw me struggling with it as I came out of the door.

"Are you planning on feedin' the whole of the island?" he goaded as he took the basket from me.

"The way you boys eat, this will likely run out by mid-day," I joked.

Sam lifted the lid and peeked inside; his eyes wide as he saw the chocolate cake I had made last night for the occasion.

"Maybe I'd better hold the basket," I teased.

We came up to the main house as Margie was just coming up the lane. She had packed a basket as well and we both laughed at the amount of food we had amassed. I grabbed her hand and told her I had something to give her before we left. We set the baskets down and headed for the barn, Mack was waiting for us and had the gift covered under a canvas drop. I told her about how much she meant to me, and how sad I was that I never got to meet her mother. I loved that she had invited me into that part of her life, and shared not only her joy, but her sadness with me.

"You've been a beacon of light to me since I came to this island Margie. You've led me home and let me know I was safe, just like your father signaling to your mother, your light lets me know I am home. We all contributed our ideas and time, and this is for you, my beautiful friend."

Mack lifted the canvas drop and revealed the carved staff with the yellow glass orb nestled perfectly in place between the three wooden prongs of the branch. The sunlight filtered through the stained-glass window overhead and the light caught the orb perfectly as it was revealed. It glowed amber as soon as the light hit it.

Margie was speechless as she slowly approached the orb and the carved staff. She ran her hands down each carving and covered her mouth as she turned the staff in her hand. She gently reached her hand up to the glowing glass and turned back to us, eyes welling up, with the most beautiful look of love in her eyes for each of us.

"It's everything. It's everything," Margie eeked out the words as she motioned for a group hug. We wrapped our arms around her and simultaneously told her we loved her. She wouldn't stop hugging us individually, and after a great deal of admiration for the gift, agreed to finally get underway. After the emotional outpouring we all filed out of the barn and headed for the dock, eager to get out on the water.

We loaded everything on the boat and set out for Sucia Island in the first warm rays of the chilly morning. The air had changed recently; there was a crispness to it that felt invigorating. Instead of the summer heaviness of salt and cedar and wildflower, it had a clean and earthy undertone, like water and fir, or a forest floor after a hard rain.

The morning was breezy, and I made my way up to the bow letting the salt spray mist me as the boat cut through the waves. The water felt cool as it landed on my face, but the sun shone down directly over us, instantly warming where the frigid waters had touched. We headed East for Sucia Island, one of Mack's favorite spots in the island chain, especially this time of year.

Suddenly Margie cried out, "Look!" and pointed off the port side of the ship. A small pod of Orca had surfaced creating puffs of mist as they drew breath and descended back into the water. There were at least 5 of them, all with different sized and shaped fins. Some of them stuck straight up out of the water like a knife blade, and some of them had a gentle backward curve to their large fin as they cut through the water. Mack reefed the sail and slowed our speed to stay in their presence for a while longer. We watched as they neared the boat, perhaps hunting but completely unbothered by our presence. They swam just aft of the ship, and we could hear them breathe again as they surfaced.

I couldn't believe how large they were in person. I had seen drawings of Orcas in books, but I had incorrectly assumed they were slightly larger than a dolphin. These animals were massive, and incredibly fast through the water. They glistened as they surfaced in the morning sunshine, nimbly cutting through the dark water and past our boat. Their speed was all the more impressive, given their absolutely massive size. The largest of the group was nearly the length of the boat, and the width of my father's automobile. We sat in silence, all of us, in awe of their presence that morning as they surfaced. Once they swam out of view, we adjusted sails and were soon cutting through the water again past Waldron Island.

Waldron Island resembled a fortress, risen from the sea, perched on tall sea cliffs. Its shore appeared impenetrable and impossible to get to from our vantage point. The center of the island was covered in old growth fir, capping the stone sides in a blanket of green. Orcas Island lay to the South of us as we passed between the two islands in the channel. Orcas Island towered above Waldron, its center showcasing several rocky peaks covered in evergreens as well. Orcas Island was much larger than even Stuart Island, and dwarfed it not only in geographical size, but also in elevation. Like so many of the islands in the Archipelago, it seemed to rise out the sea, a foundation of stone in the cold Pacific waters.

Sucia Island lay just Northeast of Waldron Island, and directly North of Orcas Island. It was a small island that was also, itself a group of islands, most of them inside of the large bay. These smaller interior islands projected like long fingers and divided the bay into channels of water that opened into Rosario Strait. The coastline of Sucia Island looked vastly different from the other islands, and I was mesmerized as we approached the entrance to one of these narrow bay channels. Instead of the grey stone that characterized so many of the San Juan Islands, Sucia appeared to be carved from sandstone. The island topography seemed otherworldly as we entered the narrow channel, and I sat awestruck from my front row seat on the bow as we crept forward.

Mack assured us it was plenty deep, even though the sea walls were so close I felt like I could touch them if I tried. The shore was carved by time and tide alone, a product of natural weathering that created the most spectacular parts of the island. Fantastic caves and caverns exposed themselves as we sailed farther into Echo Bay. Large, sculpted ridges protruded precariously far from the main bank and created irregular pockets in the rock. Smaller versions of the same chemical process of salt, wind, and water eroded repeated patterns of holes and intricate caverns in the layered rock. Stones of all shapes and sizes lay suspended in the overhanging sandstone walls, waiting patiently for time to release them back into the sea. It was unlike anything I had ever seen; it felt unreal, like a foreign land or a make-believe place only visited in dreams.

Seals lined the sandstone banks, using the native topography to bask in the sun on the natural shelves. They looked over at us sleepily as we passed by. The same madrone trees I had seen on the other islands were also thriving here, hanging from the intricate sandstone carvings, and adding to the rare natural beauty. Sea birds flew overhead, crossing the fingerlike islands from overhead, calling intermittently as they flew. Life was abundant here, and the harmony between the land and the living was delicately and intricately woven together to create something indescribably beautiful.

A small wren landed on the stanchion only a few feet from me, coming closer to investigate the new visitors to the island. It let out a shrill haunting call from its perch and I was mesmerized by the soulful melody from the tiny creature. The rest of the group was back in the cockpit and hadn't seen the bird land or heard its fervent call. She tilted her head and watched me intently. I smiled as she turned back to the sky and called again, filling the air with her unique sound. She flitted off, just as suddenly as she had arrived, and I felt so lucky to have shared that fleeting moment with such a beautiful creature. I sat for a little longer on the bow, in awe of the natural beauty and the wonder that surrounded me that morning. I was called back to the cockpit by the sound of laughter and walked back towards the stern to another kind of beauty, found only in the deep connections of chosen family.

Margie was telling Sam some story about Mack when he was little, and everyone was laughing and talking over one another. Tears streamed down Sam's eyes as Margie barely got the words out through her own fits of laughter. Mack was adding to the fun, unbothered by his younger follies, chiming in with his own additions and banter as well. I was made whole, standing there, watching my favorite people that day. I felt like I had finally found a home, a place that my soul knew intuitively, and had only longed for ambiguously. Here on these islands, with these people I felt part of something greater, and more meaningful than I ever imagined possible.

We set anchor and made it ashore safely in the dinghy. The island itself was uninhabited, although frequented by locals, and interestingly, also a favorite destination for smugglers, as Mack had mischievously pointed out.

"Speaking of dirty rotten smugglers, we should figure out what your next move is Mack... for your final run," Sam said smiling at Mack as he himself smuggled an apple out of the picnic basket.

Mack had taken out his knife and started carving a piece of driftwood mindlessly. "This one is going to be more challenging." Mack let out a sigh and blew the shavings from the wood.

"Joseph is feckin' relentless. He's checking your dock several times a day. I'm sure we'd have been stopped today if we both weren't on pass."

"It's going to take all of us Mack. You can't do this alone; we won't let you," I said and nodded at him decidedly.

We spent the better part of the afternoon concocting our game plan for the big day. The shipment was to be ready for transport to the U.S. from the drop on Pender Island next week. We decided Mr. Olmstead zipping around the island again would likely do more damage than good, alerting the Guard to a run taking place. We had to slip in and out, undetected, at just the right time.

There were four of us, and we needed to divide and conquer if we were to be successful. Sam would be on the water that night in a patrol boat. He would have information about most of the units' movements, save Joseph, who kept his patrol whereabouts and dealings private after the last run in.

Margie would be the Prevost Harbor patrol from land, ensuring nothing would come from the road. The whisky was to be hand carried to the front barn on the border of the Eriksen and MacDara property, where a cart could be loaded in secret and taken to the larger cache when it was safe. She would also keep watch on the harbor entrance, ensuring that no one lay in wait inside the harbor for an ambush.

"We'll need a way to communicate", I added. "The radio isn't an option for us, but it is something we'll have to contend with. We'll have to use light."

"Sam can signal from the boat, and I can signal with my orb!" Margie jumped in. "If there is any danger in the harbor, I'll light the orb, and you'll know not to come in!"

"I'll keep one patrol boat out of the hunt, and hopefully steer the others away from you," Sam added.

"And I'll be making the trip with you this time. I'll act as watch and help keep an eye out from the bow," I said.

"It's settled then," Mack agreed as he took his flask from his jacket pocket and passed it around.

After lunch and our impromptu strategy session, we set out to explore the island for a while. We headed across a small isthmus that led to Shallow Bay on the far side of the island. The rock formations along the shore were even more spectacular along this section of the island. Small caves had been carved out of the sandstone and were nestled twenty feet up in the cliffside. Mack told stories of coming here as a boy and playing pirate in the warm shallow water and hiding pretend buried treasure in the cave. He recalled how his father had been extremely cross with him for taking the compass and the sextant and forgetting which section of the cave he had hid them in.

This section of the bay had a large sand beach, and we spent the afternoon wading in the water and laying in the warm sand. I had wanted to continue to explore the island and hike along the large finger coves we had seen coming into Echo Bay, but the lure of great conversation on a lazy Saturday outweighed the pull of adventure I felt as the magic of the island called me to explore it. Mack promised me we'd be back, as it was also one of his most favorite places as well.

"I can't explain it, Mack. Some of these places on the island I feel as if I've been, they feel like home, almost familiar. It's like a whisper of a song, one I heard as a child, but I can't repeat the tune or tell you the words, but I know it just the same."

"Aye, I know just what you mean, I think. We've got a name for that in Gaelic, it's called Cianalas. It's a nostalgia for ancient places in which we cannae return. It's a longing for a home, the echoes of lost places, and our souls' grief for them. It's both nowhere and everywhere, like the song you know but can't remember."

I leaned into him and kissed his neck softly, thankful for how he understood me on such a deep level.

"What was that for?" he asked as he rolled over and pulled me down on the sand gently. He leaned his head down into me and kissed me softly and then again more passionately.

A loud rustling in the bushes startled us, as Sam and Margie came bounding down from the cave path. Sam cackled and made a joke about interrupting our moment. Mack gave him a look and Sam just laughed unbothered. It was time to head home anyway, if we wanted to be back in the harbor by nightfall. We begrudgingly left the sanctity of the secluded cove and headed back toward Echo Bay, and then home.

17

We Are the Foxes

The following week was spent going over plans, contingency plans, and more preparations. Margie had figured out the exact spot on Satellite Island that allowed her full visibility up Lighthouse Road while simultaneously maintaining an exposed position to be visible from Boundary Pass. She would position herself there that night and keep watch over the entrance to the harbor, as well as any car that may approach from the lighthouse. The orb would be lit if the harbor was occupied, or if anyone was coming down the road. This would be most useful as the unloading of the whisky happened when they would be most vulnerable on land.

Sam had been more alert to the chatter on the docks this week and hung around when patrols were discussed between Joseph and my father. They had recently seized a large speedboat that had been packed with whisky and contraband, not to mention several weapons. They were getting better in their mission with each search and seizure, and along with that competence, a growing confidence grew as well.

Everyone was ready, including Mack and me. When I could get away, we had spent the last few days down at the boat together changing the head sail and checking equipment. The only thing left to do was to wait, and to think. The thinking part had been weighing on me recently. I didn't like the idea of being in opposition of my father. The conflict with Joseph was fine, but it hadn't sat right with me being on opposing sides with family. Afterall, I believed in the work he did, mostly. There were much worse things than whisky being smuggled across the water. My father had stopped many bad things, and bad men, from entering our waters, and I respected him for that. The last boat they had brought in reminded me what a serious game we were involved in, and the kind of men who played it. The smuggling business was booming, and anytime money was involved there was always a new level of danger. I thought back to the Beryl-G and what had become of the people on board.

I had heard snippets from my father about the case updates as they came in from the mainland. There had been two people on board, and they were killed and thrown overboard, attached to the anchor. The ship had been loaded with illegal alcohol from Canada. Running into my father was not the worst thing that could happen out there, and Mack had been having second thoughts about me coming along.

He knew better than to tell me what I could and couldn't do, but I knew the decision to go weighed on him just as much as it did me. I reminded him that I had found my peace, in him and the farm. I had grown incredibly close to his father, probably closer than to my own father, and I had just as much of a right to fight for the things that I loved as he did. With all the things that could go wrong, a second set of hands on a sailboat at night could be the difference between success or failure, or life and death. He knew that it was true, but it didn't stop him from wanting to protect me.

Margie and I had decided to take the orb out to Satellite Island and do a test run in the dark, to ensure the orb would be visible from the boat at night. We sat together in the sand on top of the rocky cliffside and watched the sun set together. As we passed the time, she mentioned to me she had heard of open auditions in Seattle next month at the Lyon's Music Hall and I begged her to go.

"This is what you're meant to do," I told her, "You have this music inside of you, and it's beautiful and awe inspiring."

"What about Sam and my brother, and you?" she asked, "It may be what I want, but how do I leave them and this island; you all are also what I want. I couldn't bare it."

"We will figure all that out. I promise," I reassured her. "Look at what our group can do, we can solve anything. Sam and me, and your family... you can't shake us Margie, we love you too much."

She laughed and hugged me, and we sat there in the fading light, each hoping our best laid plans stayed true to course.

"I've decided to stay on the island," I told her. "For the first time in my life I feel like I'm home. This is where I belong. I haven't told anyone yet; I wasn't sure until a few days ago."

Margie leaned her head on my shoulder, and we sat together in silence, holding space for one another. I thought about all the places I had lived, and the places I may still yet live. I hoped Margie would always be with me, our paths inextricably interconnected, but I also knew she had her own path before her. I held on to this moment, and this idea of home as we sat in the silence together.

As the last rays of sunlight sank below the horizon, we readied the signal. Mack was out in the pass, watching from the bow as we lit the orb. We had brought an oil lantern and placed it gently in the wooden cradle of the staff and slowly lowered the yellow orb on top of the lantern. The orb lit up like a ball of yellow fire, and I took several steps back to admire its warm incandescent glow. We looked out into the darkness of the water and saw two small white flashes of light. Mack had seen the signal and the orb worked exactly as planned. We watched as he came closer into the harbor together, both of us not quite ready to leave the sanctity of Satellite Island.

"I can see why you love it out here," I said. "It feels like the world can't find you, concealed on all sides by the sea. Like we could just sit here motionless and stave off any future heartache or uncertainty that lurks out past the water... unseen by the devil himself." I leaned my head on her shoulder and told her, "We're not cut out for the madness of this world, we don't belong, you and I, not to that."

"What if we just sat here forever, how long would it take for anyone to find us?" Margie joked.

Mack flashed his light at us as he passed our corner of the island and I looked at Margie and laughed. "Not long," I said shaking my head. I grabbed her hand, and we carefully covered the deconstructed signal in the brush and made for the skiff. I breathed a sigh of relief knowing everything was going according to plan. I knew I couldn't control the outcome, but I also knew those that failed to plan, planned to fail. We shoved off into the calm tidal slack waters of the harbor and back toward Stuart Island.

I told my mother that I was spending the night at Margie's house, and Margie had told her father the same, that she would be at the lighthouse with me. Sam had been pacing the docks all afternoon and I had to tell him to find a project as he was stressing me out just watching him. I had packed a large bag, filled with every light in the house, spare clothes, and enough food to feed both Mack and I for a week. I still didn't feel like I was prepared, and I couldn't quell the lump that sat permanently in my throat since morning. I simultaneously wanted time to stand still and to speed up.

Joseph had been suspiciously absent the past few days, and it made me uneasy not knowing what he was up to. He had sporadically appeared, under no detectable schedule, and as suddenly as he had appeared, he would be off again in the boats. My father had been exceedingly busy as well these past few days. They had stopped a record number of vessels containing contraband and the Coast Guard was taking notice. I had heard bits and pieces of correspondence outlining increased funding, supplies, and even a visit from a high-ranking politician was in the works.

The culmination of my father's career at this outpost and my future with Mack were lining up to come dangerously close to one another somewhere out in the current tonight. I hoped they would never intersect, tonight of all nights. The sky was grey and thick with clouds, which meant less moonlight and better cover for the run. I hoped it would hold and be another ace in this dangerous game we were now intent on playing. I tried not to think about what would happen if my father or

Joseph caught us out there, especially me. I don't think either of us were prepared to deal with that kind of betrayal, either to our family or to our ideals. I hoped neither of us would ever have to test the limits of our relationship like that.

18

And We Run

The evening approached and I gathered my things and said goodbye to my mother. She waved at me from the kitchen, and I set out down the steps and up the road to Mack's. The sky was turning a deeper grey and I quickened my steps feeling uneasy as I made my way up the big hill. Out over the strait small white caps had started to form. The dry leaves rustled in the soft breeze as I rounded the corner at the top of the hill. Several leaves tumbled down the road next to me and haphazardly cascaded into the roadside ditch as I walked toward the farm. I pulled the deep hood of the wool jacket over my head and clutched my satchel closer to my body. I told myself that Mack was the best sailor I knew, and a bit of wind and cloud cover was a good thing.

Margie was waiting on the MacDara's front porch when I arrived, accompanied by Lola, who sat with her head on Margie's lap. Mack was inside staring out at the water from the massive windows of the house. I opened the heavy wooden door and he turned, broken free from his intent surveillance, and turned his focus on me as I went to him. He uncrossed his arms and I hurried into them, breathing him in as we embraced. He tilted my chin upward and gently kissed me. His eyes were the color of the water, and he looked completely calm as he gazed down at me. I felt so much of the weight and worry I had been carrying slide off me like water. He sighed as he felt me melt into him and stroked my hair gently.

"I can tell you're scared Leannan, it's alright to be," he said as his hand outlined a tendril of my hair. "We'll face this together, head on, bow into the oncoming wave, that's how we stay righted." His eyes crept back out through the glass and out to sea as the clouds darkened and swirled. His confidence transferred to me, as I sat sheltered by the tall timber frame of the MacDara house and the two people I trusted so heavily, here with me.

The light had started to fade, and we sat near the fire discussing the order of events for the last time. Sam would be leaving for his evening patrol shortly after dinner and Joseph was most likely already out on the water, scouting for boats. Margie would head out to Satellite Island just before midnight, expecting us around two in the morning. I would signal her with two small flashes of light as we neared the shore. If the coast was clear she would give two small flashes of light back, if there was danger the orb would be fully lit, and the harbor was not safe to enter.

The sun was now fully down, and the harbor was in complete darkness, save for small glints of moonlight that slipped through the cracks in the cloud cover. Margie was ready, wearing a long green cloak to protect her from the elements, and as cover from prying eyes. She would depart from the small skiff in front of their house and row to her small island outpost. We stood in front of the fire, in silence, eyes fixed on the warm embers, each focused on our specific task. Mack was first to break the silence as he looked up at us with a steely gaze, his grey blue eyes reflecting the soft orange embers from the fire.

"Before we head out, I wanted to say thank you one last time for being my friend. Truly." He took a deep breath and leaned forward in his chair as he spoke. "You know, you've both seen the good in me, as well as the bad, and you've stuck by me. All too often we meet people, and judge them, and simplify them into a one-dimensional generalization, good or bad. You've each seen a different version of me, the man, the bootlegger, the partner, the friend. And in each version of myself I've shown you two... you've chosen me, Mack, over the label. It means everything," he said as he leaned his elbows on his knees and placed his chin on his folded hands.

"Always, Dylan MacDara," I declared.

"Always," Margie chimed in. We stared at each other, moving from face to face.

"Here we go again," Mack said, a grin forming on his face, "Are you ready?"

"Let the games begin," I said, as we stood up and made our way for the door. Mack grabbed his jacket, and we flipped up our hoods as the fire illuminated everything but our faces. We walked out onto the porch into the darkness, Margie walking towards the skiff and Mack and I toward the dock. The next time we would see each other would be once it was over, and the story had unfolded. I questioned if time would paint us as villains or fools if we were caught. Perhaps a bit of both, I thought. I watched Margie's green cloak disappear into the night air and turned my attention toward the waiting boat and the dark grey skies looming out over the water.

The boat was bouncing off the pilings, sloshing water onto the dock, and groaned under the weight of the lines. The water was rough, even in the harbor that night. As we shoved off in complete darkness and silence, I thought how opposite I had felt on our day trips, so light and carefree. I felt as if we drug the entire MacDara farm from the keel tonight, a constant reminder of what was at stake, the weight of it resting on us as we pushed toward Pender Island, hopefully alone in the pass.

The turbulent water made a rough start to the night, it tossed the boat around and made everything more complicated, especially in the dark. Without a horizon to set my eyes on, I started to feel sick, potentiated by the nerves this trip induced. I pushed past the queasiness and set my eyes out over the dark water, determined to spot any ships before they spotted us. Mack and I quickly raised all the sails, and we felt the boat straighten its course and begin to cut through the water and not ride on top of it. I breathed a sigh of relief as my stomach settled and the boat picked up speed.

A light rain had started to fall, but we had a course set, full sails, and each other. Mack's face was barely visibly behind the helm, only illuminated by scattered rays of moonlight. His eyes were focused and determined, and he met my gaze with a confident smile that made me think we just might pull this off. I scanned the water every few minutes, looking for lights, and listening for engines. The sea was black and looked like a dark void, reflecting flecks of moonlight in the waves. The dark sails heaved with wind and the boat was pushed through the chop with only the rhythmic splashes on the bow as evidence of the rough waters.

We made sight of Pender Island just before midnight. The island appeared suddenly from the black water, and we turned hard to port as soon as it came into view.

"Where exactly are we headed?" I asked.

He smiled coyly and even the darkness couldn't cover the cleft in his chin and his dimples as he answered. "There's a small inlet on the outside of Bedwell Harbour. It's called Smuggler's Nook."

"We're smuggling bootleg whisky into U.S. waters and picking it up in Smuggler's Nook?!"

"I didn't name the place!" he laughed, "I guess whoever did was on to something though!"

We rounded a small point near the entrance to Smuggler's Nook and dropped sail. The boat glided along the water, following the outline of the land on the Starboard side of the boat. I watched as Mack flashed a signal with the lantern and several men appeared from the trees and bushes following the boat on its path into the nook. Mack threw the stern line to one of the men and I went to the bow of the boat and threw another man the bow line. The men walked the boat along the shore and tied the vessel off near a small hidden dock that jutted out slightly into the water.

One of the gentlemen had a large gangway that he had brought to the end of the small dock and slowly lowered it onto the rail of the sailboat. Mack jumped off the boat and onto the dock, the clandestine group now shaking hands and speaking in whispered voices. I recognized Mr. Olmstead standing near the trees as the boat was tied off. Mack walked back to the boat and offered me a hand as I jumped down from the gangway.

The men wasted no time loading the small boat with the crates of whisky. All the men were thoroughly engaged in the loading, except Mr. Olmstead, who walked over to me as the others were busy hauling cargo.

"Nice night for a sail," he said and winked at me with an outstretched hand. "I don't think I've had the pleasure of a formal introduction." He offered a wide grin from under a tan brimmed hat.

"The name's Roy," he said and offered a good natured, rather disarming smile as we shook hands. I hadn't gotten a good look at him the last time I saw him, and somehow, I had pictured him much more foreboding and imposing than the man who stood in front of me now. This Mr. Olmstead didn't look like a bootlegger. He had kind eyes and a gentle handshake. He asked me about my father, and how I enjoyed the island life. He acted as if we were at a church social and not loading crates of illegal whisky to smuggle across the border.

Mack walked over to us as the other men finished and discussed the plan back to Stuart Island. Roy told us to be careful, and that our lives weren't worth a boat full of whisky. "I'd rather see it dumped into the Salish, than have you or this fine young woman harmed in any way."

"Aye Roy, I feel the same," Mack agreed and added, "Although a boat load of whisky at the bottom of Boundary Pass isn't going to pay for next years seed and a new flock."

Roy nodded his head and patted his shoulder. "To that I'll say, fair winds and following seas my boy," and he tipped his hat toward me and walked back toward the tree line, enveloped into the darkness as he walked onto the small, wooded path.

The boat was fully loaded now, and Mack was ready to set out. "Now comes the fun part," he jested as he helped me back onto the boat.

"I may need to break into the profits when this is all over," I teased. The men walked the boat out with the lines, exactly as we had come in. One by one, they threw the long lines back on to the boat as we were free from the small nook. I gathered the lines and coiled them neatly, attaching them onto the deck rails. The weather was holding but I didn't want lines entangled in the water if the conditions worsened. I scanned the horizon continually as we left the nook, straining my eyes at every potential glimmer, or far off sound.

I was dressed warmly in the blue wool jacket, and I walked the breadth of the boat every few minutes, searching the water for signs of life, hoping we were completely alone for the journey. Mack and I didn't talk, we stayed quiet, both afraid to jinx the eerily quiet night with conversation. His eyes too scanned the water, only briefly leaving the horizon to glance up at the sails or check the heading.

We were just inside U.S. waters when I saw the first glimmer of what I thought could be a boat. My throat tightened as I stared intently out toward the object. Mack hadn't seen it yet, and I walked slowly back toward the helm as I kept it in view. Mack saw my eyes and shifted his to where I was looking. The boat veered suddenly, away from where we looked, and my stomach tightened. Mack had turned the wheel, confirming I had spotted a boat. The light grew progressively brighter as it approached and then suddenly fell off due South.

We collectively exhaled as we watched the boat turn away from our heading, and Mack adjusted course again. We were still too far from Stuart Island to signal Margie, but we were at least halfway to the entrance to Prevost. The rain had picked up and the current was moving quickly now as low tide approached. In the distance I heard a large ship sounding off a short blast, probably a commercial steamer bound for the Strait of Juan De Fuca, and into the Pacific Ocean after that. Mack kept us on course, and I kept a faithful watch on the horizon and surrounding waters as we made for the safety of the island.

A large dark outline began to take shape in the night, and I watched hopefully as the dark silhouette of Satellite Island came into view. Mack had seen it as well and signaled to me to get the light ready. As we neared the entrance before I could signal, the small yellow orb lit up along the cliffside. Mack's eyes widened, and he immediately came about with the boat. My heart started beating so loudly, and I looked back at Mack whose eyes were intently scanning the surrounding waters and the land around the harbor for signs of danger. If there were dangers lying in wait for us, they gave no signs or clues as to their location. The harbor looked as it always had, save the small orb on the cliffside glowing a somber yellow, warning us to turn back. Meanwhile, standing high on the hill cloaked in green Margie stood, exhaling relief as she saw the boat come about.

19

Marjorie's Version

Whfen Margie left both of us standing on the MacDara porch she had started walking back toward home, her mind focused on what lay ahead later that night. She ran through her plan again and again, repetitively, to the cadence of her own footsteps. She quickened her pace as she turned off the main road toward the Borcher home, resolved in her plan of action. As soon as she turned the corner of the shed, she saw it. An unfamiliar twinkle in a most familiar setting. Her eye caught the light reflected off a strange object in the water, close to the shore, just quietly bobbing in the current. She hurried down to the shoreline in front of her house, careful to stay concealed by the brush line. As her eyes adjusted, she could just make out one of the patrol boats, cloaked by the darkness, sitting at anchor. The only light visible was the strike of a match from the stern of the boat, as the occupant lit a cigarette and quickly extinguished the flame.

"It's Joseph!" Margie whispered to herself in disbelief. She slunk back up toward the house, attempting to remain unseen from the waterline. The small skiff she was to use was sitting only about thirty yards from the patrol boat, still tied up to the driftwood log near the side of their house. She sat crouched near the bushes wondering how she would get to the boat and make it past Joseph across the harbor to light the orb. Seeing Joseph lying in wait like a predator, made her job that much more important. If Mack's boat entered Prevost tonight, Joseph would be perfectly poised for the attack.

Margie sat quietly leaning up against the house neatly concealed by shrubs with only the sound of her rapid breathing as she tried to figure out how to get to the boat unseen. Joseph was in perfect position and there was no way she could creep past him. Even now, the small glow of embers from Joseph's cigarette pointed directly toward the harbor entrance, and the smell of smoke invaded her nostrils. He was too close, it felt impossible. The rowboat lay just along the shore near the far side of the house, and just to the left of Joseph's stern barely in his periphery. She needed Joseph's eyes locked away from the rear of the house and enough noise to stifle the sound of her oars... but how?

Several large thuds came from inside the house accompanied by laughter and yelling. The boys must have been having a time in there.

Jesus, if they could just settle down for 5 minutes, I could figure out a plan... I can't even think around them.

Margie bolted upright as it came to her, and her heart raced with the prospect of a remedy for her current condition. Margie turned in retreat from the water and crept along the side of the house and entered through the back kitchen door. She couldn't help but smile as she thought about the boys...

truly the biggest source of chaos and distraction known to earth. What the boys lacked in decorum and serenity, they made up for with loyalty and enthusiasm. They would do anything for her, and anything for another islander as well, especially Mack.

The boys were scattered around the main room, the youngest two wrestling near the hearth. She peered her head around the corner of the kitchen and called to them quietly and quickly. The boys sprung up, alert now to Margie's curious request. The boys filed one by one into the kitchen, asking questions all at once as they crowded into the small room.

"I can't tell you everything, mainly because there's no time, but I need you. Mack needs you," she whispered.

The boys stood upright at the call for help from Margie. Each one with an alert, protective demeanor as their sister told the boys the plan and what she needed each of them to do. The boys agreed wholeheartedly, and her impassioned plea met a determined resolve in each of her brother's eyes. Margie wasted no time and snuck out the back door and into the brush along the side of the house to wait. She saw Joseph's dark form hunched over in the moonlight, rummaging for something on the floorboards and made her move. She crept along the shoreline slowly, covered in her emerald cloak and slithered into the small skiff.

The Borcher boys were standing ready, waiting for her dark form to fill the boat to begin their part. Once she made it into the skiff the boys came barreling through the front door yelling and hollering at one another.

"You dirty rotten cheat!" one of the boys yelled as he slammed his hands on the porch railing.

"I played that ace fair and square and you know it!" the oldest Borcher yelled back as he tackled the other brother to the ground.

"I'll teach you to cheat, when I get my hands on you!" he screamed as he chased his sibling across the porch and away from Margie and the small boat.

They began to wrestle and scream, their spectacle illuminated by the soft warm glow of the open door. The youngest pretended to wail at the sight of their brothers' fighting, the sound of his screams drowning out all other sounds of the night. At the height of their performance Margie gently pushed off in the skiff unnoticed in the darkness. As Margie floated slowly away from the spectacle, Joseph never took his eyes off the knockdown drag out that had unfolded in front of him. Margie gently rowed into the dark harbor, floating gently towards Satellite Island, alone in the dark, save the sounds of her brothers still putting on a magnificent show for an enamored audience of one.

Margie had to stay low in the boat as she rowed, and ensure she made no sound as she steered toward the island. The current had caused her to drift more than she had anticipated, and Margie had to land farther East on the Island than she had planned. Joseph had delayed her, but luckily, he hadn't stopped her. She tried to remain positive as the worry set in about the delay. She tied off and scrambled up the embankment, alone in the dark and unsure of exactly where on the island she was.

She knew she couldn't use a light to illuminate the path; it would alert Joseph in the waiting patrol boat as she made her way back West to the signal point. Through the dark, she slowly pushed through the brush and the thicket in the general direction of her intended position. The island was not particularly overgrown but was littered with jagged stone outcroppings and narrow crevices cut into the terrain. Things easily navigable in the daylight, but treacherous in the pitch black. She stumbled and felt the sting of thorns as she pushed through a sea of brush in the darkness.

The going was slow and tedious, but Margie made it to a familiar trail and to the awaiting signal covered delicately in the brush. It was now approaching two in the morning and True North was due in at any time. Her hands trembled as she removed the sea grass and branches from the neatly concealed orb, hands scraped and bloodied from her passage. Her eyes jumping back and forth between Boundary Pass and the task below her. She hoped they hadn't been signaling her, cursing her slow hike to the lookout, and hoping she hadn't been too late. She carefully removed the yellow orb and lit the oil lantern, turning the knob to fully open. The oil lantern flared a deep yellow and Margie placed the yellow glass over the lantern. It lit up and emanated a sparkling golden burst of light.

20

What's Only Yours

B ack on the boat, we headed East sharply along Satellite Island away from the entrance to Prevost Harbor and away from the golden glow of Margie's orb. I hurried back to the helm and asked Mack where we would go, trying not to panic. He said that we would cut through John's Pass and stash the booze on Johns Island just across the small channel, for the night. They could easily take skiffs the following night and cut through the narrow channel to an awaiting cart. "Don't worry Leannan, I know places we can hide, we've got all night, and I know these islands a whole hell of a lot better than they do."

I nodded in agreement and ran back to the bow to keep watch. We had roughly two and a half hours before the sun would be up, more than enough time to make landfall, hide the whisky, and get back to Stuart Island. I told Mack I'd take the skiff from Johns to the far side of Stuart after we unloaded to meet up with Margie. Stuart and Johns Island were separated by a very narrow channel, called John's Pass and this way Mack could take the boat back into Prevost Harbor without me, and the skiff would be in place, hidden neatly in the brush for the small run across the channel the next night. He agreed and again, just as my confidence grew, lights appeared coming from the mouth of John's Pass heading straight for us.

There was nothing to do and nowhere to run. The patrol boat was headed directly to us, full speed ahead. Mack looked sick and ran to the skiff, ready to heave it over as a last-ditch escape pod for me, when the driver of the patrol boat flashed a light twice. Mack ran back to the helm, and I signaled two flashes back. The boat approached still at full speed until a few feet before the bow and the engines were cut. Mack cranked the wheel, and I moved the sail to the opposite side as we heaved to.

Sam yelled from the helm, "Two patrol boats on their way, one through John's Pass, the other around the Eastern tip of the island. They're coming from the lighthouse, you've got probably fifteen minutes, twenty if you're lucky. You have to go back!" he yelled.

Mack slammed his fist on the wheel, knowing the Coast Guard was closing in on him from almost every direction.

"What about the first entrance to Prevost?" I said. "You've done it in a skiff, can you do it in this boat?" I asked. "You said it yourself; nobody knows these islands better than you do!"

"The tide is already going out, we draft six feet with the keel, there's no way! It would be like threading a needle, and it's pitch black!"

"Mack, we've got to try!"

Mack looked to me and back to Sam as he bobbed in the patrol boat next to us.

"Buy us some time Sam... I'm going to thread the needle." he said as he turned the wooden wheel hard to port. I raced to the rigging and adjusted the sails, and the boat lurched in the new direction, heading back North. Sam grinned a mischievous grin and sped off in the direction of John's Pass again. I raced back to Mack at the helm and asked him what he needed. He had one hand gripping the wheel and the other reached out to grab my hand.

"This is madness, you know that right?" he said. "There's a fair chance we end up on the rocks. If we do, you have to take the skiff and disappear before the patrol boats get there. Promise me."

"You can do this. We can do this," I said staring intently at him, knowing full well I would never abandon ship or him, tonight of all nights.

The alternate shallow entrance to Prevost Harbor sat on the East side of Satellite Island. A massive rock outcropping sat dead center of the shallow channel, with swirls of water already circling the craggy rocks and reef that lie just below the water's surface in all directions. We reefed the sails, as the current would give us all the push we needed as it flowed through the small channel and out again through the main channel farther West. Mack slowly turned the wheel, and we made the delicate push into the perilous channel. Mack positioned me on the bow, and I stared into the dark water just in front of the boat, ready to alert him to any visible rock that would impede the boat.

The boat crept along the channel, the shoreline barely visible in the first hints of morning light. I heard the keel make its first scrape on the sea floor and I winced at the sound. Mack's hands were white knuckled on the helm and we both scoured the water line trying to make out exposed rocks and orient to the channel landmarks as we floated in. The keel caught again, and the stern of the boat kicked out to the starboard side and then bobbed over the underwater blockage. Mack turned the wheel sharply, but without sails and speed, the boat was slow to respond. I grabbed the oar from the skiff and shoved the bow away from a large rock that was looming directly in front of us. The weight of the boat felt impossible as I pressed my body into the butt of the oar and leaned out over the rail precariously.

The maneuver realigned the boat, and we were drifting again, free from the obstacle. The boat groaned as it slid, mere inches from the craggy sea floor, knocking against rocks as we made our slow approach into the harbor. Mack watched the shore for cues and turned the helm abruptly keeping the boat precariously moving forward. We passed the large center channel boulder, and the last large reef scraped against the side of the boat as we narrowly passed. The only sound now was water gently lapping at the bow and Mack loosened his grip on the wheel and flashed me a feral smile.

"Jesus, Mary, and the carpenter, I think we did it!" he exclaimed, looking wildly over the side of the boat and back through the small inlet we had just passed through.

I took a deep breath and readied the lines for our approach to the small dock, unwilling to jinx our run of luck on early celebrations. The dock was tucked into the near side of the harbor, and barely substantial enough to tie up to. It would do for a short stay in calm weather, and that's all we needed currently. Once docked, even if a patrol boat passed, we wouldn't be seen from outside the harbor from the snug enclosure of the small cove. The sun was still not up, although the glow of dawn was already visible over the tree line. The sound of patrol boats just outside the harbor could now be heard as we pressed slowly into the dock. I leapt from the boat and quickly tied us off. Mack raced below and began depositing crates of whisky on the deck for us to offload. The cache was just up a small trail, set neatly next to Mr. Malby's stone and we raced back and forth lowering the crates into the cache until the boat was empty and we were out of breath.

By the time the whisky was safely stowed, the sun was making its first appearance through the tree line, and the rest of the harbor was coming into view. We shoved off and made our way up the harbor, shielded by Satellite Island, deep inside Prevost and feeling protected. I threw my arms around Mack as he steered the sailboat toward his family dock, feeling the first ripples of security as we put the night's events behind us. I let out a long breath I felt like I had been holding all summer.

Simultaneously, Mack and I spotted the danger that had been previously obscured by darkness, that we had both naïvely been so oblivious to. Our eyes widened and we both gasped as the anchored patrol boat came into view. We could make out a small form near the tiller, his back to us, eyes fixed on the main entrance to Prevost Harbor, patiently waiting for his prey.

The wonderful thing about sailboats is the silence while they move; the only sounds are the gentle lapping of water as the bow cuts delicately through the water, and the occasional luffing of the sails if the wind changes. We came up on the patrol boat early that morning without a sound. As the ship came into the periphery of Joseph's gaze, Mack, with one hand around my waist and the other on the helm broke the silence. "Morning Joe, beautiful morning for a sail."

Joseph looked as if he had seen a ghost, his eyes wide and then quickly filled with rage. He looked wildly towards the entrance to the harbor and back to where we had come from, trying to make sense of our arrival. He trembled with rage and disbelief; his mind unwilling to accept what his eyes were seeing.

"We'll meet you on the dock if you'd like to search the boat again. I'll make coffee. How do you take yours?" Mack made a small wave and then cast his eyes back on the awaiting dock, his arm loosely on my waist. I reached up and kissed his cheek and leaned into him giggling as we approached the dock. Joseph fired up the engines and raced past us, throwing up wake and pushing the wooden boat into the pilings as we tied up. Mack and I burst out laughing, freeing the pent-up worry and fear we had held onto all night.

We sat on the edge of the boat together for a few moments, in disbelief of what we had narrowly escaped and the sweet satisfaction of our victory. We were cleaning up the boat when Margie came flying down the road and raced down the dock in the full light of the morning. Her eyes searching for answers, unable to speak after running all the way to the dock.

"It's done, we're safe, everything is ok!" I yelled as we hugged. As soon as she caught her breath, she told us all about Joseph lying in wait in the harbor and the staged fight with her brothers, trudging through the island in the dark... all of it.

"I thought we were goners so many times!" she exclaimed.

Mack told Margie about Sam's warning and our unhinged decision to use the East entrance to Prevost. Margie screamed when we told her, knowing full well herself, the mine field of rock and reef there.

"I can't believe we pulled this off!" she said as she hugged me again. After our emotionally charged debrief, we walked down the dock toward the main house, remembering we had to make an appearance at home shortly. I told Margie I would walk her home, thank her brothers, and head back to the lighthouse myself. We said our goodbyes to Mack and started walking down Over the Hill Road toward the Borchers, finally feeling clean and relieved that it was over. A dew had settled over night and the pasture was covered in sparkles as the morning sun cast its early light. The island looked alive and vibrantly glowing as we headed toward Margie's that morning.

"Do you smell that?" I asked Margie.

"No, what?" she replied, as I twirled around looking for the grey telltales of smoke, hoping I was mistaken.

Just above the tree line, a small swirl of smoke was slowly ascending into the sky. It was coming from near the front of the MacDara property, close to the road, right where the family barn stood. Back toward the dock Mack was running at full speed toward the road.

"I'll get the boys!" Margie yelled as she ran for home. I took off back toward the MacDara place and followed Mack's path to the fire. Smoke was billowing out of the hay door when I arrived, crackles and pops sounding off from the interior of the barn. Mack was pumping water furiously and yelled to me to get to the lighthouse and get help. I took off down the road in such a panic, I failed to see the front bumper of my father's car, tucked neatly into the brush near the airfield, with Joseph leaning on the hood smugly.

I had just made the turn up the road to the lighthouse when the car crept forward and turned in behind me. I had been running so frantically, I hadn't heard the Buick tires on the gravel until he was very close to me... until it was too late. Joseph stomped on the brakes and leapt out of the door next to me. He grabbed me from behind, nearly squeezing the breath from me as he drug me toward the idling car.

"You think you fucking won?!" he snarled at me.

I tried to fight him off, but his large frame overpowered me as his eyes dripped with rage. He threw his arms around me and lifted me easily into my father's Buick as I kicked and screamed futilely. He pushed me deeper into the car and jumped in behind me, raising his hand in a fist as I reached for the door.

"I know you helped him hide whisky today. God damn it! I know it's in that barn!" he screamed. "Well now I won!" he yelled, out of control with rage and fury, pointing at the smoke as it rose through the sky. "Look what you made me do." He grabbed my chin and forcefully turned my face to the sky.

"Maybe you're the problem Willow, hmmm, maybe you should disappear," he said decidedly and threw the car into gear. *Oh my god he's going to kill me* I thought. He produced a pistol and flashed it at me, before placing it on the dash directly in front of him. "Last known whereabouts, consorting with bootleggers..." he announced, crafting his alibi as it came to him. I knew I had seconds to act.

I grabbed the wheel and yanked as hard as I could toward the right. Joseph countered the movement with an even harder pull to the left and the car fishtailed wildly. The sleek blue Buick careened off the gravel lane and plummeted down the roadside embankment. The car bounced erratically down the hill, in a spray of gravel and dust, and slammed into a tall fir tree about thirty feet off the road. The car was filled with dust as it settled, and I choked as I tried to catch my breath. Joe was bleeding form his head and slumped over the steering wheel. My eyes searched the interior of the car for Joseph's gun. The seat was covered in glass, and the gun was nowhere to be seen. It must have been lost in the commotion, hopefully flung from the car on impact. Time was running out to get out of there. It was time to run. I hadn't noticed the blood running from my shoulder. I never felt the slow pooling of crimson on my forearm, which had taken the brunt of the collision. I had slammed into the dash on impact but fueled by terror, I used Joseph's current moment of incapacitation to try and extricate myself from the tangle of glass and debris. The door wouldn't open so I shimmied out the shattered window, collapsing on the ground beneath the car as I made my escape. He was awake.

A pained gasp emanated from inside the smashed vehicle as I quickly made it to my feet. The sound propelled me toward the road. Joseph tried his door, but the accident had smashed the front end so badly he couldn't pry the driver door open either. I could hear him rummaging around behind me as I scrambled up the embankment, glass shards clanging on the metal as they fell. He slid out the passenger window like a snake after me, but I had already made it back onto the road and quickly ran for the lighthouse.

I screamed for help as I ran, but there was nothing between the lighthouse and the car, only towering sea cliffs and acres of forest. I turned the corner at the top of the hill and realized hopelessly he would catch me before I made it to the house. I would never make it. I turned off sharply from the road, hoping I could signal someone from the tall cliff if anyone was outside at Turn Point. I ran down the moss-covered trail and burst into the clearing at the top of the cliff, scanning for someone, anyone, at the lighthouse to signal.

My mother was hanging washing, and I screamed and waved to her to get her attention. *He would be around the corner any second now.* I ran to the far side of the cliff, hoping to hide and stall for time, or possibly circle back on him. I could hear my heart beating in my chest, and my breath rapid and erratic. I crouched low against the small rock outcropping hoping for a miracle. My fingers dug into the moss and earth instinctually trying to grasp at the island like a lifeline, the dirt working itself under my nails as I clawed at the earth in terror. Like clockwork, I caught the ominous form of Joseph in my periphery walking toward me, his head lowered, blood dripping from his forehead onto his shirt. He stood near the top of the rise staring at me, looking almost possessed as he adjusted his sleeves, the blood pouring from his head. He smiled eerily when he saw me.

"Get away from me!" I screamed and backed up until I had nowhere to go.

Joseph wiped the blood from his head and laughed at me as he did. He reached for a cigarette and lit it, blowing smoke at me, his hand trembled with rage. The crimson blood spilled between his knuckles following the path of least resistance as it streamed down his arm onto the ground. He pointed the cigarette at me, speaking softly at first, his voice a forceful whisper.

"Do you see what you did? You wrecked everything; you threw it all away." He paused and lowered his eyes like a monster. "FOR WHAT?!" he roared, eyes red with rage. He took another long drag of his cigarette, looking down at it in his hand as it undulated with fury. He chuckled maniacally to himself. His demeanor had changed so dramatically, I didn't even recognize him as he spoke. This monster couldn't be the same person I danced foolheartedly with at the beginning of summer. My mind replayed the sequence of events that led to this moment, to the unraveling of him and the exposure of his small evil core.

"You would have made a lovely bride," he said as his eyes met mine and he nodded rhythmically. I knew for certain as he looked at me and then back out over the water, he planned on killing me right here. His transformation was even more terrifying as the rage left his face and the certainty set in. I had nothing to defend myself against the maniac in front of me, other than making a break for it or leaping into the waters below. The thought crossed my mind as he crept closer and closer to me, with only the high sea cliff and the open strait at my back. I might survive the leap if I controlled the jump. I knew if Joseph had his way, he would ensure I was incapacitated prior to throwing me off the cliff, breaking an arm or knocking me out with his fists. I scrambled to my feet, certain that the next few moments were life or death and made a break to the left.

Joseph reached into his waist behind his back and produced the small pistol. He casually pointed it at me as he took another drag from his cigarette and asked, "Was it worth it Willow? All of this…?" The gun halted any efforts of escape. He shook the pistol in a circular motion as he continued his diatribe. I scanned the path behind him, frantically looking for an exit, but he had me pinned against the cliff. I turned my back to him, left with only one option, nosing right up to the edge of the cliff. I stared straight out over the water, following the horizon with my eyes, unable to look down for fear I would hesitate. I could hear his footsteps approaching behind me and knew what I had to do. I drew in a shaky breath, steeling myself for the unthinkable. Just as I motioned forward, I heard a scuffle behind me, a soft moan, and saw Joseph flail forward past the side of me and off the edge of the cliff. His body still reaching out to me as he cascaded down the cliff, knocking into the wall as he tumbled, and splashed into the water some 200 feet below. The gun had been torn from his hand as his body met the jagged rock of the island and it plunged into the water, swallowed hungrily by the sea.

I turned around sharply to see my mother, hands outstretched, breathing heavily, and wild eyed. She threw her arms around me and pulled me fiercely back from the ledge. She embraced me shaking and grabbed at me wildly, each grasp a reassurance that I was indeed alive and unharmed. She had seen me frantically gesturing from her spot in the garden and ran the entire way up the hill. When she saw Joseph with the gun she had rushed him, not thinking twice, and thrown her body into him as his back was turned and he approached the ledge. I stood in disbelief as I realized what she had done, and what would have happened had she not. She held me shaking, refusing to look toward the ledge, only pausing to run her hands over my arms and back, repeatedly telling herself that I was ok.

One by one, my father and Mack appeared, both out of breath, looking equally terrified, respectively. They ran toward us, my father demanding answers, still in a state of shock, trying to process all that had happened, scanning for Joseph around the cliff face. I met my father's eyes, looked toward the cliff and pointed. "He's gone, good riddance," I said calmly. My father ran to the edge of the cliff and scanned for any signs of life in the frigid water. The water churned methodically below, swallowing up the evil that had descended into its depths. The rhythmic currents unchanged by the foul interruption of his body as my father learned of Joseph's true nature. The kelp swayed gently back and forth, quickly recovered from the sudden intrusion of Joseph's frame as it plunged into the frigid water, leaving no trace of him behind.

My father turned away from the cliff and looked at me solemnly, with more remorse and terror in his eyes than I had ever seen. Gone was the imposing, inflated posture of a sea captain, replaced now with a terrified father, contemplating the almost loss of his daughter. My mother cried woefully and ran to him, and they embraced and pulled me toward them. Mack stood off to the side, still looking harrowed, but his countenance fading mostly to relieved. My parents eased their embrace after ensuring I was in one piece, and I ran to Mack throwing myself into his chest and feeling the safety of his presence. I felt myself breathe for the first time and let go of the knot of fear that had been choking me since I had seen the first wafts of smoke. He shook as he held me, tears welling up in his eyes as he too realized how close I had come to death.

We sat for a few moments just holding each other, when my father approached, hand in hand with my mother and he said, "I was wrong about you son. The way you look at my daughter is the way a man looks at a woman when he would give up his own life to protect her. The way her mother and I do." He looked at Emily, his wife, with new eyes as she had risked her own life, without hesitation to protect their child.

He stretched out his hand to Mack and Mack reached out his hand to the captain. "Aye, I would die for her, but my plan now is to live for her, Sir." He met my father's eyes with an intensity that made my father say, "I believe it Dylan...I believe it."

"What about the barn?!" I remembered.

Mack said he had heard my cries and left the barn burning to run to me. "I'm sure it's ashes now," he said squinting, looking back toward the tree line home. He too hadn't given it a thought until just before he heard my screams coming from the road. "The barn faded to nothing at that moment."

"I'll get the rest of the men and some hoses, and we'll meet you there," my father offered. We split up, my mother and father heading back to the lighthouse, and Mack and I made for the barn.

When we arrived, we found the Borcher boys, Sam, and Margie extinguishing the last smoldering embers of the barn fire. The large red barn had miraculously survived, thanks to their quick work. They had arrived on the scene just as Mack had heard my screams and left the fire burning to find me. The structure had remained mostly unscathed, as a pile of hay inside the barn had been the ignition source, not the actual barn. The boys had been able to pull the flaming pile out of the barn as it lay on an old canvas sheet, and it burned itself out eventually. The smoldering hay was littered with a few alcohol bottles, no doubt staged by Joseph to falsely incriminate Mack in the event he had been mistaken about the whisky's location. The flames had just started to spread to the wood structure when the flaming ball of hay was hauled out from inside the smokey barn. Other than smoke discoloration and some minor damage, the barn had withstood the fire and would outlast Joseph's vengeful spite.

We spent the greater part of the afternoon cleaning up the fire debris and talking to the neighbors and each other about what had happened. The small island community had always rallied around each other, and this incident was no different. Word had spread across the island and several folks came to offer a hand, but mostly to hear the tale. Before the sun had set, handshakes were made and offers of help had been solidified for clean-up and restoration. Only a few stragglers remained, retelling the incident to each other to savor the excitement.

Once the ash and emotion had settled my father suggested we all head for home. He had invited Mack up to the house that evening once the barn matter was settled. I began the walk home in the low light with my parents, still trying to process the events of the summer, and how they had led to the here and now. I told them to go on ahead, that I needed a few moments alone before heading back. It seemed like years had passed and so much had changed from that first evening in spring, when I first set foot on the island.

The move to Stuart Island had nearly killed me, but as I headed for the lighthouse, for home, it struck me how much more alive I was inside. Cold gusts filtered through the trees and the salt air rushed past my skin as I walked, stripping away the smoke odor, cleansing me with each forward step. The island was inextricably a part of me now. Each thread of it ingrained in my being, intertwined and woven into the story of my life like an invisible drawstring, pulling me into it. I placed my hands on my arms to shelter from the cold and smiled at the slivers of dark earth that were wedged under my fingernails like medals of valor. I looked out onto Haro Strait and watched as the water pushed through the islands—like the life blood it was. It's pace slow and rhythmic, taking and giving, imperceptibly shaping this remote section of the Northwest. I smiled to myself, fully enveloped by the island and wrapped in a kind of peace that I wore like armor now that I had it. Looking out past the water, into the vast wilderness of the Pacific Northwest, a small wren sung out in the distance, her call softly drawing me back from battle, and I felt the embrace of home.

Acknowledgements

A huge thank you to my family and friends for their encouragement and support. Mario, thank you for the countless hours 'making it work' when I just wanted to write; your technical prowess is unmatched. Thank you for the hours of research, and bringing the manuscript to the finish line. Kathy, Lori, and Patty, for your friendship, support, and encouragement. Andrew, Julie, and Brittany for being the first people to read it, unedited, and not crushing my spirit; your kindness was a gift. Jade and Samantha, thank you for baby stepping a new author through the maze of publishing. Thank you to Addie Thompson, without whom this book would not be sitting in your hands. Thank you for your guidance, the hard work, and most importantly, your unwavering support in this endeavor. A big thank you to Bob for your amazing cover design, your creativity brought this story to life visually, and I am eternally grateful for every yes throughout the design process.

Thank you to The Turn Point Lighthouse Preservation Society for keeping the legacy and history alive in that magical place. Your work inspired mine, and for that I am forever grateful. My acknowledgement to the TPLPS also comes with a plea for mercy for the creative liberties my characters created, which perhaps blurred the line between fiction and history too deliciously. Lastly, to the lyrical mastermind that is Taylor Swift, whose music is the soundtrack to an examined life.

About the Author

Jennifer Reinhardt was born and raised in the Pacific Northwest and currently works as a Registered Nurse in the Puget Sound Area. She is a mother, wife, avid adventure seeker, and next level Swiftie. When not writing absolute literary bangers, she can be found on her sailboat True North, with a glass of wine in hand, chasing the sun and trying to pet stray cats.